SOUTHERN SASS . . . AND MURDER

"Wake up!" Mama shouted at my ear.

"I'm tired," I groaned, rolled over and pulled the blankets over my head.

"Marygene Francis Brown, I'm not telling you again," Mama said.

I jolted upright, suddenly aware my mama meant business. Wait a minute, Mama was *dead*. I rubbed my face with my hand, feeling the grittiness of dried mascara. "Lord help me, what a nightmare." Mama was about to bless me out for something or another. In her mind, I had always been guilty of something.

"This isn't a dream, child," Mama flipped on the lamp next to her. She was sitting in the beige Queen Anne chair across the room, wearing her yellow dress with white daisies and matching yellow belt. Her brown hair was curled and styled closed to her head like she always wore it.

I didn't speak, completely amazed with how vivid this dream was.

"I don't have much time, so I'll be brief." That was Mama alright. She was efficient. "There's going to be a murder at the diner tomorrow." She leaned forward. "Close for the day."

"What? Close the diner?" I covered a yawn with my hand. *Am I really seeing this?*

"Listen to me, young lady! Neither you nor your sister needs to go to work tomorrow." She faded away.

I blinked hard and stared at the empty chair . . .

Southern Sass and Killer Cravings

Kate Young

KENSINGTON PUBLISHING CORP.

www.kensingtonbooks.com

KENSINGTON BOOKS are published by

Kensington Publishing Corp.
119 West 40th Street
New York, NY 10018

All Kensington titles, imprints, and distributed lines are available at special quantity discounts for bulk purchases for sales promotions, premiums, fund-raising, educational, or institutional use. Special book excerpts or customized printings can also be created to fit specific needs. For details, write or phone the office of the Kensington sales manager: Kensington Publishing Corp., 119 West 40th Street, New York, NY 10018, attn: Sales Department; phone 1-800-221-2647.

ISBN-13: 978-1-4967-2145-7
ISBN-10: 1-4967-2145-4

First printing: June 2019

10 9 8 7 6 5 4 3 2 1

Printed in the United States of America

Electronic edition:

ISBN-13: 978-1-4967-2146-4 (e-book)
ISBN-10: 1-4967-2146-2 (e-book)

Chapter 1

My phone rang for the umpteenth time this morning. After a brief glance at my cell, I hit the speaker button on the steering wheel. "Hey, I didn't get cold feet. I'm doing this." My lips creased in a grin, proud my tone sounded confident, even to my own ears.

"I'm so glad to hear it, Marygene." My friend Yvonne sounded relieved I hadn't chickened out, that we were both moving back home around the same time. We each had our issues to sort out, but the two of us would feel a bit stronger together.

"I just passed the Peach Cove welcome sign." They'd repainted the giant peach since my last trip home for Mama's funeral two years ago.

"I'm so jealous. I can't wait to be welcomed by that glorious peach. Two more days and I'll be home too. Do me a favor. Roll down the windows so I can hear the wind." My hair whipped around my face the exact second she said dreamily, "Oh, I can hear it now. Don't you love that salty air?"

I sampled the air before agreeing.

"Hello, my beautiful island," Yvonne sang. "Do you miss me?"

A chuckle escaped my lips.

Yvonne was doing her best to cheer me up. It was working. "You did have a heart-to-heart with Jena Lynn, didn't you?"

Returning home with my proverbial tail between my legs was difficult enough, without an extra helping of guilt from my sister, and that was exactly what I'd received when I made the phone call. There was no way I was going to mention or discuss Peter and my messy divorce at that time.

When I didn't respond, she continued, "You're going to have to find out if she signed those papers. In your current situation, you don't have another option. You need an income stream."

I made a noncommittal noise.

"You're so stubborn. Listen, I'm at my attorney's office now. I'll see you in a couple of days. Maybe less. Be brave."

I'd fled Peach Cove only a few short years ago, determined to make a new life for myself in Atlanta. "Established Around 1854, Population 2,003," the sign now read. The island never changed much. The large number of original settlers migrated from the Carolinas to the small island off the Georgia coast and never left. Once folks were born here, they usually died here.

Yvonne had moved to the city a year earlier pursuing her interior design degree. In my case, I planned to follow my dream of attending Le Cordon Bleu. Luckily, Nanny had left me a little inheritance that would cover most of my first-year expenses. Yvonne, God bless her, fully aware of the tumultuous relationship Mama and I had, had given me a standing offer of rooming with her and splitting expenses. It worked out that the proximity of her apartment proved convenient for the both of us. A month after my first semester began, I'd secured a job working for a prestigious caterer. During one of those functions is where I'd first met Peter. Little did I know then that he'd turn my life upside down. I'd left the island a naive young woman and returned a little battered yet wiser.

Jena Lynn had been running our family business since our mother's passing, and because, in her mind, I had effectively abandoned our inheritance, she was eager to buy me out. When we were younger, she worked tirelessly at perfecting her skills in the kitchen. For me, it had just seemed to come naturally. As you could imagine, that had been a point of contention between us. Now, The Peach Diner was my lifeline.

I came to a stop at a red light at Cove Square, where most of the businesses in town were situated, including The Peach. Pedestrians, from shoppers to diners to those enjoying the bluegrass bands that set up on the corners to play, filled the square at all hours. Today was no exception. A flash of brilliant red hair to my right drew my attention toward the paved brick crosswalk. A face I'd not seen in years came into view.

"I can't believe it!" I cried and laid on my horn.

A couple of seconds later, my fiery-haired friend, with a personality the size of Texas, waved like a loon before she threw herself against the hood of my car to peer through the windshield. A giant smile spread across her sun-kissed face, her emerald gaze twinkling. "Marygene! Hell's bells! It is you!"

"Betsy! It's been ages!" I laughed.

Betsy Myers was a unique character who, by some folks' standards, was an acquired taste. To her friends, she was larger than life. Boisterous, completely outspoken, with a generous spirit and a heart of gold.

"How's things?"

She huffed. There was always something going on with Betsy. "Long story." She gestured to her ears.

I got it, there were nosy people everywhere. I grinned as she practically crawled through the window to give me a hug.

"Seeing you has made this uncomfortable day bearable," I said as she carefully extricated herself from the window.

She glanced at my backseat crammed with clothes, obviously tossed there in a hurried fashion, and scrunched up her face in a distasteful way.

"Wow! Things didn't go so well, huh?"

I shrugged.

"Men, whatcha going to do?"

We shared a loaded glance. *Men are pigs,* our eyes were shouting.

The truck behind us started honking the horn. The light had changed, and we'd been too preoccupied to notice.

I waved to Betsy. "I better go. I want to show Jena Lynn I'm raring and ready to work."

"Okay. You moving back into your mama's place?" At my nod, she continued, "Terrific! My shift is about to start. I'll see you at the diner." Betsy was a lifer at The Peach, employed at the diner since the day she turned fifteen and begged Mama to hire her. She never gave any inkling she had any intention of ever doing anything other than wait tables. It was good to have reliable help.

Once parked, I took a couple of deep breaths and checked my reflection in the rearview mirror. The bruise on my neck had nearly faded, thank God. Today was the first day of my new life. *Peter Hutchinson will not break me.* The night we'd met he'd been so charming, projecting confidence that I'd found so alluring. I'd lost myself in the illusion. Shame consumed me when I recalled my infatuation. What a cliché. Older man finds desperate younger woman who's struggling to find herself. Younger woman is enthralled by older man and his attentiveness. A few extravagant dates via private jet where he showered me with affection and I fell hard. Only a few short months later, he popped the question. I should have listened to my friends when they cautioned me about how fast things were moving. Yvonne mentioned that Peter isolated me from those I held dearest. I hadn't seen it. Maybe I hadn't wanted to see it.

I got out of the car and gave myself a once-over. My khaki shorts were a little rumpled from the drive, but the peach polo I wore with "The Peach" embroidered above the left breast still fit well. My fake-bake tan gave me a healthy glow. It would be good to have access to the beach again, because tanning beds were a poor substitute for natural vitamin D. As I raised my face toward the sun, I invited the rays to seep into my pores, the warmth healing.

Okay. One foot in front of the other. I can do this. I tightened my grip on my wristlet and crossed the bricked street.

The tinkling of the door signaled my arrival in The Peach. With a deep inhale of the married aromas of all the food being either fried, scattered, or smothered was such a comfort. It was as if I'd never left. For the first time, I actually took in *my* diner. From the age of ten, Mama had Jena Lynn and me wiping down tables and cleaning gum from underneath them. I had worked about every single job in the diner. That I knew it so well brought me an overwhelming sense of calm. It was strange how something you'd run from your entire life could feel like a comfy fit in the end. There was no evidence of my ex here. He'd spent his childhood and teen years in New Jersey. That would account for his lack of manners, my Nanny would have said. God love her, she'd been a Southern snob. *Marygene, if a man ain't*

Southern born and bred, he ain't worth spit. In my current predicament, I had to laugh.

Nanny would have despised Peter. A month into the marriage, I'd discovered he struggled with alcoholism, just like Nanny's husband had. It was my nanny's words that came rushing back to me last night. *A man that raises a hand to a woman should be DRT* (dead right there). God, I missed her. But being inside the diner, I felt like she sort of was here, cheering me on.

Our diner was decorated in a fifties motif with its black-and-white checkered floor tile that set off the peach vinyl booths and chairs with a white stripe down the center. The long counter, where I'd spent many years of my life doing homework, ran the length of the room and was fitted with eighteen high chairs. The walls were adorned with old photographs of the town and townspeople, with the back wall dedicated to Peach Cove's high school football team.

My sister, Jena Lynn, walked out of the bakery side of the kitchen located behind the grill line. She lifted the glass dome lid and began stacking peach rolls neatly on the decorative white display plate. I gave her a weak smile. My sister's light brown bob was tucked neatly behind her ears, and she had a light dusting of color across her cheeks.

"Want a glass of peach tea?" She gave me a tentative smile that didn't quite meet her amber eyes.

"Yes, please."

My half-brother, Sam, peeked through the service

window, spatula in hand. I waved. Both of us had inherited our father's gray-blue eyes and easily tanned skin. Over the years Sam and I had sort of settled into an awkward brother-sister relationship. The sibling rivalry we had down, the close connection part, not so much. Maybe that could change.

I was on my way to round the counter to greet my brother properly, when Betsy lumbered into the diner. "Gawd, it's hotter than Hades today." She was fanning herself with an old magazine. She greeted a couple of customers on her way over to me. "Y'all, ain't it great to have our girl back home?"

Several customers nodded and smiled. Their welcome was appreciated.

"Sorry I wasn't here to be your buffer. I had to run into the pharmacy. Was it awkward with Jena Lynn?"

"Sort of."

"I wish you'd told me sooner about that SOB." I opened my mouth to respond but she cut me off. "I hate it, but I get it. I'm just glad you called me yesterday and I'm here for you now. It'll get better." A lump developed in my throat as I fought emotion. She smiled, understanding shining through her eyes. "Well, your hair looks fab. Those highlights really add dimension." She ran her fingers through my shoulder-length layered cut. "Not that your blond locks weren't already the envy of the island."

I'd spent a fortune on the highlights and style in one last-ditch effort to hold on to the mirage of the life I was living. "Thanks."

"We need to have a wine-and-dine night, to catch up on all things on the island. Bet you could use one."

"Right you are, Bets," I said as Jena Lynn deposited a glass of peach tea on the counter and I took up purchase of a free stool next to old Mr. Ledbetter, followed by a healthy sip from the glass. Sweet but not too sweet, with a perfect amount of peach flavor. Tasted like home.

"Good?" Betsy tied on her apron.

"Delicious," I groaned and grinned.

Mr. Ledbetter patted my hand. "I bet Jena Lynn is glad to have you back. Those peach rolls of hers sure could use some pop."

"I told you I was still tweaking the recipe." Jena Lynn's mouth contorted in a disapproving grimace.

"Well, they smell wonderful from here," I said placatingly, not wanting to remind her of any old competitions between us.

Unfazed by her admonishment, he held up his mug. Obligingly, she refilled it. Betsy took the sugar caddy in front of him and replaced the missing packets. She eyed me with amusement as he pointed to the framed newspaper print on the wall.

"You haven't changed a bit," Mr. Ledbetter's smirk caused his sagging dimples to deepen.

Betsy hooted with laughter, and I gave them a wry smile. It was known around the island that I had the gift of an expert's palate. It was true I could tell you what was missing from a recipe or what needed to be adjusted that would send the dish right over the top. If a dish needed a dash of this or a dessert called for a hint of zest or perhaps a splash of vanilla, I was your gal. In my junior high years, like a lot of kids, I had gone through an awkward chubby phase. Fortunately for them, most pubescents aren't subjected to having those years captured and published by their hometown's paper and then framed in the family diner. I cringed at the image of my face, round as a MoonPie, grinning while taking a large bite of Mama's blueberry cobbler and captioned beneath the picture, "The Peach's secret weapon Marygene Brown will never allow a dessert to be served without her stamp of approval." Ugh. Next to that little gem was another framed print of me. My arms were thrown around Alex Myers, then captain of the football team. I'd been wearing his letterman's jacket and we were in the lip lock of the century.

"Well, we've had perfectly ripe peaches in abundance since the Fowlers took over the McKenna orchards, year before last." My sister saved me from the moment of embarrassment. "We've started selling preserves by the jar. Oh, that reminds me. I've been working on a new berry crumb bar recipe. Something about it isn't quite right. I'd love to get your opinion on it."

"Of course. I'm here to help." I meant it.

"You get that order straightened out?" Betsy asked Jena Lynn as she began wiping down the laminated menus.

With a roll of her eyes, Jena Lynn nodded, "They're sending a rush order. Cami in the order department claims they received a call from me canceling the order yesterday."

The loud rumbling of a tow truck pulling up in front of the diner diverted our attention.

"What's going on?" Jena leaned over the counter, attempting to gain a better view.

"I don't know." I got up to investigate with Betsy and my sister on my heels.

The bluegrass bands were in full swing as I charged out onto the sidewalk. The usual crowd appeared to be enjoying the music. They clapped and tapped their feet to the beat. All were witness to the tow truck loading up *my* Prius!

"What do you think you're doing?" I shouted over the band to the coverall-clad man with grease-stained hands and leathery skin.

Not an ounce of empathy was visible on the man's face as he handed me a slip of paper. "I have an order here to repossess this vehicle." I didn't even read the specifics, stunned by the name *Peter Hutchinson* scribbled at the bottom of the order slip.

"That lowlife high-handed jerk!" Apparently, my ex's reach extended to the island. "My things are in there," I choked out.

"Marygene! You didn't unpack when you first got home?" my sister asked.

I said frantically, "I haven't gotten there yet." Now I was second-guessing my decision to visit the diner first. My face began to burn and the crowd around the diner grew.

"Can't she at least get her stuff out of it before

you haul it off?" Jena Lynn asked the man, her tone demure and annoyingly calm.

Surely he would show some compassion, but my hopes were dashed when he spoke. "Once it's loaded, I can't unload it until I reach the destination on the work order." He spat a wad of chewing tobacco near my feet. "Sorry. Just doing my job here, ladies."

I poked him in the chest with my finger. "Well, your job just plain sucks!"

The man literally shrugged me off and stalked around the truck, his heavy work boots pounded against the street. His nonchalant disposition added fuel to the flames. I glanced back toward Jena Lynn and Betsy then to the flatbed. My sister was vehemently shaking her head. Betsy gave me an enthusiastic two thumbs-up.

Up the side of the flatbed I went. The doors were locked but I'd left the windows down.

"Hey! Get off there!" the man bellowed as I crawled through the passenger-side window. I reached into the backseat and flung what clothing I could grab out toward Betsy. She was scooping up the items as fast as I was throwing them down.

"Not without my stuff!" I shouted back as he revved the engine, threateningly.

Our eyes met in the side mirror. I narrowed mine in a silent dare. He *dared*. The truck lurched forward, flinging me into the dash. Determined not to be beaten, I scrambled back over the console and made another grab for my belongings. Betsy screamed my name, shouting something about the deputy sheriff right before I was flung forward again. I deemed it wise to bail on the rescue mission. I hit the ground with a thud, glad to have landed on my feet. Betsy and I high-fived. *Ha!*

My victorious mood lasted for less than a minute. All eyes were on me. Half of Peach Cove Island's population had just witnessed my breakdown.

Chapter 2

Betsy and I shoved everything I'd retrieved into the backseat of her car. "Y'all go on! Ain't nothin' to see!" Betsy shouted as I tried desperately not to lose my stomach's contents.

Heat was radiating off my face.

"It's going to be all over the island now," Betsy told me, the corners of her mouth turned down as she gave a regretful sigh.

"I know," I groused. "That was one of the things I never missed." Living on a small island had its disadvantages, like everyone always knowing your business.

"Well, if anyone asks me, and I suspect they might, being the most important witness and all," Betsy wrapped an arm across my shoulders, "you are a total rock star."

I certainly didn't feel like a rock star, but I appreciated the sentiment.

"I've had just about enough of this," Mr. Ledbetter

said when I walked past Felton Powell, the deputy Betsy had warned me about a few moments ago.

I snorted, not making eye contact with them as Betsy hustled me into the diner.

"Oh, honey," Heather Lawson said as she rushed through the front door after us, nearly colliding into two tables. She enveloped me in a massive hug. Heather graduated a year behind Betsy and me, but our mamas were close friends. She was tall, dark haired and too thin these days. As The Peach's fill-in waitress, she eagerly worked every shift Jena Lynn had available.

I hugged her back, taking care not to squeeze too hard—her edges were sharper. "I'm sorry I haven't kept in touch" was all I could think to say.

Heather released me and immediately cut me off with a "Pfft. Don't you start that. You went off to spread your wings—good for you, I say. But it's mighty fine to have you back home with us. Jena Lynn has kept us apprised of your life." Concern etched her brow as she noticed the bruise on my neck. Startled, I stood like a deer in the headlights as my hand covered the evidence. "You decide you want me to send some boys to put a beatdown on that ex of yours, you just say the word." She leaned in and whispered, "I'm so proud of you for leaving. You ever need someone to talk to, I'm here." She raised her hands. "No pressure, though. And my offer still stands." Heather gave me a wink I interpreted to mean she would gladly send her brood of brothers over to put a hurting on Peter. They were probably the reason her ex was MIA. I must admit, it was tempting.

"Thank you. I'll keep your offer in mind," I whispered, and she gave me a solid pat on the back.

"Was the car in his name?" Jena Lynn asked, her eyebrows raised, causing that little wrinkle between her brows to deepen.

I nodded and she gave me an admonishing look. She didn't have to quote the words of my Nanny. They rang loud and clear. *You can't trust a man to take care of you. You've got to take care of yourself, child.* Nanny was right, and that was what I was attempting to do. "It seems I'm still a work in progress."

"Y'all go on back to your tables. A round of peach rolls on me!" As of this moment, Betsy was my hero.

I was relieved when everyone had gone back to their respective tables to finish their meals. Several customers paid their checks and took their freebie to go. I received several pats on the shoulder in passing. Pity—I hated it. I scrounged up a smile for them.

"You didn't have to do that," I said to Betsy, overwhelmed with her generosity.

"Don't worry. Jena Lynn won't make me pay." She folded her hands in a praying fashion toward my sister, who reluctantly gave her a nod of agreement before she laughed. Betsy had that effect on people.

I reclaimed my seat at the counter next to Mr. Ledbetter. Seemingly unaffected, he was devouring his BLT quite happily now. He clapped me on the back and pulled me closer, not quite in a hug but near enough, without it feeling awkward. The old man was heavyset, with gray hair. In his day he'd always had a reputation of being a ladies' man. To look at him now, you'd never have guessed it.

"Take my advice," his raspy tone lowered, "play hardball. Take the man for everything he's worth. Make a statement you won't be played for a fool." He leaned back. The metallic taste of anxiety was in my mouth. He took a sip from his mug. "The past always has a way of coming back and biting you in the keister."

Betsy took a right on Orchard Street, which had rows of grand, historic colonial-style homes with large front porches. It was picture-perfect, with nice manicured lawns and budding flowering trees. There was comfort here, along with the stability that couples sought out when they were ready to settle down and start a family. Mr. Johnson was picking up sticks out of his driveway that had fallen off his large oak tree, much older than my twenty-seven years. He threw his hand up in my direction, and I responded in kind. The smell of fresh-cut grass marked the coming of summer, and I had to smile. Today was one of those balmy days on the island, with a clear blue sky and lots of sun that made me glad I lived in the South. The air was thick down here most days, but our saving grace was that wonderful breeze coming off the Atlantic.

"When did Felton Powell get back into town? And get a job with the department?" I asked. "Last I heard he was living in Savannah."

"He's only been back home a couple of weeks. Your daddy was awful nice to hire on another deputy." The Peach Cove Sheriff's Department consisted of two officers, including the sheriff, my biological father, Eddie. The other was Betsy's cousin Alex. With Felton now aboard, that made three. It was ample; the crime in Peach Cove mainly consisted of petty thefts, with teenage perpetrators.

Honestly, I was surprised Felton had returned to the island. Of all the kids I grew up with, he had the most difficult childhood. He was always making noises about getting off this island.

"He and Heather hooked up a few days after he got back," Betsy said.

I nodded, not really caring. Betsy took a right onto Cloverdale, the winding sandy road compacted with shells, which Mama insisted we never pave. Slowly, she navigated through the canopy of Spanish moss–covered trees until the old farmhouse that had been in our family for ages came into view.

"Weird, huh?" Betsy put the car in park.

"Yeah," I agreed as we both began gathering up my salvaged belongings from the backseat.

Two stories of peeling white wood siding stood before us. The large wraparound front porch had been restored two years before Mama died. It looked good. The hanging baskets were now barren of late spring blossoms, and the grass needed a mow. The yard guy was scheduled for tomorrow morning, so Jena Lynn had informed me. The old brown late-sixties model Chevy pickup that had belonged to my late Paw-Paw still sat off to the side.

Jena Lynn had offered it to me to drive. I stared at the rusty, muffler-less behemoth and sighed. It wouldn't be pleasant, but it would get me from point A to point B.

"You gonna be okay financially?" Betsy asked when we reached the front porch.

"Yeah. I've got my savings account at the community bank here in town. I can get by on that until the divorce is finalized, then I'll buy a new car." I inserted my key into the front door and gave it a good nudge. Humidity did a number on everything around here.

I took a stifling breath of stale air into my lungs and stood for a moment in the foyer. Jena Lynn had updated a few things and painted the wood paneling white, which brightened the living room up a great deal. Mama's old plastic-covered red-and-blue plaid couch and loveseat remained, as did the La-Z-Boy recliner.

Everywhere I looked I saw my mother. "I can almost feel Mama." A little shiver slithered down my spine.

"Yeah, it's creepy."

Betsy and I strolled into the kitchen. I glanced up at Mama's picture in the hallway. Why she had left the old place to me, I'd never know. The business was in Jena Lynn's and my name, why not the house? I'd been floored at the reading of the will. I was sure thankful to have it now.

The kitchen sure could use some sprucing up. The hardwood floors gleamed, but the green Formica countertops were an eyesore. I'd probably have to gut the entire kitchen if I ever decided to sell the place.

A quick peek into the bag Betsy had brought revealed several bottles of wine, assorted cheeses, cold cuts, an array of olives, and a good loaf of French bread. I smiled approvingly and went in search of a corkscrew. Her decision to run into the market before she drove me home had been an excellent idea. I could use a glass, or three, of wine.

She moved into the living room with our cheese board. "Marygene, you bringing the wine?" Betsy called and I carried two glasses and a bottle into the living room.

"Your ex going to contest the divorce?" Betsy asked.

"He says he won't if I can see reason, but let's talk about something else."

I sank down onto the couch just as Betsy said, "Hey, did Jena Lynn mention your daddy today?"

"Of course. She was disappointed that my biological father and I hadn't already had a joyous reunion." I took a deep sip from the glass. "How am I supposed to have a healthy relationship with the man?" I was the daughter of Edward Carter, a fling of Mommy Dearest when she and Jena Lynn's father were having problems and again, when Daddy died—correction, Jena Lynn's daddy died—when I was eight. She and Eddie had had a tumultuous relationship for as long as I could remember. Clara Brown believed a relationship with a plebeian—the town's sheriff—to be beneath her. Once considered to have a lineage of aristocracy, the Brown family fell from grace when Nanny's husband lost himself and his fortune in moonshine and gambling. My enterprising Nanny used her talents and the money she had left to open The Peach. Still, Mama always pretended she was a cut above. It was ironic that what had saved Nanny then was saving me now.

"Well, he did finally tell you," Betsy reminded me with a snicker.

"Right, because dropping a bomb on a sixteen-year-old the way he did was completely normal." I poured myself another glass and suppressed a shudder at the memory of a red-faced Eddie stomping out of the house when my half-brother Sam and I came home from the movies.

"Well, at least he didn't catch you making out with your brother." Betsy shoved two slices of capicola into her mouth.

"Yuck. That would have never happened, even if Sam and I weren't related."

Betsy laughed so hard she nearly choked. I supposed the situation was funny, if it had happened to someone other than me. I laughed anyway.

"Wake up!" Mama shouted at my ear.

"I'm tired," I groaned, rolled over, and pulled the blankets over my head.

"Marygene Francis Brown, I'm not telling you again," Mama said.

I jolted upright, suddenly aware my mama meant business. Wait a minute, Mama was *dead*. I rubbed my face with my hand, feeling the grittiness of dried mascara. "Lord help me, what a nightmare." Mama was about to bless me out for something or another. In her mind, I had always been guilty of something.

"This isn't a dream, child," Mama flipped on the lamp next to her. She was sitting in the beige Queen Anne chair across the room, wearing her yellow dress with white daisies and matching yellow belt. Her brown hair was curled and styled closed to her head like she always wore it.

My scalp tingled.

"I see I have your attention."

I didn't speak, completely amazed with how vivid this dream was.

"I don't have much time, so I'll be brief." That was Mama all right. She was efficient. "There's going to be a murder at the diner tomorrow." She leaned forward. "Close for the day."

"What? Close the diner?" I covered a yawn with my hand. *Am I really seeing this?*

"Listen to me, young lady! Neither you nor your sister needs to go to work tomorrow." She faded away.

I blinked hard and stared at the empty chair.

Chapter 3

To my surprise, the rust bucket fired to life after I turned the engine over a mere six times. *Ugh*. Massive amounts of smoke billowed up from the non-existent exhaust pipes, burning my lungs and nearly suffocating me. I had to keep the windows rolled down to allow some fresh air into the cab, since obviously the truck didn't have air-conditioning. It wasn't even seven in the morning, and already my thighs were sticking to the cracked black vinyl bench seat. As I attempted to shift gears on the steering column, I longed for my climate-controlled Prius. Shells and sand spun out from under the tires on my long driveway, clanging against the sides of the truck. I had no idea how fast I was going because the speedometer was no longer functional. I'd have to simply guesstimate.

The gawking commenced when I turned onto the square and circled it to try and find a vacant space near The Peach. My only saving graces were the giant dark glasses and head scarf I'd taken out of Mama's room. In this disguise, I prayed no one would recognize me. When I finally found a space, I cut the engine off, tossed the scarf and glasses onto the seat, and darted from the truck. I gave the door a giant bump with my backside and hoped it would close. Not that I waited around to see if it latched. If someone wanted to steal it, more power to them. A coughing fit took hold as I dashed through the cloud of smoke toward the diner. So much for arriving incognito.

The second I crossed the threshold, Sam came rushing around the counter, grill spatula still in hand. He was famous around the island for his Sam's Surf and Turf Burger, which he obviously named after himself. He charged right past me toward the window and shouted, "You drove Mad Max!"

Great, now everyone in the diner would know it was me polluting the square. The name he'd given the truck in his teens, around the time he'd begged Mama to give it to him, never rang true from my perspective. Rust Bucket was far more suitable.

"Hi, Marygene. So nice to have you back home." I put my hands on my hips and glared in his direction. "Wow, you're looking well. Have you lost weight?" I asked in a mock falsetto. "Why thank you, Sam, and yes, I think I have lost a few pounds. Stress, you know."

He flushed. "Sorry. I am glad you're back," he said and gave me a side hug before rushing back around the counter toward the grill.

"And FYI," I called after him as I tossed my purse

on a vacant stool at the bar, "I've changed his name to Rust Bucket."

That got a few chuckles from a couple of elderly men at the counter having their breakfast.

Sam peeked through the open service window to give me a horrified look. "You blaspheming female. How dare you defile my baby?" He winked before he disappeared from sight.

I gave my head an amused shake. If Rust Bucket was his baby, no wonder he was still single.

I tied on an apron, poured myself a mug of coffee, and waved at Heather, who was hustling this morning, before heading back into the kitchen.

"Marygene!" my sister called. "Is that you?"

"Mm-hmm," I mumbled around a mouthful of coffee.

Sam was flipping a stack of pancakes and tossing a potato waffle on the waffle iron. My mouth watered as I gazed longingly at the shredded potatoes, cheese, and herbs closed into the iron. He tightened his American-flag bandana on his head. He had aged some. Tiny crow's-feet were visible now. He pulled out the waffle, plated it, and sprinkled chives and extra cheddar cheese before placing it in the open window. He certainly was a pro now.

"What's new with you?" I asked with genuine interest.

"Same ole stuff mostly. Though, I bought me a fishing boat last spring." His countenance lit up like a lightning bug.

Bay fishing was a town pastime. There was nothing better than slathering up with tanning oil and lying out on the deck of a boat. I sighed. I would have to get out on the water at my first opportunity.

"That's great. You'll have to take me out sometime." I patted him on the shoulder, moved past the commercial sink the staff used to wash up, and went into the bakery side of the kitchen.

Jena Lynn was dumping a giant lump of yeasty dough onto the perfectly floured stainless-steel worktable. It didn't spring back as much as it should when it hit the surface. Something was off with the elasticity. The peach rolls weren't going to be as light as they needed to be.

"How's Zach?" Zachary Atkins and my sister had been together since her freshman year in high school. Mama had expected wedding bells and pressed for years. I suspected she was the reason Jena Lynn hadn't taken the plunge. Mama's overbearing nature evoked rebellion.

"He's fine. He and his dad are in Atlanta until next week. When he gets back, we should have a big Sunday brunch. Like we used to." Sunday brunch was huge in our family. It was the only day the entire family had off during the week. The diner had closed every Sunday since its inception. "The bars are on the counter." She paused. "What?"

"Nothing." I made my way over to where the crumb bars were.

The fragrant berry scent informed me the fruit was perfectly ripe. I picked up the refrigerated bar and took a bite. The delectable crust had a nice texture and buttery flavor. The bar had a solid flavor profile and a nice crust-to-fruit ratio. It was a decent bar, good even.

"Tell me." Jena Lynn's irritated tone let me know she was referring to her dough.

Since it was too late to do anything about that now, I told her about the bar instead. "Well, they're good." I placed the bar back on the plate. "They would be great with some lemon zest to freshen them up, reduce the sugar because the fruit is sweet enough, and add a dash of cardamom. Replace the cornstarch with flour. It makes it too gummy. Then it'll be perfect."

She closed her eyes. "Cardamom. Marygene, I don't know how you do it."

I smiled.

"How'd you sleep last night? In the old house, I mean. Was it odd?" She spread peach preserves over the perfectly buttered dough.

"I had a dream about Mama last night." I took a sip from the mug. "It was so real."

"Tell me."

I related the dream to her, but I held back about why Mama had insisted we close for the day. The thought still creeped me out.

She laughed. "Weird how our subconscious stirs things up. But Mama would never suggest closing the diner." There was something odd within her gaze. "You know there is no such thing as ghosts. Mama's in Heaven. It's all in your head."

"Didn't mean to upset you."

We settled into an uncomfortable silence.

"You didn't. Mama loved you. She wanted us both to run the diner and follow in Nanny's and her footsteps."

Did that mean she expected me to run the diner with her now or just become a regular employee? I bit my lip, unsure how to broach the subject. After all, I had been the one to suggest the buyout in the first place, or maybe that had been Peter. Huh. Now, it all made sense. If I sold my half of the business, then I would have had nothing to fall back on financially, further trapping me within the confines of my miserable marriage.

Jena Lynn let out a sigh. "Don't stand over there looking pitiful. Get over here and hug my neck."

We embraced.

My sister smelled of burnt sugar and deep-fried foods. "I tore up those documents the second I received them. That man was bad for you."

She had no idea.

"You never should have run off after you and Mama had that misunderstanding. You weren't thinking clearly when you jumped into marriage with that older man."

I was unable to hold back my tears of gratitude. "You're right, and I can never thank you enough." Jena Lynn had always had her hands full with Mama. A responsibility that we should have shared. The guilt I felt because of leaving her weighed so heavily on me that I could never burden her with my troubles. Besides, there were moments when Peter was sweet. It wasn't a total nightmare the entire time.

Sometimes, when he was sober, he behaved like a complete gentleman. I'd been consumed with the desire to help Peter, despite the fact that he never wanted me to visit my family. The possessiveness, I'd convinced myself, was because he loved me so much. *That wasn't love.*

She hugged me for a few seconds more, then stepped back, her expression full of pain. "This may not be the time, but I think we need to clear the air."

I took a deep breath, bracing myself for the onslaught ahead. "You're right. We do."

She exhaled, "I'm just going to jump in."

"Okay."

"The constant tension between you and Mama was unbearable for me. I know you don't want to hear this, Marygene, but the two of you clashed because you were so much alike." I opened my mouth and her hand shot up, "Let me finish."

"Not in every way, but your stubborn streak comes from her. Neither of you were willing to give an inch. I know that wasn't all on you. Still, it affected me." Her face held this strange expression. "When you left, I had to find a way to deal with her, and after we found out she had cancer that affected her moods, I chalked it all up to that and forgave her. With you gone, I was left to deal with . . . well . . . everything. It was hard."

My mind went back to that awful day. Mama and I had had one of our major blowouts, where I had wanted to discuss culinary school, again, and broaden my horizons. We'd had more discussions, or should I say arguments, than I could count regarding my vision for the diner—well, the expansion thereof. I never wanted to change The Peach. But I'd dreamt of opening a catering side to the business, tailored to special events, that offered higher-end cuisine. Culinary confections were a passion for me and Mama had been well aware of that fact. To this day, I still can't fathom why she'd been so averse to my dream.

When I informed her that I'd been accepted into Le Cordon Bleu, she blew a gasket. She called me a deserter and an ingrate. Mama had abandonment issues, and when I told her I wasn't leaving her, just going to school, her eyes were wide with shock at the mere mention of her issues. I still recall the tears streaming down my cheeks as she railed at me. I was just like my biological father, stubborn and selfish. "You don't need me anyway!" she'd shouted. Then she said the unthinkable . . . that I'd been a mistake.

If she believed the consequence of her affair with Eddie was a mistake, then fine. Those were her regrets and as much as they pained me, I refused to suffer under her verbal assaults another second. I wanted my own life. And I'd told her so.

So, I left, leaving my sister alone with our mother. A pang of regret pierced my heart.

"Jena Lynn, I've been a total witch. My life in Atlanta was a disaster, yes, still, that gave me no right to behave the way I did or allow Peter to influence my decisions about the business. I should have considered the responsibilities my leaving would add for you. Please forgive me." I moved closer and reached out and grasped her hand. "I love you and have been a horrible sister. That crazy, self-pitying Marygene is gone now, and I'm here for you. Okay? I will do my best to forgive Mama, for you. I'll happily make loads of dough, help you create culinary masterpieces that will get us a visit from the guy on the Food Network you love, and swear I will give you all the credit!" I smiled. "Deal?" That had been another dream of hers, to get The Peach on her favorite Food Network show.

"Deal," she said, and we got busy.

Sam strolled out of the kitchen just as I was finishing up lunch. The door tinkled, and a few late lunch arrivals entered. He leaned against the counter, nodding to the people who had entered. "Y'all take a seat anywhere." After they were seated, he said to us, "Did y'all hear that the turtle hatchings are going to be filmed?"

We all shook our heads.

"Yeah, a big film crew is in town. Kinda exciting, huh?"

"It is. Nothing ever happens on this island," Betsy said.

"I thought years ago when that other crew came to the island to investigate, they said we didn't have enough population for it to be worth their while," I said.

"Guess we do now." Sam's name was called and he rushed back to the kitchen.

Betsy huffed and perched on the edge of the seat next to me. It was two o'clock, the slow time of day for us, and I could tell by the way she was gawking at the leftover fries on my plate, she was starving.

I brushed her arm with my fingers. "Order your lunch. I'll take that table for you."

Since the diner's doors opened, employees were always allowed to eat for free. It was one of the perks, along with discounts for pies and cakes for holiday functions. We really were like a big family. The Peach family is how Nanny referred to the staff, and it stuck.

The relief on Betsy's face was gratitude enough, but she thanked me anyway. "You're a lifesaver. I got in late and didn't order breakfast before the rush started."

"Didn't sleep well?" I asked.

"I kept having that dream. You know, the one where your section is full and you can't get the food to the table fast enough?" I nodded and she handed me her ticket book and pen. "I hate that dream. Some comfort food is what I need."

"Good idea." I hopped off the chair, snatched two freshly cleaned laminated menus, and strolled to the table. "Afternoon," I greeted the two gentlemen who'd taken up residence in the back booth. I placed the menus in front of them.

They were definitely out of towners. Their choice of cabana-style clothing gave them away. I surmised they must be the film crew or producers of the turtle-hatching project.

"Afternoon," the one with ash-colored hair and square-framed black glasses said.

"Can I get you both something to drink while you look over the menu? Our peach tea is freshly made."

He nodded with a smile. "Never had peach tea before. I'm game to try it."

I turned my attention to the smaller man with a large broad nose and dark black hair.

"I'll have a Sprite." He didn't look up from the menu.

"Coming right up," I said as cheerily as I could manage.

After I deposited both drinks on the table, the man with glasses asked, "What's good here?"

"Well, our Surf and Turf Burger is real good." I pointed to it on the menu. "It's a ground sirloin burger stuffed with seasoned blue crabmeat served on grilled ciabatta bread, or you can get them as sliders. Some people prefer the smaller burgers, easier to manage."

"Sliders sound great!" He handed me the menu after I scribbled it down on Betsy's pad.

"You want fries, onion rings, or french-fried pickles with that?"

"Fried pickles."

I took his menu and glanced toward his companion.

"I'll have the grilled seafood salad. Hold the avocado," he said in a monotone voice as he shoved the menu toward me, still not making eye contact.

Mr. Personality. I hung the ticket on the wheel for Sam.

My sister was beating butter and sugar in the commercial mixer when I came back into the bakery side of the kitchen. She had a look of panic on her face.

"What is it?" I asked.

"The order still hasn't arrived. I've been assured it will be here before six a.m. tomorrow, but I'm on pins and needles. This has never happened before." She picked up the half-empty bag of confectioners' sugar she'd placed on the worktable.

"You're using a new brand these days?"

"No. I found this in the supply closet. I wasn't expecting to find any, but with only half a bag here, I must have used it before and found it satisfactory."

She held up the bag for my inspection.

"Maybe it got brought in with your last order by mistake," I offered.

"Maybe. I just wish I could remember how it mixed." She pursed her lips. "Well, I've got to use this for Mr. Ledbetter's chocolate frosting. It's traveling and I'll need to stabilize our usual frosting since we won't have the proper chill time. I hope it doesn't need too much extra sifting." She inspected the fineness of the product. "Heather took a to-go order from Rainey Lane this morning. A chocolate mango beer cake. She's coming in around three and they're going to celebrate her husband's big acquisition deal with Mr. Ledbetter."

"But don't we have chocolate mango beer cakes in the refrigerator?" We always had cakes on hand. This recipe was a variation on Nanny's stout cake.

Jena Lynn and I experimented when mango beer came on the market one summer. We added coconut and raspberries, and the mango beer cake was born.

"You thinking about Mama's face when she tried our cake for the first time?" I nodded and she grinned with the memory that our obstinate Mama had loved it. "Well, to answer your question, we do have several in the fridge, but Rainey Lane made me promise to make a fresh one for them. Like made a few hours before she picks it up kind of fresh. She's lucky I found this. Otherwise, she'd be forced to accept a day-old cake."

Typical Rainey Lane.

"Order's up, Marygene!" Sam called, and I hustled to grab my order.

My customers were happy, their glasses were full, and I was holding it together. I took a seat at the counter next to Mr. Ledbetter, who always seemed to be here.

"How ya feelin' today?" Betsy asked the old man as she sat down next to him to eat her lunch.

"I'm feeling really good." He leaned over to me again. "I had to have both knees replaced a few months back."

"Sorry to hear that, but glad you're doing so well now," I said. "I hear your son and Rainey Lane are coming in to celebrate with you."

I feigned interest. Rainey Lane and I never were all that close. Rainey Lane Echols, at the time, now Ledbetter, was a tall, perfectly built brunette who'd always been the belle of the ball. She plagued Betsy, Yvonne, and me from the first day of kindergarten until the very last second of our high school graduation.

He snorted. "That ole gal is nothing but a spend-thrift. She and my ingrate of a son deserve each other."

Betsy and I exchanged a wide-eyed glance.

"Now they're coming here. Like I need another headache after all that ruckus with those idiotic developers last week."

"More developers were in town?" I asked.

"Uh-huh, but your sister gave that gal a good chewin'-out at the town hall meeting. I was right proud of her. Over my dead body would I leave this island. Peach Cove is my home. I was born on this island and, by God, I'm going to die on this island!"

The island never changed much, and residents wanted to keep it that way. Despite this, the occasional developer showed up periodically and tempted families with handsome sums in the hopes of buying their properties. They were obsessed with making Peach Cove the latest all-inclusive resort destination.

"Amen!" an older couple in the corner cheered him on. "You tell them, Ledbetter!"

"See, they know what I'm talking about." He waved to them. "Why anyone in their right mind would want to move into that crime-ridden city is beyond me. Besides, I like my villa at Sunset Hills." He finished off his coffee and placed a ten on the counter. "The place is swarming with lonely ole ladies just begging for my attention." He waggled his eyebrows at me, and I nearly choked.

"You watch that kind of talk. Disrespecting women. You should be ashamed." Yvonne's mama, Ms. Brooks, who I'd not noticed earlier, interjected her finger between Mr. Ledbetter and me.

To the old man's credit, he shut his mouth.

"I mean it. It's talk like that that'll get strychnine put into the well." Had she just threatened to poison him? "You'd do well to sleep with one eye open."

She patted me on the shoulder next. "Take care of yourself, little Marygene. I'll have Yvonne call you when she gets home. And steer clear of that one." Her head jerked toward Mr. Ledbetter.

The crowd at the counter watched her storm out the door.

"Remember what I told you?" He hitched his thumb over his shoulder toward the door. "It always comes back to bite ya in the keister." Mr. Ledbetter chomped his teeth together and smacked his backside. "It's a good thing I'm wearing my denim britches today or that woulda hurt."

I lost it, laughing so hard my ribs hurt.

"Hey, Jena Lynn," he turned to my sister, "bring me a slice of that cake. My son and his bridezilla can eat some at home."

After I composed myself, I got up to refill my customers' drinks. Still chuckling, tea pitcher in hand, Rainey Lane Ledbetter walked in, plastered to her husband's side.

"Don't you just want to rip out each one of her

ugly bleached platinum blond hairs by the root?" Betsy propped next to me at the counter after dropping her plate in the bus tub.

Her comment caught me so off guard I gave a bark of laughter. I disliked ostentatious Rainey Lane from the top of her dark roots down to her red designer pumps. My cell rang softly with a familiar ringtone, and my hand froze over the pocket that held the phone.

"You okay? You look pale," Betsy asked.

"Fine," I croaked weakly. "This developer Jena Lynn told off," I lowered my tone, "was she upset after the ordeal?"

Jena Lynn was the sensitive type. She hated confrontation.

"Hard to say. But that woman was vicious. She told Jena Lynn, in front of everyone, that she better watch herself." She leaned closer. "Jena Lynn called her a lying bitch."

My mouth dropped open.

Jena Lynn never cursed.

"That woman was cold, she—"

A scream erupted, causing me to drop the tea pitcher. The contents splattered the feet of the patrons in the back booth.

Mr. Ledbetter slumped over the counter.

"Somebody help him!" I yelled.

The old man appeared to be struggling to breathe. I prayed that someone knew the Heimlich. I rushed over to him, intending to give him a couple of hard pounds on the back. He fell forward.

We both went down onto the floor. His left hand

had a death grip on my right hand. He pressed something into my palm.

He gurgled next to my ear, "Don . . . trus . . . anyon . . ."

Everything exploded into chaos. Betsy called for an ambulance. Heather was in tears. Jena Lynn was shaking all over as she stared at Mr. Ledbetter, who was now foaming at the mouth beside me.

Someone was shouting, "Call nine-one-one!"

I sat there helplessly. The man from my table was on the floor next to us now, trying to revive the unconscious old man. Rainey Lane and Carl were standing off to the side, faces drawn in panic. Carl began yelling, calling out his dad's name. The other patrons were staring on from their tables in utter shock.

I longed for the sound of sirens as tears streamed down my cheeks.

The man from my table made direct eye contact with me. His square black frames slid down his nose. His face was grim as he panted, "This man is dead."

Chapter 4

My shopping basket was full when I rounded the corner to the toiletries aisle of Mason's Market. I was operating on autopilot after the ambulance had hauled Mr. Ledbetter away.

Yvonne was standing in front of the nail polish display. "I've been trying to call you!" she shouted and dashed toward me. After an awkward hug, both of us holding baskets, she said, "I got home two hours ago and was bombarded with bad news."

I nodded. "It was awful. I just can't get the image of that poor man out of my head." I swallowed over a lump that had developed in my throat.

"I can't even imagine. You poor thing." She lowered her voice as an elderly woman passed by. "What did they say happened to him?"

I twirled a stray strand of hair around my finger. "I overhead Carl telling Felton that his dad mixed up his medications sometimes, so maybe it was that."

"Maybe. Did Peter really have your car repossessed?" She gasped upon confirmation.

"I'm too shaken up to go into it now." I stared at the shelf that held the shampoo.

"Oh, of course." She shook her head, her blond curls bouncing. "How insensitive of me." She brightened. "I guess I have to get used to this again. You're bound to run into everyone at the only grocery store in town."

"That's true." I was thankful for the subject change.

"Do you like passion pink or lilac rose?" She held both shades of nail polish, wiggling the bottles.

"Lilac rose, definitely." I picked up a bottle of hydrating shampoo. Menial tasks. That was what I needed right now.

Yvonne looped her arm through mine as we continued to move through the store. She was a couple inches taller than me. She was wearing a blue-and-white Lilly Pulitzer dress tonight. We essentially were the same size, despite the height difference. I wouldn't mind borrowing the lovely sundress, along with the white heeled sandals that made a dainty little clip-clop sound when she walked. We strolled toward the checkout lane, where I plunked my basket on the small conveyer belt.

"You want me to drive you home?" She put her bags in the trunk of her cute little red convertible.

"No. I've got to get Rust Bucket back home."

When she appeared confused, I explained. She nodded, cringed, then hugged me. "You're going to get through this, and when you do, you'll come out on the other end a force to be reckoned with."

"Thanks for that."

Before we parted ways, she casually mentioned

Alex Myers, saying she'd run into him and he'd asked about me.

"I'm not even divorced yet. Plus, he's with Olivia Townsend." I glanced down the street. "Last I heard, anyway."

She opened the car door. "Not anymore. They broke up a few months ago."

"Not that it matters. I'm not ready to consider another relationship."

Alex and I had been attached at the hip from junior high through our early twenties. I'd thought he was, *the one.* It hadn't ended well.

"No, but you will be."

I waved bye as she drove away.

The warm breeze was nice tonight, and before poor Mr. Ledbetter's passing, today had been good. I'd been surprised how much I enjoyed churning out pastries and fresh bread. After I was granted free rein in the kitchen, Jena Lynn had become giddy at all my suggestions and ideas. She'd even gone so far as to encourage me to experiment, which gave me high hopes for our relationship moving forward. Everything here was simpler, slower paced. Down the street, Harold's Hardware Store had its front door open, and the faint strains of eighties music reached me. To the left, a smiling Bonnie Butler was locking up her boutique for the night. She threw her hand up and wiggled her fingers in the air as she strolled to her car.

The Peach in the center of the square was lit up bright; the glossy painted peach on the sign was glimmering in the moonlight. The tables by the windows were full, and, from what I could see, the counter was too. Betsy was hustling tonight with a full section. She balanced her serving tray with ease as she placed the plate on the table at the window. Her high ponytail swung around as she refilled glasses. She paused, pitcher still in hand. She was waving like a loon as she leaned over her male customer. "Hey, Marygene!" I could read her lips.

I waved back as the customer said something that must have been harsh because she wagged her finger in his face. The rest of the table roared in laughter as she spun on her sneakered heels toward the kitchen.

As I climbed into Rust Bucket, my mind drifted back to the night before. Mama. Her prediction came true. How could that be? I'd heard of people having weird dreams before the death of a loved one or someone close to them, but this, I couldn't wrap my head around. I remembered that what Mr. Ledbetter had given me was in my pocket. I smoothed out the crumpled piece of scratch paper and examined the series of letters and numbers scribbled there in blue ink, AP081587F. Why had Mr. Ledbetter given this to me?

The aroma of coffee percolating and freshly baked chocolate muffins brought a smile to my face, even after the horrible events of yesterday. I slogged into the kitchen, where my sister was fist deep in dough. Shadows were visible under her eyes.

"Didn't get much sleep last night either, huh?" she asked.

"No." I reached the commercial coffeepot and proceeded to pour us each a cup. "Seeing poor Mr. Ledbetter zipped up in the body bag . . ." I shuddered and we sank into silence.

Jena Lynn continued her task of removing muffins from the pan and let the subject drop. "The new order came in this morning, thank God. Our stock shelves are overflowing. I gave the delivery guy a piece of my mind too. That mix-up was unacceptable." Chewing out the delivery guy wouldn't do a bit of good. It was the equivalent of shooting the messenger.

"You spoken to Eddie yet?" She brimmed with optimism.

I pushed my hair out of my face. "I'm going to."

"Good. He loves you, you know." She checked the croissants in the proofing box.

Of course I knew he did. I loved him too.

"Don't let a bad decision on his and Mama's part ruin the relationship you can now have."

"You're right."

She smiled.

"I promise I'll call him after work today."

Sam strolled in without a word and went to fry himself some breakfast. He didn't like to talk before coffee either.

Jena Lynn and I went to sit at the counter and have a pastry before customers started arriving. And, for the first time in years, my sister and I were on good terms.

Sam took a seat next to me as Betsy shuffled through the door. "I had the worst night." Her eyes were red rimmed and began to fill up with tears. Maybe her bad night had more to do with Darnell than Mr. Ledbetter.

Jena Lynn's face was unreadable. "You okay, Betsy?"

You had to tread lightly with Betsy. If you joined the bash-Darnell bandwagon and then they made up, like they always did, you'd be on her bad side. One minute she was a basket case, sobbing and carrying on, the next she was ready to knock your lights out for bad-mouthing the man.

I slid the entire box of pastries Jena Lynn and I had been working our way through over to Betsy.

Betsy sat her plus-sized figure down next to the container. "I've had it, y'all. Yesterday was a wake-up call for me. Life is short. This time, it's really over."

Jena Lynn and I exchanged a weary glance.

Betsy glared from my sister to me. "I mean it! Y'all know that little gal Kelly Crawford that works down at Tuckers?" Tuckers Jiffy Lube was the only gas station and mechanical shop in town.

Jena Lynn's face contorted in disapproval.

"You referring to that scantily clad girl who runs the register?" I asked as Jena Lynn hopped up to retrieve the coffeepot.

"That's the one." Betsy curled up her lip in disgust.

"That girl is barely legal!" I was outraged.

"I know! I'm going to tell her granny. She'll take a hickory switch to the girl when she finds out what she's been up to. She was all over Darnell." Betsy wiped her nose with the back of her hand. She was right about that. Her granny wasn't the type to spare the rod; she parented old-school style.

Jena Lynn's tone rose as she stirred raw sugar into her coffee. "You caught them?"

"Well, I called him after what happened with poor Mr. Ledbetter—"

We shook our heads.

"—told him I was going to be late 'cause I was taking that extra shift. Guess he thought late meant real late 'cause when I got home, they were rootin' around on *my* couch, the one my meemaw gave me last spring when she had her house redecorated."

We sat in stunned silence.

"I threw his junk out last night. And when he still didn't budge from the TV"—she paused for effect—"I set it all on fire, right there in the front yard." She leaned back and crossed her arms over her expansive chest.

"That's harsh." Sam stacked his empty plates. "Maybe it wasn't Darnell's fault." Jena Lynn and I gave him a disapproving glare. He appeared oblivious to his offense, and the moron had the audacity to reach into the container for a cream cheese Danish.

"Sam, if you value that scrawny hand of yours, I'd pull it out real slow or you'll be drawing back a nub," Betsy warned.

"Sheesh!" Sam jerked backward. It was obvious he didn't doubt her for a second. He marched toward the kitchen and dropped the plates in the bus tub with a loud thud.

"He should know better. You don't touch a gal's

comfort food in a time of crisis," I said, and my sister nodded in agreement.

Jena Lynn patted Betsy on the arm. "Ignore him, Bets. He's a man."

I stood. "And if I may be so bold as to speak for all the women of the world who have been unfortunate enough to be in your shoes, we applaud you."

A satisfied smile spread across Betsy's lips. "Thank you." She took a little bow. "That's why my eyes look like they do. Smoke got to me." She leaned in closer. "I threw all his high school football trophies into the blaze while he was hollering at me. The whole neighborhood came out to watch."

I chuckled. The thought of Darnell Fryer running around watching all his belongings go up in smoke was hilarious. I wished I'd been there. "Did anyone try to step in and help Darnell?"

"Hell nah. He owes his buddies so much money from borrowing to pay his gambling debts, the ones that came out brought their camping chairs and watched the show while tossing back a few cold ones." She got up from the counter to scoop a glass full of ice and filled it with Diet Coke from the fountain. "Y'all, I gotta lose this weight now I'm back on the market."

Betsy was one of a kind.

The jingling of the door and flashing blue lights broke into our little powwow, and, for the second time this week, my world was rocked. Edward Carter, my biological father, had a powerful gait. Being the sheriff did that to a guy. He was a little grayer than the last time I saw him. His grayish blue eyes, the exact same shade as mine, surveyed the room before landing on me.

When he reached me, he hesitated a moment. We both bobbed around like chickens, him wanting to hug me and me thinking I'd pass. We'd been close once during a few years' spell when Mama let him hang around without kicking him out every other month. That had been before I'd been told the truth. What he'd seen in that woman I'd never know.

"Eddie, what's up?"

We settled into an awkward side hug.

"I came by the house last night and tried your cell a few times," he said.

"Sorry. I meant to call you back." I felt a tad childish.

He nodded before getting to the point of his visit. "A forensic team is on its way here. There seems to be some suspicion surrounding Mr. Ledbetter's death." He released me. "Where's your brother?"

I pointed to the grill line.

"Sam!" he called.

"What's going on, Dad?" Sam raised his eyebrows and joined us.

"What do you mean, suspicious?" Jena Lynn asked at the exact same time I did, "Where did this forensic team come from?" Peach Cove certainly didn't have one handy.

His deputies, Felton Powell and Alex Myers, walked into the diner, dressed in their brown uniforms. They both nodded when they saw I'd noticed them. Where Felton was bald, tall, and lanky with a pudgy middle, Alex was on the shorter side and sturdy. He had untamable black hair that curled around his ears, and the most animated dark eyes I'd ever seen.

"The team is on loan from the state. The body has been scheduled for an autopsy. We won't know anything until the reports come back. I received a call from a buddy who's a statie. He gave me the heads-up that Carl Ledbetter is using his connections to have the process expedited, and they want the diner searched and evidence tested."

"Oh, my Lord!" Betsy rose from the counter. "Surely they don't think one of us killed the man!"

"Now, Betsy," Eddie put a hand on her shoulder, "no one said anything about murder. Carl has had a shock, and he wants answers. It happens sometimes when a death occurs suddenly."

But the mere mention of murder and a forensics team on the way here did mean someone certainly had their suspicions.

Eddie opened the door to admit the team of uniformed men loaded down with equipment. I wondered what they had in their little cases. None of the men made eye contact with me as Eddie asked us to step outside.

"I don't like this," Betsy said as we stood outside the diner.

The way the team had swarmed in, as though they were busting Colombian kingpin Pablo Escobar, had us all on edge. We watched as a couple of guys carried out large open bags full of our baking supplies. How were we supposed to run a diner without the ingredients to fill orders? Jena Lynn couldn't stand still.

"That order just came in, Eddie," Jena Lynn said. "None of those supplies have even been touched yet." Jena Lynn's bottom lip quivered as she watched the bags being hefted into the back of the giant black van.

We were starting to draw a crowd.

"Calm down," Eddie placated, but Jena Lynn wasn't soothed. "The supplies can be replaced."

I wrapped my arm around her shoulders and pulled her back from the van.

"What are we going to do?" Her voice shook.

Before I could answer, Bonnie Butler had made her way over from her boutique. "Eddie, what in tarnation is going on? Who are all these people?"

Eddie took the older woman off to the side to have a word with her. I watched him nod at Alex, who had popped his head out of the door. Alex went on crowd-control duty.

"This is bad," Betsy stated the obvious as she moved to the other side of Jena Lynn, her face pale.

"I know," Jena Lynn hissed. "It won't even matter that we didn't have anything to do with the death. With all this commotion," she flung her arm in the air, "rumors will fly and people will be afraid to eat in the diner."

"What's going on?" Heather hurried to cross the street, weaving around pedestrians, her apron tossed across her left shoulder.

Once I filled her in, she was beside herself with worry. "We are going to be able to open, aren't we?"

Unshed tears were visible when she'd spoken. "I've got my youngest's asthma appointment with that specialist scheduled for next week. My deductible has skyrocketed."

Jena Lynn wrapped her arm around Heather's shoulders. "Don't worry. We'll figure something out. I won't let you lose that appointment. It took months to get him in."

I stepped aside as my sister consoled Heather. Her tone sounded much stronger.

Sam was pacing up and down the sidewalk grumbling to himself. Betsy was gnawing on her fingernails, and Mama was standing beside the van. *Mama?*

"I told you. Why didn't you listen?" Mama scolded. *Heaven help me.* I turned my back. "Betsy," I whispered out of the corner of my mouth, "Do you see her?"

"Who?" Betsy asked as quietly as I had.

With my right hand, I reached across my body and pointed over my left shoulder.

"Bonnie? She's gone." Betsy was staring straight toward the van. She would have to see Mama. She was standing less than half a foot away.

"I know this is going to sound crazy," I turned around, "but, Ma—" My voice died in my throat. She was gone. I needed a breather. "Be right back."

With my lower back resting against the masonry wall in the alley, and my hands on my knees, I took a couple of deep breaths. My pulse jittered. Had I really seen her? Heard her? Perhaps my brain was addled by sleep deprivation and a twisted imagination. No, she'd been there.

"Marygene," Alex said and I glanced up, panting. "God, are you okay?"

"Well . . ." I couldn't think of how to phrase what I was experiencing. "I've just been . . . I think I'm losing it, Alex." I wiped my clammy hands on my shorts. He was in front of me now. Familiar and safe. I threw my arms around him and buried my head against his chest.

He responded instantly, holding me tightly. I'd think about this later, second-guessing my actions and motivations and the complications that could arise, but right this second, I couldn't have cared less.

Chapter 5

The next day all of us who had been present the day Mr. Ledbetter died were called down to the sheriff's department for interviews. The old department building, located adjacent to the town hall, was in major need of renovation. The station had been built to last, utilizing hardy Georgia red clay bricks.

The office was small as precincts went. I'd always told Eddie the place reminded me of something out of an old seventies police show, with its drab wood-paneled walls and white-tiled flooring. There was enough room for about twelve people, if they didn't mind getting cozy. Rearrangements had been made to the room to accommodate the crowd. Eddie had to borrow folding chairs from the Peach Cove Baptist Church for seating. The chairs were lined up and down the perimeter of the walls.

I was seated between Betsy and my sister. Heather sat on the other side of Betsy, with Sam next to her. If it hadn't been our slow time of day when it happened, Eddie wouldn't have been able to seat everyone. The Davidsons, who had been contemporaries of Mr. Ledbetter, sat on the opposite side of the room, looking bleak. I recalled them cheering him on in his determination to live out his days on the island. Two other couples sat near them. For the life of me, I simply couldn't remember their names.

The front door opened and in walked a cantankerous Ms. Brooks, escorted by Yvonne.

"Sorry we're late," Yvonne said to Alex, as he held the door open for them. "Mama had a doctor's appointment." Yvonne gave us a little wave as she and her mama took the only vacant seats available across the room.

"Did you hear that Yvonne put in a bid for the old Palmer place?" Sam asked.

The Palmers were our cousins on Mama's side.

"Nate told me," my brother went on. "She made the offer a few days ago."

That must have been what delayed her homecoming. She'd told me about her appointment with her lawyer but not that she'd spoken to my cousin Nate. I had been so preoccupied with my own ordeal, I'd neglected to ask the specifics.

"To live in?" Betsy asked.

He shook his head. "Nah, for her interior design business. That's what Nate said."

Yvonne leaned forward, obviously overhearing bits of our conversation.

Sam was loud. I mouthed congrats to her. She brightened, her smile gracious.

"Nothing is done yet," she mouthed back. "But it's looking good."

Her mama asked her a question, and the two engaged in a low discussion.

"I heard Carl has a detective coming in to head up the investigation," Jena Lynn said to me. "This is just getting worse and worse for the diner."

"Eddie will get to the bottom of this." I picked a bit of lint off my sister's shoulder. "I wonder if the autopsy is completed yet." This was obviously not an accidental overdose as I had first assumed. They wouldn't have hauled us in here if it was. I clasped my hands in my lap, trying hard not to fidget.

If Mr. Ledbetter's wife were still with us, she would be the first suspect. I turned my attention to Carl and Rainey Lane, standing in the back of the room. Rainey Lane appeared unsteady in her white open-toed sandals. Perhaps she was medicated. Carl had his arm wrapped around her waist. He wore tan linen slacks and a pale yellow button-down shirt that matched his wife's sundress. He scrutinized the room, and I wondered if he viewed us all as suspects. Did he realize that, from this side of the room, he was on the list?

"Are you listening to me?" Betsy bumped her shoulder against mine.

"Sorry. What were you saying?"

She scowled. "I was saying they've gotten the autopsy back. Carl put in a call. His dad was moved to the front of the line."

Carl appeared to have a lot of connections.

"Alex told me Mr. Ledbetter had internal bleeding." Alex was Betsy's first cousin on her mama's side. I highly doubted he would come forth with that sort of information.

I raised my eyebrows. "Did he really?"

"Well, to be honest, I overhead him talking on the phone to Felton last night. We were at my meemaw's." She'd been snooping. Typical Betsy.

Like me, she had a curious personality. I moved my head closer to hers.

"I caught bits and pieces then put it all together. I told him about what Ms. Brooks said." Of course, she did.

"He asked about you. You know, he and Olivia broke up."

I shrugged a shoulder. I wasn't sure what Alex thought about yesterday. Eddie had called him, and we'd been forced to part swiftly.

My mind drifted back to Mr. Ledbetter. What was internal bleeding a symptom of? Strychnine? I hated to think it. Had Ms. Brooks and the old man had some sordid past I was unaware of? I fought the urge to get out my cell phone and google a symptom checker. His ramblings about the past coming back to bite you ran through my mind. What were the numbers and letters references to? I glanced at my little pink paisley Vera Bradley cross-body bag, knowing I should hand it over to Eddie, but the old man had instructed me to trust no one. He could have easily handed the paper over to the sheriff's department. He obviously had reason to believe he needed to pass the information along to someone he trusted. Or maybe he had just been given this information and had yet to figure out what it meant.

I twirled a curl of hair around my index finger. *There's going to be a murder at the diner*, Mama had warned. Goose bumps traveled up my flesh.

When I noticed we were attracting attention, I shushed Betsy, as she weaved her own theory. My customer from the diner had a pair of those half-lensed glasses perched on the tip of his nose today. He caught me staring. There was something within his gaze. What information did this stranger possess? He also had a watchful eye on all in attendance. What he must think of us. This certainly wasn't an accurate impression of our island and townspeople.

A heavyset man wearing a dark jacket came into the room. He was taller than my father. Eddie began relaying information to the man. His back was to me, so I couldn't read his lips.

"Folks," Eddie addressed the group, "This is Detective Davis Thornton from the Atlanta PD. He's going to be asking you all a few questions, one at a time." It made sense that, with a bizarre crime like this, they would need outside intervention.

"How long is this going to take?" the old man, whose name I couldn't recall, asked. "The Braves are playing at 1:05 today. They're away until Sunday."

"Sorry to inconvenience you." Eddie paused and pinned the man to his seat with a dead stare. "But, I believe the death of a neighbor to be far more important than you making it home for the first pitch. Wouldn't you agree?"

The old man made a grunting noise and folded his arms across his chest. His wife gave him a disapproving glare.

"Detective Thornton, you have the floor." Eddie stepped back between his two deputies. Both men's faces were impassive, though I could tell they were both energized by a case such as this. I'm sure neither one of them ever believed they'd *catch* a murder.

The large man scanned the room. He spared a few extra seconds on every face. His scrutinizing gaze was uncomfortable as it landed on me then moved on to Betsy. She sucked in a breath then released it when he moved on.

"Afternoon, folks," he finally began. "We have a homicide on our hands here."

Several shocked gasps met the detective's bombshell of an announcement. My sister started crying. I reached out and took her hand.

"It's going to be okay," I whispered to her as I gauged the reactions of those in the room as inconspicuously as I could manage.

The face of the man from the diner altered. Excitement? Anxiousness? Curiosity? Mr. Personality who had dined with him appeared bored.

"Like your sheriff said, I'm going to have a talk with you one by one, and one of these deputies will be taking your statement."

I glanced behind him at Felton and Alex. Felton was trying not to appear excited. Alex, on the other hand, looked uneasy. He shifted his weight from boot to boot. He gave me a half-smile when he caught me staring.

"You'll leave your contact information with the deputy, in case I need to speak with you again later." He nodded to Carl and Rainey Lane. "We'll begin with you and your wife, since you're both grieving your loss. Deputy Myers, you're with me."

"I warned him," Ms. Brooks said.

"Mama, hush." Yvonne's face flushed.

"Well, I did. Somebody got tired of his ways. Served him right, I'd say." Ms. Brooks unwrapped a peppermint she'd extracted from her purse and popped it into her mouth.

Yvonne was whispering furiously into the woman's ear.

"My money's on her," Betsy whispered.

Mine wasn't. Poisoning had to be premeditated. Especially in the way Mr. Ledbetter had been. Someone probably mixed up his meds on purpose. Although, with the search and seizure at the diner, that didn't make sense. My stomach lurched. He could have easily been poisoned or bludgeoned to death in his villa with no witnesses. Someone wanted his death to be public and tragic. Why at the diner?

Lord help us, we had a murderer on the loose in Peach Cove.

Chapter 6

Two hours passed before the detective's large hand engulfed mine. Detective Thornton asked me a series of questions regarding my relationship to the Ledbetters and my duties at the diner. What had Mr. Ledbetter eaten that day? Who prepared the food? Who served it? Was I in charge of ordering supplies? Was I aware of anyone who had a grudge against Mr. Ledbetter? None of it felt real. I didn't hand over what Mr. Ledbetter had given me. I didn't know the detective from Adam, nor did I trust him.

"How much longer do you think the diner will have to stay closed?" Sam asked when I came out of the interview room. "He said the forensic team needs about a week or so. I hope they won't keep it closed for longer than that."

He needed the paycheck. Everyone who was employed at the diner did, including my sister and me. None of us were wealthy, and the financial strain this would put on us would be painful.

"I spoke with Felton while he was outside having a smoke," Sam said.

He and Felton had played football together.

"What did he say?" I asked in a stage whisper and leaned against the back wall in the hallway.

"Not much. Just that some test had come back positive and everyone was waiting on the toxicology report. Dad said it usually takes a minimum of two weeks for that, but since Carl could get a rush on the autopsy, he felt confident he'd had the report expedited as well. The Ledbetters must have some serious connections."

If the Ledbetters had connections in high places, and utilized their contacts, that meant they didn't have any confidence in the island's law enforcement to handle the case objectively.

"I'll see ya." Sam stalked off.

Slowly, I moved down the narrow hallway under the fluorescent yellow lighting. Lockers snaked around corners. I paused when I spied Alex in a cubicle taking Betsy's statement or a condensed version of the one I assumed she gave the detective. She was moving her arms and acting out the scene of the crime dramatically. He noticed me and began to rise. I kept moving. Eddie would be disappointed in me if I withheld anything. The interrogation process was something I wanted to avoid in the future. Withholding evidence would certainly not aid me in that endeavor, but when I'd found him, he was getting chewed out by the old man fuming about missing his game. He'd instructed me to go home. So that was exactly what I did.

I had a pot of gumbo going on the stove. Bacon, dill, and Gouda cheese scones were in the oven. Since my sister had still been waiting to be interviewed, I planned on running them over to her house later. I was positive she hadn't given dinner any consideration.

After I listened to the voice mail Peter had left, I felt melancholy. He wasn't budging on solely retaining the property, and he had no intention of selling, citing that, with the current housing market, we'd lose money. I was thankful that I'd had the presence of mind to have a prenup drawn up in regard to the diner and Mama's house. His voice brought back memories I wanted to forget. Not to mention I was tired of him humiliating me. The first time he'd come home after having a few too many, hurling insults about my lack of refinement or straitlaced personality, I'd been shocked. I'll never forget standing there staring at the "stranger" in our bedroom. I cried as I attempted to help him into bed—the vile words spewing from his lips. *He just needs to sleep it off.* I kept telling myself that everything would be okay in the morning. That night he'd broken my finger: *It was an accident. He hadn't intended to hurt me.* But every time he drank, more accidents followed. Flowers, jewelry, and promises of change came after each incident. But change never occurred and his possessiveness grew.

I'd put a call in to my attorney. He was out, but his secretary was still in the office. She informed me that my attorney was already aware of the car situation. At this point, I would agree to sign almost anything, just to be done with this ordeal. I told her so. She said she'd relay the information.

I was in the kitchen making a glass of iced tea when there was a knock at the front door. Tea sloshed over the rim of the glass.

"Shoot!" I stooped to wipe up the mess.

My nerves were on edge as I made my way through the living room. I opened the door, surprised to see the man from the diner.

His lips turned up in an uneasy grin. "Remember me?" Like I could have forgotten so soon.

"What are you doing here?"

He held his hands up defensively. "I should've called first. Listen, my name is Roy Calhoun." Putting a name to the face was always helpful. He pushed his square black frames up on his nose. He wasn't imposing. He didn't have shifty eyes or a menacing demeanor. Nevertheless, this stranger had no business being on my front porch.

He reached into the front pocket of his plaid short-sleeved, button-down shirt and pulled out a card. "I'm a reporter for the *Atlanta Journal Daily*. I'm covering the turtle project."

I didn't take the card he was extending.

He put the card back in his pocket. "I saw Mr. Ledbetter put something in your hand. You didn't tell the detective about it."

How did he know that? Had he observed the transaction on his way to aid the old man?

"I was questioned after you. The detective would have asked if I had been privy to the information if you had."

Would he have? Or is this man trying to trip me up? Could he possibly have had something to do with Mr. Ledbetter's death?

"I have absolutely no idea what you're talking about. I need to go." I moved to close the door.

His hand braced against the top of the frame forced it to stay open.

"I'm not here to cause you any trouble, but I did lie to the detective."

I contemplated his words as I peered at him through the crack in the door. "What are you after, Mr. Calhoun? You planning on writing a piece for the paper?"

He didn't look away when he spoke. "I'm thinking about it. There's a story here. I'd like to get your take on how all of this will affect your diner." The glint in his eyes spoke volumes, reminiscent of a dog chasing a chew toy. This man was champing at the bit to discover what I was hiding.

Well, the way I saw it was I had two choices: I could tell him, "No comment," and hope he wrote a positive article, or let him in and hope my words were a positive influence. Reporters were a pain in the butt.

Stepping back from the door, I said sweetly, "You want a glass of tea or something?" Nanny always said you could catch more flies with honey.

"Yeah, that'd be great." He followed me into the kitchen.

Out of the corner of my eye, I saw him look around. I was sure it seemed odd a woman in her late twenties would be living in a home obviously decorated in the late eighties. The fuchsia rug in the living room and the hunter green curtains were a dead giveaway. Redecorating wasn't high on my list of priorities.

"It's my mama's old house." I filled the glass full of ice then pulled the pitcher of tea from the fridge. "You want lemon?" I poured him a glass.

He waved off my offer as he took the glass from me. "Something smells good."

"Scones and gumbo."

"I haven't had gumbo in ages." He eyed the stove. If he was fishing for an invite, he would be sorely disappointed. His attention turned back to me. "What did the old man give you and why didn't you hand it over?"

"I thought you wanted to ask about the diner?"

"I do. The man died in your diner."

"You said you lied to the detective?" I took a deep sip from my glass.

"I did. I don't have all the facts yet, but I intend to." He seemed to be studying me, as if I were some riddle he needed to solve. When I didn't comment, he continued, "The man obviously suspected that his days were numbered. He was carrying something around with him. Something I'm assuming of value. Information or a clue? Then he chose you." His glasses slid down his nose, and he pushed them back up with his index finger.

I laughed. "I think you've got this built up in your mind, Mr. Calhoun. And that would make a great story for you to sell. But . . ." I took another sip and watched him over the rim of the glass.

He had leaned forward, listening intently.

"It was nothing. He handed me the napkin he had in his hand when he groped for help." I sighed. "I was the one next to him. You see, there was nothing to tell the detective, and that's why I didn't mention such a trivial thing." My tone was even as I lied.

"I don't believe you." He stared so hard into my eyes I felt he was crawling through my sockets to reach my brain.

I could almost see the wheels of suspicion turning within his head.

"Sorry to disappoint you. It was a freak thing. Now, if you'd like to take a seat, Mr. Calhoun, I'll gladly give you The Peach Diner history lesson."

He placed his glass on the island. It hit the surface with a little thud. "It seems we've wasted each other's time. Thanks for the tea." He left a card on the island before he left.

When the engine sounds diminished, I grabbed my cell and went down my list, calling and warning our employees not to talk to the reporter. All we needed was more bad publicity.

"Proud of ourselves, aren't we?" Mama said from behind me and my cell phone went flying.

Mama was seated at the kitchen table, dressed in that same dress with the flowers. "Pride cometh before the fall," she chastised. "You think you have it all figured out, don't you? Can handle this on your own. Lying to the man with such ease. You should be ashamed."

"I *must* be losing my mind," I said.

"I would think so, putting Gouda cheese instead

of cheddar in the scones." She shrugged. "I suppose that's a nice substitution."

"It's an improvement, not a substitution," I grumbled before I realized I was responding. "I *am* losing my mind." I pinched myself, hard. It hurt.

"Stop being so dramatic. You didn't have any trouble believing in Nanny's gift." She folded her hands together on the table. Her French manicure was perfect.

Nanny had always been what we down here refer to as superstitious. She firmly believed in spirits and premonitions, while still holding to her Baptist doctrine. Some would say the two conflicted. Nanny disagreed, always saying, "They believe in angels but not in other spirits. God doesn't have to explain all his ways to them. Blind is what they are."

"You said all of that was 'complete and utter nonsense.'" I began pacing.

She sighed. "I stand corrected." That was difficult for her to admit, I knew it. Her painted red lips pursed. "Sit down, Marygene. You're making me nervous." She fluffed her hair. Even in death, Mama was worried about her appearance.

I obeyed. "Okay." I took a deep breath.

Nanny had said that those of us with "the gift" had the ability to see those who had passed. When they needed our help anyway.

"Why are you here?"

She glanced upward. "Like I said before, they only give me small increments of time, so I'll be brief." Her glance turned to a glare. "I'm trying to tell her now, Mama."

I smiled. "Nanny is there with you. Why couldn't I get her?"

She focused back on me with a serious expression. "It's complicated. Now listen, your sister is going to be charged for the death of Joseph Ledbetter."

"What are you talking about?" I leaned forward.

"Jena Lynn inadvertently poisoned the man. All the evidence points to her." Mama's image started to fade. "Help her . . ."

"Mama, wait!"

She was gone.

Chapter 7

Ten minutes later I was hauling tail back into the sheriff's department. Jena Lynn's car was still parked out front. My heart rate became erratic as I took the steps two at a time.

The cubicles were empty when I rounded the corner, running smack into Alex and Eddie having a heated discussion. Whatever they were discussing had Eddie's face contorted in disapproval.

"What's going on?" I was unable to hide the trepidation in my tone.

Both men turned in my direction. Eddie's eyes held a wild glint. The only other time I'd seen that look was when he knew it was over with Mama and there was nothing he could do to alter it. Control issues were a family trait. When he nodded to his office and moved there swiftly, I followed.

Alex took my hand right before I made it to the door. "I'm here if you need me," was all he said, his dark gaze locked on mine for a couple of beats before he released my hand and moved with a purpose toward his cubicle.

I swallowed hard and crossed the threshold to my father's office, closing the door behind me.

Eddie was leaning against the front of his desk, his face weary. His office was a small twelve-by-fourteen-foot space, containing a metal desk, a couple of chairs, and an old-school filing cabinet off to the side. On his desk were two old picture frames holding a picture of a much younger me and a fishing picture of Eddie with his arm around Sam's shoulders as he held up his catch, both men beaming.

Despite the issues he and I had over the years, he'd been the only semblance of a father I had growing up, and right now that was enough. Jena Lynn's earlier words echoed back to me. *He loves you. Don't let a bad decision on his and Mama's part ruin the relationship you can now have.* Shutting him out for so long weighed heavily on me.

"Why is Jena Lynn's car still outside?" I choked out over the lump in my throat. "I didn't see her anywhere." My knees were wobbly.

None of us in Peach Cove were accustomed to this sort of investigation. How could this have happened *here*? We lived on an island where people didn't have to lock their doors and children could walk to school by themselves.

"She's still being questioned," he said, and I felt the sting of tears.

He handed me his handkerchief, and I wiped

my nose. Eddie was the only man I ever knew who carried one.

"Sit down." Eddie kissed the top of my head and helped me into a chair. "Listen to me. You did really well in your interview, pumpkin, and I'm proud of you." He paused. "The report just came back."

"And?" I fisted the handkerchief. My mind raced. Mama's words, the odd order being canceled, and the unknown brand of sugar. *Please don't say it was in the sugar.*

"Arsenic. The bag of powdered sugar contains high levels of the poison."

My heart sank with the confirmation that Mama was a spirit and Nanny was right all along.

"I don't understand," I said.

"Someone laced the sugar with rat poison, and that poison was fed to Joseph Ledbetter," he said in a controlled tone only he could manage.

I stared, unblinking for a couple of seconds. "I followed all of that, Eddie, but who would dare tamper with our supplies? There must be some mistake."

"The tests were conclusive."

"Okay," I tried to grasp the situation, "then what can we do?"

His tone was gentle. "You don't remember anyone unusual hanging around the diner that day, do you?"

"There were the men in town for the turtle-hatching project and the reporter." He knew about them. They'd been questioned as well. "What about Ms. Brooks? She threatened him right in front of everyone."

His face softened.

Right, I was grasping. "But isn't that reasonable doubt? And what about Charlie? Did anyone talk to him?" Charlie Wallace, the diner's janitor, began his work after the diner closed for the night.

He hadn't been there this morning, and he certainly wasn't here now. Every muscle in my body tensed. Could Charlie have done this? And if so, why?

"We can't find Charlie. Jena Lynn said he cleaned the night of the incident, but with the diner being closed, she hasn't needed his services. His neighbors haven't seen him."

I chewed on my bottom lip. There had to be a way out of this. "Isn't the family always suspected in crimes like these? Carl would have motive. Jena Lynn doesn't."

"We're considering everyone, pumpkin."

"Do you know if Charlie might have something against Mr. Ledbetter?"

"Joseph Ledbetter had issues with a lot of people." Eddie's face was set in hard lines. "He certainly never concerned himself with pleasing his fellow man." My birth father had two very distinct tells I'd picked up on over the years. One when he got quiet—that was when you were in real trouble—and two, when his eyes softened, you were about to receive extremely bad news. He patted my hand, and I prepared myself for the bomb he was about to drop. "Everyone who worked in the diner had access to that storage room."

I nodded to signify I was following along.

"But Jena Lynn is the only one who used the poison."

"But Jena Lynn is here and Charlie is missing!" If that wasn't clear evidence, I didn't know what was.

"We're looking for him."

"Is Jena Lynn being arrested?" I became light-headed.

"Right now, she's a person of interest," he said, as if that would lessen the blow.

I deflated. "Mama, you were right," I mumbled.

"What was that?"

"Nothing." I stared at my fingernails. They looked terrible. I'd been picking away at the polish.

I started to plead my sister's case, to insist Eddie go before her and sing her praises to the detective and assure him she wasn't the one responsible. Realizing how juvenile that would sound, I refrained. It wouldn't matter what Eddie told the detective at this point. The evidence was all he would care about.

"Well, I guess someone needs to locate Charlie and get to the bottom of this mess."

My thoughts went back to what Mr. Ledbetter had given me. I should give it to Eddie. I glanced back at my lap. He closed his fist over both my hands.

"What is it?" he asked and I hesitated.

Why was I hesitating?

I blurted, "Mr. Ledbetter gave me something right before he died."

"What was it?" He was in full-blown sheriff mode now.

"It was a scrap of paper with some letters and numbers written on it. He said not to trust anyone with it."

"You didn't tell Detective Thornton?"

I cringed and he frowned.

"Where is it?"

"It's at the house in my purse." I expected him to scold me for forgetting my purse and driving here without my license, but he didn't.

"I'll come by the house and pick it up. Don't get your hopes up. It probably isn't anything we can use in your sister's defense."

It *was* important, it had to be.

"And," I began, "that reporter, Calhoun, he saw Mr. Ledbetter give it to me. He came by the house asking questions."

"He had no business showing up at your house."

I agreed with him one hundred percent.

"I'll have a word with him. All we need is some reporter sticking his nose where it doesn't belong."

"Can we reopen the diner?"

"I'll find out. You take your sister home and try to relax." Eddie brushed my cheek with the back of his knuckles. "You're my daughter, pumpkin," he whispered. "I would cut my left arm off to save you from pain."

Oh God, I'd been so horrible to him. He'd always reached out, calling and sending me cards on my birthday. He came to every school function that I could remember, even before I knew that he was my father. The resentment grew throughout the years and since Mama passed, I'd taken it all out on him. Intentionally ignoring his calls and not involving him more in my life. *No more.*

"Things just got all messed up. I'm sorry, Eddie."

He sighed. "I never should have let your mama talk me into keeping the secret that I was your father."

He pulled me to my feet and held me against his chest. I took in his scent of Old Spice and Irish Spring soap.

"I called Zach. He's on his way back and asked if you would stay with Jena Lynn until he gets home tonight."

I nodded against Eddie's chest.

I had Jena Lynn tucked away in her bed. The poor thing was understandably overwrought. At first she tried to be strong for me, but, in the end, she broke down. Her last words before she drifted off to sleep were, "Why can't we reopen the diner?" She reminded me that the tainted sugar bag had only contained enough for the frosting for one cake, which was odd. Rainey Lane had asked specifically for a fresh cake. That call forced Jena Lynn to use the powdered sugar. That led me to believe that someone must have impersonated my sister and phoned the company to cancel her order. The only people who would know those numbers and schedules or at least have access to them were employees. The words *don't trust anyone* played over and over in my mind. I hated to suspect the staff. Betsy was definitely out, no question about it. Heather took the call from Rainey Lane. I'd have to consider her.

The detective would want to close this case fast, and evidence to convict would be all he would search for. Mama had said Jena Lynn would be charged. As of this moment, she was only a person of interest, but I feared worse things were brewing.

I was sitting on the front porch of Jena Lynn's and Zach's beach house, going down a list of people to consider, when Zach drove up. He was a huge guy, standing a foot taller than me, with broad shoulders and a wide neck. He was the love of my sister's life.

"She's asleep," I said as he took the steps two at a time. "I gave her one of those sleeping pills she took when Mama was ill."

"Are they still effective?"

"I called Doc Tatum and she phoned in a refill."

"I just can't wrap my head around any of this," Zach said.

"I understand." Silence. "Hey, do you remember any weird rumors about Mr. Ledbetter floating around when we were younger?"

His face was weary. "Nothing more than he was a rounder and had a lot of women. Some of them married, I think. Did they find Charlie?"

"Not yet," I said, bewildered.

"They better, even if he isn't guilty. He could certainly shed some light on the situation. You need a ride home?"

I stood and stretched. "No. Sam and Felton dropped off Rust Bucket."

"Rust Bucket?"

I pointed to the old truck parked across the street.

"Ah, that's right. I think Jena Lynn mentioned

you were driving Paw-Paw's old truck." He had his hand on the doorknob.

I could tell he really wanted to get to my sister. "I'll call and check on her in the morning."

He reached out and touched my arm. "She was really happy about the two of you making amends."

I gave him a sad smile.

Chapter 8

I was snuggled in my bed, wrapped in a blanket cocoon, with the air on full blast.

"Wake up!" a loud voice shouted, and a hand grabbed my shoulder.

Jolting awake, I nearly leaped out of my skin and probably would have if the blankets hadn't held me hostage. My brother, Sam, was looming over me, wearing a navy Magellan fishing shirt and shorts.

"Good Lord, Sam! You scared me half to death!"

His shoulders were moving up and down in silent laughter.

"What are you doing here?" I squinted, shielding my eyes from the bright sunlight shining through the window and bouncing off the white bedroom furniture I'd grown up using.

"You didn't answer your cell, and the house phone has been disconnected." He tossed my robe onto the bed. "I have news."

"Coffee," I grunted and rubbed my eyes in an attempt to clear the cobwebs.

"I'll go start the pot."

Desperate for caffeine, I sat up, staring at the now-empty doorway, then flung my feet over the side of the bed. Sleep had eluded me until well after three a.m. My brain wouldn't shut down. I'd spent half an hour calling to Mama. She never showed. I snatched my cell off the bedside table—yep, it was dead. In hindsight, I shouldn't have instructed Jena Lynn to disconnect the landline.

"Cute," Sam said, as I stumbled into the kitchen.

I glanced at my fruit-covered sleep shorts and T-shirt and shrugged. They weren't stylish, but man, were they comfy. I secured my robe and ran a hand through my hair, making me suddenly aware that I had major bedhead going on. The benefits of being single.

"You going fishing?" I croaked, when the aroma of a steaming hot brew greeted me.

"I was. Can't now." My brother thrust a mug into my open hand, and I sat down at the table. "They found Charlie last night." He took the seat across from me.

"Oh, well, that's good, isn't it? Now maybe we can get some answers."

Sam's face looked grim. "His boat is docked next to mine. When I got out there, I thought, what the hey? I went aboard. I found him. Dead."

My mouth fell open. "Did someone kill him?"

Sam averted his gaze. "They said it looks as if he had a heart attack."

"But . . . you're not sure you believe them?" I cradled the warm mug between my hands.

"It was the way he was lying. Like he'd fought with someone." Sam busied himself with stirring sugar into his mug. "I don't know. Dad said it appears legit."

Charlie's cause of death wasn't sitting well with either of us. The department had been searching for him. Surely the man's boat would have been searched first, after his house, that was. And even if it was a heart attack, it was mighty convenient he just happened to have one during the investigation. Perhaps it was a bit presumptuous of me to question the prowess of our boys in blue, but this was too important not to. "Did they tell you when his boat was first searched?"

"It had been searched a couple of times. I had to give another statement." My brother's left eyelid drooped a bit, giving the illusion of a dramatically smaller eye, his tell for exhaustion. "I'm just so sick of all this."

"Me too."

Eddie hadn't come by last night, so I was still in possession of the evidence. I suppose he would make a trip out later today, but I had questions now.

"What are you doing?" Sam asked as I gulped the contents of the mug and abruptly stood.

"I'm getting dressed, and we're going down to have a chat with our father."

The floorboard of Sam's truck was full of Coke cans. They kept rattling together and hitting my ankles with every turn. I should have worn my Nikes instead of flip-flops.

I kicked a couple cans. "Do you ever clean out this truck?"

He opened his mouth. I was certain he had a smart comment to hurl my way, but the flashing lights stunned us both into silence. Jena Lynn was being taken out of the black Lincoln by Detective Thornton in cuffs, and Zach was being restrained. Fury radiated off him, and Alex, who was doing his best to hold him back, was looking a little uneasy.

The two men had known each other their whole lives. It was like brother being forced to turn on brother. I hated this! I didn't wait for Sam to park. I leaped out of the truck when he slowed down to go around the corner and ran full speed toward the department.

Felton Powell grabbed me, his meaty hands gripping my rib cage a little too tightly as he held my back against his pudgy midsection. "Just let them do their job, Marygene. None of us like this, but it's out of our hands now."

I stared up at Felton. Rays of sunshine reflected off his shiny bald head. I found this momentarily distracting.

"I thought she was just a person of interest. What changed since yesterday?" I forced out through a dry throat.

"Evidence was recovered from her hard drive," Felton whispered in my ear and walked me around the corner and out of sight. "We found a bill of sale for arsenic in Jena Lynn's name, bought with her credit card."

I stared at him, attempting to process the information. "Okay. Maybe she bought it to kill pests," I mumbled almost incoherently.

"She bought it from some shady online site. If she needed it for rodents or something, she would have gone to the hardware store in town." Felton turned to leave.

Has everyone gone insane? I grabbed his upper arm. He glared down his nose at me.

"If the item was bought online, anyone could have gotten her credit card information and used that to frame her."

"I've got to go. I've said too much already." Felton left me standing in the alley.

The cement held me as tightly as if it were quicksand. I forced myself to move, lifting my head and squaring my shoulders as I marched up the department steps. Someone had to answer for this.

The phone was wedged against Eddie's ear when I barged into his office. He motioned for me to sit, then his finger went to his lips. I obeyed. He was discussing something about legal fees. When the conversation concluded, he opened with, "Your cell phone went straight to voice mail." He *had* tried to call me and give me a heads-up.

"It's dead. Sam came by and woke me up." I relayed what I understood via Felton then lifted my palms. "That detective can't possibly believe Jena Lynn did this."

"Felton shouldn't have told you anything." He

gave me a loaded stare that I read loud and clear. Eddie would protect his deputy and I respected that.

"I was mistaken. He didn't tell me anything," I said.

Then he confirmed what Felton had told me was accurate. "The evidence against her is, in my opinion, circumstantial. She has no motive."

I felt better hearing that.

"However, she is going to be charged."

"She can't be. We have to do something," I shrieked.

"Calm down. I put a call in to an attorney I know in Savannah. He owes me a favor and I called in to collect. This was done before you, Sam, or Jena Lynn were interviewed. Alex was on standby to barge into either of the rooms during the interrogation if necessary. He was instructed to notify Detective Thornton that your attorney was on his way and you would be waiting for him before you answered any more questions." Eddie was doing his best to look out for us all, yet Jena Lynn was still going to be charged.

"He should already be here. He was parking when we hung up." Eddie ran both hands through his graying blond hair. He had the shadow of a beard and his uniform wasn't pressed.

"We need to tear this island apart and find the person responsible before anything goes to trial."

"And you know I will," Eddie reassured me. "This case is going to have to be handled delicately."

Sam flew into the office and slammed the door. "Did y'all see that Jena Lynn is getting booked?

That attorney out there said you called him and he's saying that it's okay. How can that be okay?" Sam was swinging his arms, his hands fisted.

"I did call him, son. Let the man do his job."

Sam snorted and began swearing a blue streak.

"Now calm down, both of you. I have more bad news."

Terrific.

"Detective Thornton is petitioning the court to keep the diner closed a while longer."

"Why?" I asked while Sam said, "They can't do that!"

"It's been presented as a safety precaution for the island's residents. Since Jena Lynn has no obvious motive, they're making a case that perhaps she was targeting more than just Joseph Ledbetter."

That detective was trying to nail my sister and bankrupt our entire family in the process! Sam was livid. I was more focused on what he hadn't said. If they were making the case that Jena Lynn had acted alone, they should allow the rest of us to reopen the diner since she was in custody. They weren't, and that spoke volumes to me.

It was obvious when Eddie confirmed I was putting the pieces together. "Both of you go home." His face closed when I opened my mouth to protest. He wouldn't be indulging my brother or me any further. "This department is going to be under major scrutiny. We just don't have murder cases 'round here."

He was right. I understood that, but this was Jena Lynn we were talking about.

"You're her sister and I'm your father," he put his hand on my shoulder. "They're going to be scrutinizing my every move. Now, I don't think we're going to be overrun by staties or anything, especially with all those riots going on in the city."

Atlanta had issues with droves of people protesting after a trial surrounding a police officer that didn't go the way the people thought it should. They'd shut down major intersections and expressways. It was a mess, and I grieved for those affected.

Sam grumbled and groaned but, in the end, we both knew Eddie wouldn't budge. Plus, he was correct. Our presence in the precinct would only worsen matters for my sister. I left the office, shoulder to shoulder with my brother. Well, my shoulder to his rib cage, but my head was held high. I made Eddie swear to let me know about the bail hearing the second he found out the court date. That attorney he called in the favor from better be extremely good. My insides were so twisted up, I didn't know what to do.

Sam and I parted ways after we left the sheriff's department. For all I knew, the detective suspected he and I were both in on it, or at least had prior knowledge, but there was no sense worrying Sam with this suspicion. Especially when there wasn't a darn thing he could do about it.

The Peach had been cordoned off with new yellow police tape this morning. The sunlight danced on the polyethylene plastic in a taunting way. A holy anger welled up within my gut at the sight. This place had been built and run by the blood, sweat, and tears of *my* family for a hundred years. I had to do something. I couldn't just sit by and allow the diner to remain closed or my sister to go down for the crime. Jena Lynn would get her precious diner back, even if it killed me.

Moisture beaded on my forehead and between my shoulder blades, and I still couldn't move from this spot. It was a muggy morning. One of those on the island where salt from the Atlantic stuck to your skin and made it itch. Your hair was always wet with perspiration around your neckline, ears, and forehead. A storm could be brewing over the ocean and make landfall at any time. Or it could simply change directions and move around us. That was what this felt like emotionally too. That life as we knew it hung in the balance, victims of this violent situational storm.

A few pedestrians passed by, avoiding eye contact. I heard whispers behind me.

I fought the urge to shout, "My sister is innocent!"

"Marygene." Felton put a hand on my shoulder. "Eddie sent me out here. Why don't you let me take you home?" He awkwardly wrapped his arm around my shoulders. He always was a real unusual guy when it came to girls. He stepped away.

"Okay. Thanks, Felton." The moment's awkwardness made me uneasy.

"Sorry." He stared down at me, his expression unreadable.

"There's nothing to apologize for."

"I guess."

Poor guy always had it hard growing up. The

rumors surrounding his mama weren't pretty. His daddy hadn't been an upstanding member of the community either. I was proud of how well Felton had overcome his trials.

"This is hard on everyone."

He rubbed his bald head. "Yeah. We finally got Zach to calm down. He wouldn't go home, though. Alex is talking him off the ledge. That's why he didn't come out here. He wanted to." He made direct eye contact with me. Was that supposed to make me feel better? "My car is this way." He pointed down the block.

We walked in silence. I was having an internal strategy session on how to effectively convince Felton to help me get to the bottom of this. Especially since the consequences could be steep if the detective got wind of his involvement. Felton could lose his badge. Eddie would be furious with me if he knew I was even contemplating recruiting his deputy. If he said no, there was always Alex. They both knew Jena Lynn. Her innocence surely wasn't up for debate.

"I can't believe Marygene Brown—well, I guess it's Hutchinson now—hasn't aged a day." He held open the passenger side door.

I slid into the car. "It's Brown. I never changed it. But, that's nice of you to say. Although, the last couple of days I feel like I've aged ten years."

He reached over and patted my shoulder.

"The divorce close to being final?" He pulled around the square.

"That's what my lawyer keeps saying." I sighed.

"But, if it doesn't, I may become a widow really soon." I crossed my fingers, making a joke to try and lighten the mood. It wasn't until the last word left my lips that I realized how inappropriate it had been under the current circumstances.

I was relieved when he laughed.

Chapter 9

"I guess this wasn't the homecoming you imagined," Felton said as he wrapped both fists around the steering wheel. That was the understatement of the century. "Heather said you are living at your mama's old place?"

"Yeah, on Cloverdale." I turned in my seat to face him. "So, what brought you back to the island?"

He glanced my way before focusing back on the road. "Well, you know, life in Savannah didn't exactly work out as I planned."

Nothing ever does. "I know Heather is glad you're back."

He rubbed the top of his head. Nervous habit? It was new.

"What made you shave it?"

"Huh?"

"Your head. I was curious why you decided to shave it all off?"

He took a left out of the square. "Oh." His laugh sounded forced. "I have the Powell hairline. The result was inevitable, so I just went with it."

"Well, it suits you."

"Sorry you're having to deal with all of this," he said with obvious sincerity.

"It's mostly Jena Lynn who's having to deal. Surely Eddie will be able to get her out of it." I prayed that was true. Talking about this felt surreal.

The rest of the way we rode in silence, with only the sound of the scanner continually reminding me of the mess my sister was in. When Felton pulled down the long driveway, I let out a heavy sigh. My arms and legs felt like they weighed a ton. All of this was taking its toll.

"Want to come in for a glass of tea?" Even though life was unraveling at the seams, he'd gone out of his way to take me home, so the least I could do was have him in for a glass of iced tea. Southern hospitality didn't wane during a crisis.

"I'll take a cup of coffee if you have it. Just give me five minutes to make a phone call and I'll be in."

I nodded and opened the car door. The smell of rain was in the air, and the dark sky was filled with heavy clouds. That storm might happen after all.

Four large suitcases and several large boxes sat on the front porch. A note was taped to the first box.

Mary,
   I had the housekeeper pack all your clothing and basic items she believed you would need. See, I can compromise. I do hope we can reach an agreement before we both become financially destitute.

Peter

Obviously that secretary hadn't relayed my request to end this. Not having the bandwidth to deal with this now, I rolled the bags into the foyer. Then I shoved the boxes in beside them.

The house felt emptier than usual. I glanced up at the stupid family photo on the wall, my sister beaming back at me. Jena Lynn must be beside herself. Then a thought hit me. It could have been me who made the cake. Not in a million years would it have occurred to me that the sugar could have been tampered with. Honestly, I would have rather it been me instead of my poor sister. Could it be possible that someone was simply targeting my sister or the diner? No, that didn't make sense. *Think, Marygene, think.*

I shuddered at the thought that Jena Lynn could have sampled the frosting. If she had, it could have killed her. Who knew how much was too much?

I plodded into the kitchen. Jena Lynn had left her notebook on the table the last time she was here. I closed it and moved it onto the large hutch Mama had kept all her porcelain knickknacks in. The little clown holding a balloon while petting a puppy began to rock. Spooked, I leaped backward, gawking as the Precious Moments figurine next to it fell forward, clanging against the glass.

Was I crazy or had those things just moved on their own? "Seriously, Mama. These parlor tricks are beneath you." I slowly spun around in a circle, "If you know who is behind this, tell me." Nothing. "Help me, dammit!"

Still nothing.

A trinket fell forward against the glass. My tone was unsteady. "Fine. If you're not here to help, then leave!" It would be just like her to cause trouble when Jena Lynn and I were getting along so well. Why would she come by and caution me and then disappear? She was useless. In the kitchen, I grabbed a santoku knife from the knife block and raised it toward the ceiling. "If you're here and refuse to show yourself, to help me save Jena Lynn, then I swear to all that's holy, I will stab myself just so I can die and cross over and beat the ever-loving fool out of you!"

When nothing happened, no lights flickered, a pot didn't come flying off the rack toward me, I was satisfied that if she received the message, I'd effectively scared her off for now.

I had the coffee scooped into the filter and was filling the pot with water when the screen door clanged shut. Water sloshed over the top of the coffee maker. *Get a grip, Marygene.*

Felton strolled into the kitchen and parked himself at the table without a word.

"Coffee should be ready in just a minute." I made sure my tone was even.

"Thanks." He folded his large hands on the table. There was a tan line where a wedding ring would be. Heather hadn't mentioned he was recently divorced. Not that it was a big deal or anything, but the information could be useful. Finding the common denominator was my specialty.

I poured him a cup of coffee and set it on the table in front of him.

"I spoke with the sheriff. He wanted to make sure you got home okay. He said he'd come by and check on you later."

To get the scrap of paper, I assumed.

"You guys getting along better these days?"

No sense in letting him in on our family business. "You take cream and sugar?" I placed a plate of pastries I had individually wrapped in cellophane, a habit of mine, in front of him. I bake when I am stressed—eat too.

He hesitated for a moment, and I snorted in disgust, took a turnover, and bit into it. Then he reached out, grabbed one, and devoured it in two bites, flakes of buttery pastry left on his lips. "Black's fine."

Apparently, he had his doubts about me. I was beginning to become annoyed with Felton.

Taking a seat across from him, I watched him chew, swallow, and take a sip from the mug. When Felton caught me staring, he quickly glanced away. What motivated Felton? It sure would be advantageous to us if we had someone other than Eddie on the inside helping us with this case. But did I want someone who had doubts about my sister's innocence?

"So . . ." I began.

"I can't talk with you about the specifics of the case. Please don't ask me to. You should know better, with your dad being the sheriff and all."

In my humble opinion, I deemed his response a little snippy and uncalled for.

"I wasn't going to ask anything inappropriate," I muttered, hiding my growing agitation. He'd been so forthcoming earlier. Eddie must have issued a warning. I should have known better than to divulge my source. "You divorced?"

A few years back, his grandmother had told Jena Lynn he'd been engaged to a woman with means whose father was some big-shot attorney in Savannah. Felton had been working for him after he received his degree in criminal justice.

He took another sip from the mug and set it on the table. "Divorced."

"Sorry to hear that. It can be difficult having to start all over again."

He shrugged, not elaborating further.

"Heather seems really happy."

"She's been helpful to me."

I was sure that would make Heather happy. "Hey, I want you to know I'm here for you, if you need to talk. Coming back to the island couldn't have been easy for you."

His jaw clenched. Uh-oh. "I left the past where it belongs. I have every right to be back here. Same as you."

"I didn't mean that."

Felton was touchy about his past. I never should have gone there.

"I just meant, with the divorce and all." I pushed the plate of pastries closer to him. "The department is already investigating other possibilities, right? Surely you guys have some leads."

He made a face, showing me his distaste for my

inability to respect his earlier request. "Marygene, please," he said softly and scooted his chair uncomfortably close to mine. "I like you. I always have." He reached out and took my hands. "This is hard on you. I get that. But I have a job to do and I plan on doing it."

What was he getting at? Did he believe Jena Lynn was guilty? Did he think I was involved? I was so taken aback by his statement, I was momentarily at a loss for words.

He continued, "I'm going to give you one piece of advice, and I can't elaborate further. It might be best for you to go back to Atlanta." My back stiffened and he tightened his grip on my hands. "Just until this whole thing is settled."

The back door burst open, and Betsy came rushing in. "Oh, my sweet Lord, Marygene! I just heard! It's all everyone's talking about. Some of those idiots even believe Jena Lynn is guilty. I can't—"

She spied Felton holding my hands. He released his hold and rose to his feet.

"Felton, I wondered whose patrol car was parked outside. You better not be arresting her!" Betsy wagged her finger in his face. "She ain't got nothing to do with Mr. Ledbetter's death, and neither does Jena Lynn. Everyone at the diner is innocent! You should be ashamed of yourself. Does your granny know you're over here persecuting God-fearing Christians for deeds they haven't done?"

God bless her. Betsy was so outraged she was ready to take a swing at him.

"He's not arresting me. Eddie asked him to escort me home," I told her.

"I'll see you later." He reached out and squeezed my arm in a reassuring sort of way. "Think about what I said." He gave a curt nod toward Betsy.

When the door closed, Betsy peeked out the window. "I just can't believe it. Poppy Davis who works over at the Beauty Spot said the Ledbetters brought in some fancy-shmancy attorney from out of town." She turned toward me. "Someone big from the DA's office to prosecute Jena Lynn."

I pinched the bridge of my nose.

Chapter 10

"This stinks to high heaven." Betsy paced the floor next to the counter, where she'd just placed the bags she'd carried in. "I brought wine."

"How is wine going to help?"

"Honey, wine always helps." She uncorked a bottle and poured two tall glasses full. "I bet the Ledbetters had him whacked because he was costing them money. Or it was Ms. Brooks. You heard her threatenin' him, all brazen-like. They should have arrested her wrinkly old ass instead of Jena Lynn." Betsy gulped down the entire glass.

"You better not let Yvonne hear you say that. I am planning on having a chat with Ms. Brooks, though, I certainly don't believe she did it. She obviously has dirt on the old man, and, to establish a motive, we have to find out all that we can."

"You know, I'm going to have a talk with Alex. See if he can do some investigatin' on the side for us."

I held my hand up. "I don't think that's wise. We don't want to get him in trouble with Eddie."

"We won't. I saw him lookin' at you while we were all waiting to be interviewed. He seems over you trying to kill him now."

I closed my eyes and tried to count to ten—I made it to three. "I wasn't trying to kill him!" I slammed my hand on the table for emphasis.

"You hit him over the head with a wine bottle and kicked him in the nuts before shoving him overboard." Betsy smirked. She was always reminding me of why he and I hadn't worked out. Even though he was her cousin, she hadn't been on his side. "Not that your treatment didn't serve him right, for allowing Rainey Lane to paw all over him. You should have flung her overboard. She deserved it most."

"Oh, right, blame Rainey Lane, yes, she's an evil, conniving narcissist, but Alex wasn't doing much to shake her loose. In fact, he had a little smile going on."

"Marygene, don't be like that. It's been years, and you were broken up at the time."

"I'm not upset about it. I just don't like it when everyone portrays him as the victim," I muttered. "I've been over him for ages."

"You always hold grudges. It's not healthy."

"No, I don't." *Do I?*

She scrunched up her face in disapproval.

Okay. I was being completely foolish now. There was no way I was going to sit back and harbor sore feelings while my sister rotted away in prison.

"Yeah, okay, go ahead and call him. But feel him out about the case. Don't go asking him to break any rules. He might say no." I finished my glass of wine in two loud gulps. "I'm going to do a little digging on my own."

"Good idea. 'Cause if the island believes Jena Lynn is guilty, no one will want to eat at the diner again."

I held out my glass for a refill.

"I don't trust that detective. He was really rude to me."

"Me neither," I said.

Betsy's face scrunched up. "This is bad, Marygene. You could lose the business, and I'd be out of a job. It's hard to find work on a small island like Peach Cove." She chewed on the inside of her cheek. "I don't want to move to Savannah. It's full of tourists."

"Right, and just like everyone has mentioned on numerous occasions, this is the first murder this department has had to investigate. We have no confidence in Detective Thornton. He's an outsider, who is only after a guilty verdict. He doesn't care if she's guilty or not. And Felton actually had the audacity to tell me to leave the island."

Her mouth dropped open. "The nerve."

"How can we possibly rely solely on the efforts of the department with that detective at the helm?"

"We can't!" Betsy agreed.

"Exactly." The wine was going to my head fast. "No one is more motivated to find the killer than me. And where the sheriff's department's perseverance may wane, mine will not." Not that I believed Eddie would give up, but I had to face facts—his hands were effectively tied. Mine, if I stayed clear of the police, were free as a bird.

"Let's examine what we know," I said.

Betsy took a seat next to me. "Okay, I'm listening."

"Someone canceled Jena Lynn's order and put that poisoned sugar bag in the supply closet."

She nodded and took a sip from the glass.

"The bag of sugar Jena Lynn used, I'd not seen in there. You?"

"No, but I don't go in there often."

"Well either it was placed there the night before or in the wee hours of the morning, or maybe—"

"Or maybe she overlooked it," Betsy supplied.

"Charlie was working the night before, and now he is conveniently out of the picture."

"Poor Charlie. He was such a nice man." Betsy's tone was laced with sorrow. "What did Eddie say about Charlie's death?"

I tapped my forehead. I'd completely forgotten to ask any questions regarding Charlie. "I was solely focused on Jena Lynn when I was at the station." I made a mental note to have a chat with Eddie.

"Poor Jena Lynn. I hate to think of her behind bars." A tear leaked from Betsy's eye and traveled down her cheek.

"I know," I choked out. "But we have to be strong for her and focus. Eddie is looking after her."

Betsy nodded and wiped her face.

"I have another piece of evidence I'm going to tell you about."

Betsy sat forward.

"You have to swear not to mention it to Alex until Eddie does. I've told him about it. He's supposed to come by and get it."

"What is it?"

"When Mr. Ledbetter slumped over on me, he shoved a wadded scrap of paper into my hand. He had a death grip on my right hand, Bets."

She stared at me in disbelief.

"He whispered to me not to trust anyone." I relayed the letter and number sequence. I'd memorized it after I decided to give it over to Eddie.

"What does that mean?" She stared, unblinking.

"I don't know. Another thing is that the reporter, Roy Calhoun, who was eating at the diner saw him give it to me. Or he suspects he gave me something." I gave her a quick summary of what was said the day Calhoun dropped by unannounced.

"What if he's involved and he's worried you have information that will put him away?" Betsy made a point that I hadn't thought of.

"What about fingerprints on the sugar bag?" she asked at random. "Maybe his are on it."

"They probably wore gloves. I would have." *Think like a murderer. Now, how does a murderer seek out his victims?* It depended on the type of murder. "I think we need to go through all of Mr. Ledbetter's belongings. There must be something in there to decipher what the letters and numbers are referencing. He probably wouldn't have given it to me if it wasn't a clue to the truth.

"The more I think about it, the more I believe the reporter Calhoun was right," I said. "Mr. Ledbetter must have known his time was coming. But why? I mean, if you think about all the murders that take place, the common threads are usually a couple of things."

"Money, love, or obsession," Betsy supplied.

"Right, plus greed, ambition, jealously, or perhaps revenge. This doesn't feel like a crime of passion. I don't see some widow taking him out because he isn't a one-woman man."

Betsy laughed.

"I know the old goat wasn't loved by everyone, like some of our elderly are, but," she sighed, "he was honest, and that is a quality I appreciate in a man. He called it like he saw it."

I wasn't so sure about the honest part. He wasn't so honest in his behavior when he was cheating on his wife in his younger days, or so I'd been told.

I poured myself another glass of wine.

Chapter 11

The ringing of my iPhone startled me into consciousness the next morning. I'd stayed up late drinking wine and strategizing, so it felt as if I'd just drifted off. It took me a second to orient myself. The large mahogany bedroom furniture was much nicer than the white girly furniture I grew up using. Ah, I was in Mama's room—no, scratch that, *my* room. I vaguely recalled Betsy's and my conversation when I'd announced I was kicking Mama's ghostly butt out of the house by moving into her room.

Betsy and I had been drinking on the back porch, enjoying the breeze, and I'd officially worked myself into a tizzy with all the *what-ifs* going through my brain. "What if I can't find the killer, Betsy?"

"You will. We'll investigate everyone if necessary."

An eerie howling had commenced through the trees.

"Oh God, do you believe in spirits?" Betsy had slurred, after having a few too many.

"I think I do." I sat up straighter on the swing. "I believe Mama is haunting this place." I told her about Mama predicting a death in the diner and my sister being charged with the crime.

Petrified, Betsy shouted, "I can't sleep in no haunted house, and I'm too tipsy to drive home! We've got to do something about your spook mama!"

"We do! She hasn't been any help, and when I tried to summon her, she never showed."

"Typical," Betsy snorted.

"Well, I'll kick her out! I can move into her room and spread all my good juju. My room's too small and doesn't have its own bathroom." Yes, that was exactly what I should do. "You hear that, Mama? I'm kicking you out!" I said to the porch ceiling with a chuckle of satisfaction.

"I'll get some sage and burn it in *your* new room!" Betsy shouted upward.

"Let's do it!" I hopped off the swing so quickly that I missed my footing and slipped, hitting my head against the porch rail. "Ouch, sweet baby Moses! I'm still taking that room!" I shouted at Mama and shook my fists toward the sky. I stood and rubbed my aching head. "She always had to have the last word. Well, not tonight!"

I kicked the porch spindles several times, just in case she was near, then stamped my feet.

"Get her, Marygene! Get her good!" Betsy had encouraged and started doing a little stomping of her own.

No wonder my head was aching now. Alcohol,

Betsy, and superstitions didn't mix well. My hand fumbled around on the bedside table until I managed to find the still ringing phone.

"Marygene, you awake?" my brother asked.

"Barely," I mumbled, my face smashed into the pillow.

"Well, make some coffee! You've got to go to the emergency town hall meeting and stand in for Jena Lynn."

I sat up. "What are you talking about? What meeting?"

"The mayor is hosting a meeting with the business and large beachfront property owners this morning. Those real-estate developers are close to a majority vote this time."

The mayor never held an emergency meeting for developers. Why would he start now? "These are the same ones that failed to get enough interest a couple of weeks ago?"

"I think so. I got a heads-up call from a buddy of mine at the courthouse. Jena Lynn is unable to attend, so you should go. The Peach needs a representative. It starts in half an hour. Zach will meet you there."

Something else to worry about. *Great. Just great.*

I showered and dressed in record time, choosing my cream linen pantsuit and white heeled pumps.

It had taken me ten minutes to find a place to park and haul it into the municipal building. The doors were closed in the largest courtroom, and I could hear voices inside. I was late.

I decided to go around and sneak in through the side door. The heavy steel door creaked as I slipped inside. The room was jam-packed. Heads turned in my direction. Embarrassment overtook me and my face burned.

Zach was seated over on the left side of the room. I scurried toward him, my head down, and slid onto the bench.

"You're late," he whispered.

"Sorry. But I'm here now."

Zach was alone, so I assumed he was the one representing his family's construction company.

The woman at the front of the room was tall and lean, with the darkest black hair I'd ever seen. She had a condescending air about her. She was giving the usual spiel. How nothing in our lives would change once the resorts were in place, except we'd be rich. That tourism would be a wonderful thing for our island. Our beaches would be protected and well kept. The increase of foot traffic would keep local businesses afloat. *Blah blah blah.*

I'd never been one to get involved in island politics. Now I would fight tooth and nail to keep my family's business the way my nanny wanted it. In *our* family with *no* outside interference.

Nanny and Mama had fought the investors their entire adult lives. Now it was time to take up the torch and be the responsible business owner Nanny had always believed me to be. I wouldn't let her or my sister down.

When the woman finished, the mayor, Bill

Gentry, stood. He was a small, gray, round man in his late fifties. He always played Santa Claus at Christmas. The suit fit him perfectly. "Thank you, Miss Waters."

"Tally, please."

Mayor Bill smiled. "Now, this meeting will remain civil." His voice boomed. "I open the floor for questions."

"Is that the woman Jena Lynn had it out with?" I asked Zach.

He gave me a tight nod. That Jena Lynn had stood up to a woman like that made me even more proud of her.

"Have you spoken to her? Jena Lynn."

"She's getting bail." I let out a huge sigh.

Ms. Brooks stood. "You said the offers you sent out would be increased by twenty or twenty-five percent?"

Yvonne sat next to her mama.

"If we can get a majority vote, then the offer will be increased to twenty-five percent," Miss Waters replied. "Plus . . ."

Ms. Brooks leaned forward and cupped her hands beside her ears.

". . . a signing bonus of ten thousand dollars to those who agree without stipulations."

I snorted. She was making a deal with the devil.

I couldn't believe Ms. Brooks was entertaining the notion.

"What counts as a stipulation?" Bonnie Butler,

owner of Bonnie's Boutique, the storefront next door to the diner, asked.

Miss Waters smiled. "Things like needing an enormous amount of time to pack and move off the premises." Enormous being two weeks.

"Don't you even think about it, Bonnie!" Gerald Collins shouted. "We discussed this at length a few weeks back. Now, after the Ledbetter murder, they're swarming like vultures and preying on our fears."

"An island resident reached out to us, and we would like to extend our aid, Mr. . . . ?" Miss Waters asked smoothly.

"It's Collins and I ain't buying that for one second. These big-city developers don't give a rat's ass about us! They want to take our birthright from us and use it to line their pockets. I vote no!"

"Me too!" A chorus of voices went up.

"Calm yourself, Gerald," the mayor warned.

A sudden hush fell over the crowd when Carl Ledbetter stood. This was the first time I'd noticed him among the audience. "My daddy loved this island. But even he saw reason in selling."

That wasn't what Mr. Ledbetter had announced to an audience at the diner the day he died.

"He was ready to sell, with the stipulation that he could live out his days in his villa." Carl took a minute to compose himself. "Did he always feel that way? No." Carl gave his head an exaggerated shake. "But he was up in age and, after the hurricane swept through several years back and he experienced a loss like a lot of people did, he began to wonder if the island could sustain itself without the aid of investors like Tally, who would bring in tourists' revenue."

The room was thick with mixed emotions. The weight of it made it hard for me to breathe.

"Carl, you should be ashamed of yourself. Your daddy's body ain't even cold yet and you're betraying him!" someone shouted from the back of the room.

"Don't you believe a word he's saying!" Poppy Davis, owner of the Beauty Spot, said. "Joseph Ledbetter would never have agreed to sell!"

Carl's face reddened. "What you people saw was a lovable and private man who didn't speak his business outside the family." Oh, he was laying it on thick now. Mr. Ledbetter used to let the world know his convictions.

"I'm grieving. My daddy was killed by a member of his own community." Carl pierced me with an accusing glare. "I'm here for him. To carry out his wishes and to save this island from ruin."

Before I knew what I was doing, I was on my feet. "You—" I cleared my throat. "You know good and well that Jena Lynn isn't responsible. She would never have hurt your daddy. She cared about him. Just like she cares about all of you. This island means everything to her," I said to the crowd and dried my palms on my capris. "She views y'all as her family." Some made eye contact with me, but not all. I was a bit disheartened.

Zach pulled on my arm, urging me to sit.

"My sister was the one going by Mr. Ledbetter's villa checking on him after his knee surgery."

Betsy had informed me of that. That got a few smiles and head nods.

"Where were you, Carl?"

Carl's brow beaded with perspiration. This wasn't a man overwrought with grief. This man was desperate. *Why?*

"Jena Lynn wouldn't hurt a fly!" someone shouted.

"This isn't the time or the place, Marygene," Mayor Bill said. "The case is under investigation. We need to leave this to the authorities."

Felton, who had been standing at the back of the room, started making his way to the front.

I ignored the warning glare he shot me. "She's innocent and everyone with a brain here knows it! Over our dead bodies will we ever vote to sell!"

Miss Waters gave me a cunning smile. A worthy adversary, her eyes were shouting.

That was when I recalled the threat she'd hurled at my sister. Did she make good on her threat to make my sister pay for calling her out? Would an investor go to such lengths to secure a deal? If so, she would need an accomplice, someone who knew the diner well and Jena Lynn's routine. That person had to be someone I knew, someone close to my family. My blood ran cold.

It hardly registered when Carl began speaking again.

Miss Waters and I were still locked in on each other when everything spiraled out of control. People were on their feet shouting. She gave me a little nod, which I took as a concession for this round of the fight. She knew as well as I that no vote would be taken today.

Chapter 12

Betsy came trudging down the stairs late that afternoon. She had slept the day away. She gave no indication she was feeling the aftereffects of last night's wine-drinking binge. She was quiet as I told her about the meeting. Her bottom lip poked out slightly before she said, "I can't believe you didn't wake me. I'm your wingman."

"You can be my wingman and drive me to the square in the morning. I want to talk to Poppy and then maybe Ms. Brooks."

She followed me into the kitchen, where I made a sandwich for each of us.

"I'll call Yvonne later and see if her mama's up for a visit."

"I'd just pop in," Betsy said. "You don't want her to have time to fabricate a story."

"I'm not worried about that." If anything, Ms. Brooks would probably be more likely to embellish than hold back. When the cheese was melted, I pulled the sandwiches from the griddle and plated them.

"You know, only a fool would buy what Carl was selling. Old man Ledbetter would never sell out." I handed her a plate and tossed her a bag of chips.

"Agreed. What did you hear about the confrontation between Jena Lynn and that Tally Waters?" I sat down at the table and took a bite of my sandwich.

"Only what I told you at the diner. Jena Lynn was hoppin' mad, though. That woman called her a couple of times to increase her offer." Betsy popped a chip into her mouth. "She came into the diner a couple of times too. Went on and on about how great the Sam's Surf and Turf Burger was."

"Which I'm sure Sam ate up."

Flattery got women everywhere with Sam.

"Yeah, he took her out too."

"What?" My brother dated the woman who had it out with Jena Lynn? He never said a word about it. Maybe that was why he didn't offer to go with me this morning. Could my own brother be inadvertently aiding this woman? It wouldn't be all that difficult for her to manipulate Sam. He wasn't stupid or anything, but he was weak when it came to women.

Betsy nodded. "Yep. She's scary, if you ask me. She has cold, lifeless eyes. Like a zombie." She gave an elaborate shiver and got up to refill her glass. "Want a Coke?"

"Sure."

"What kind?"

"Don't care."

She handed me a Sprite. "That reminds me. I waited on her the first time she came in. She was a real snot. I asked if she wanted a Coke or some tea? She said Coke, so I asked her what kind. She and her assistant started laughing. Went on about how Southerners referring to all soft drinks as Coke was absurd. They laughed like I wasn't even standing there. I could have slapped the spit out of her. But I'm a professional. Didn't even spit in her food."

I nearly choked on the chip I'd been chewing. "Good for you," I said when I managed to catch my breath.

"Anyway, she and Sam only went out a couple of times. That was before Jena Lynn gave her what for." Betsy drained her glass.

"She probably thought he could influence Jena Lynn."

Sam and I were overdue for a conversation.

"I'm going to get my laptop and do some googling on Tally Waters. Then I'm going over to see Jena Lynn."

"Good idea. I'll drive you to see our girl." Betsy said.

"That'd be great, thanks." I got up from the table and retrieved my laptop from one of the boxes that had been sent over. I'd opened them to see what the housekeeper deemed worthy to pack. She'd chosen well. Especially if she'd been restricted to just a few boxes.

"How's she holding up?"

"Eddie said she's hanging in there. She'll feel

better when she sees us." I sat back down at the table and typed Tally Waters's name into Google. She had a Facebook page; sadly, it was private. The only information visible was her divorced status and place of employment. Her other social media pages were much the same. I found a couple of write-ups about her success within her company. After a few more searches, I closed the computer no wiser regarding the woman on a mission to shake up our lives.

I wiped the steam from the bathroom mirror. It was 10 a.m., and I had received a call from my attorney at 9 a.m. with the news that Peter had signed the papers and, as of that moment, I was a free woman. It was the good news I needed after yesterday.

I didn't have to feel bad anymore. Peter's opinion of me no longer mattered. There would never be another trip to the emergency room with a broken finger or a black eye that I was forced to explain away as an accident. That part of my life was over and I had no intention of allowing anyone to control me again. Ever. Two and a half years of ups and downs. The last accident, my bruised neck, brought an end to my denial that he would change. I no longer believed the lies he told about the demon I'd brought out of him. His sickness was on *him*. And dammit, I knew my worth! I was my nanny's granddaughter. *A survivor.* It was in that moment that I knew I had to come home, rip Peter out of me by the roots, rebuild my relationships with my family, and start anew.

Perhaps the marriage had jaded me in some way. I was more suspicious of people. That was why Mr. Ledbetter's warning had rung true. I had trust issues on top of my trust issues.

I stared at my reflection. What did people see when they looked at me? A strong, independent woman in her prime? Perhaps they saw a young woman trying to find her way. Heaven forbid if they still saw Clara Brown's indiscretion.

I firmly believed my trials in life had strengthened me. I *was* a survivor. A trait Betsy and I shared. And it was what connected us on a level only women like us could understand. Would Jena Lynn be stronger after all of this? Perhaps. Though, her situation was completely different.

I pulled out my hair dryer from under the sink and retrieved my makeup bag from the second drawer of the vanity. Even though I didn't feel like making myself up, I had to. The bags under my eyes were a dead giveaway I was having trouble sleeping. Not that anyone would blame me. But there were people I needed to speak with today, and showing up with a face like a raccoon wouldn't do.

Down the hardwood stairs I went, in a pair of white capris, a turquoise top, and jeweled flip-flops just as there was a knock at the front door. I was expecting Betsy.

It was Eddie. He was dressed in his weekend clothes, navy cargos and a Hawaiian fishing shirt, quite a contrast from his usual uniform. It was a relaxed look, yet his posture was stiff. It took years off him.

"Come in," I said the second I opened the door.

He did, closing the door behind him. "I hear you started a ruckus at that meeting yesterday."

"No more than Nanny or Mama used to."

He grunted in response as he followed me into the kitchen.

I poured a cup of coffee for each of us. "Jena Lynn out on bail? I hated having to visit her in custody. Poor thing tried to be strong, but it was clearly visible to me just how frightened she is."

Eddie had made sure she was as comfortable as possible while awaiting arraignment. She was never even put in the general population, and for that we were all eternally grateful. Not that the little jail was overrun or anything, but my sister didn't belong with convicted criminals, no matter how petty the crime.

"Yes. Zach put up their beach house for the bond."

"Good." I turned and leaned against the counter.

I didn't ask about the case. He wouldn't discuss it with me openly. Rumors of Detective Thornton's influence were everywhere.

"Hey, what do you know about Tally Waters?"

"Not much." He leaned over and took a pastry off the white pedestal stand. "She's the representative of the Malcom Investment Corp. Why?"

I'd found out that much from my Google search.

"You know she threatened Jena Lynn?"

Eddie pointed his finger in my direction. "Don't go poking your nose in, Marygene. Let us handle the investigation. I'm not going to let your sister be convicted."

"So, you have leads then?"

He grunted again.

"Don't be like that. That detective thinks she's guilty. He isn't going to want to hang around here while you investigate other leads, now is he?"

"This is my job, little girl. Don't you go telling me how to do it." His tone was gentle yet firm. "Where's the paper Ledbetter gave you?"

I pressed. "He probably has his suspicions about us, too, you know?"

"The paper." Eddie held out his hand.

After I retrieved my purse from the breakfast table, I unzipped the side pocket and held the thin folded square between my fingers. I wasn't sure why I was hesitant to hand it over. I'd already taken pictures of the front and back with my cell and memorized the numbers. I turned to face him; his hand was still out. "The only people who could have known about the delivery that day to cancel it were those closest to her." I held out the paper, which he took from me with a napkin and placed in a little ziplock bag. "Diner employees."

Eddie showed no emotion; he had probably thought of this too.

"Charlie would have had access to that information. It wouldn't take a rocket scientist to find the order forms and numbers on the computer at the diner. Her credit card information would be simple to copy. Jena Lynn keeps her purse stowed in the bottom drawer of the desk in the office. It's awfully convenient that Charlie isn't around for questioning."

"Charlie died of a heart attack. We don't have

any proof that someone else placed the order." He regarded me with what I hoped was respect. "But it's a case that can be made in court."

"You're working that angle?"

He didn't respond.

"Felton and Alex are working it with you?"

He leaned forward and kissed me on the forehead. "Trust me. I'm doing everything I can." He put his mug down on the island. "Go see your sister. She isn't as strong as you are. And, Marygene," his tone was serious, "stay out of this."

Chapter 13

"Hey, Bets." I slid into the cream-colored leather seat of her red Camaro. "I'm a divorcée!"

"Woot! Woot!" Betsy cheered and we high-fived. "Now you can buy yourself a decent ride." She turned around in the front yard and drove down the driveway.

"I'll probably run into Savannah to that big car superstore and pick out another Prius." Betsy took a left on Cloverdale.

"You don't want another Prius. Buy something flashy and fun. In fact, I can run you over to Keith's Car Palace. Keith will get you a great deal. I bought mine from him." She caressed the steering wheel. "I love my baby."

It wouldn't hurt to take a gander at what Keith had in stock. The lot was tiny and his inventory limited, but he always had decent deals. Plus, he wouldn't dare sell any lemons. That would kill his business. Reputation was everything on the island.

"I hate to be a buzzkill." Betsy furrowed her brow and pressed her lips together as she reached between the seats. "Did you see this?" She deposited a copy of *The Island Gazette* in my lap.

Jena Lynn's face was plastered on the cover. The headline read, "Death by Chocolate." Underneath that was, "Local business owner indicted for murder." The article went on to describe the scene of the crime. With some colorful foodic additives, such as "killer cravings" and "dining experience not so peachy for local man."

"Are you freaking kidding me?" My mouth went slack. There was a tingling in my chest.

"It's bad, I know." Betsy reached over and gave me a pat on the shoulder. "This is going to be so bad for The Peach, even after we exonerate Jena Lynn." Betsy sounded so confident that we would succeed.

My fingers fumbled on the power window button on the doorframe. Several gulps of salty air later, I managed to calm down. Who had the audacity to write such an article? I nearly burst a blood vessel when I spied the name of Roy Calhoun. He didn't even work for the *Gazette*. His paper was out of Atlanta.

"It gets worse," Betsy said. "Page seven."

A nervous laugh left my lips. "How could it possibly get any worse?" I fumbled through the pages. Tally Waters had been interviewed. She stated that the investment group was excited about the prospects of igniting the economy and restoring the island to its glory days. She was photographed with Bonnie Butler, owner of Bonnie's Boutique, and Carl and

Rainey Lane Ledbetter. "We are close to a majority vote" was written under the image.

My phone buzzed in my wristlet. "Are we in *The Twilight Zone*? What is wrong with everybody?" I dug out my phone.

"Feels like it," Betsy agreed.

The text on my phone read, "I can explain the article. Let's meet tonight at 8:30. I'm at the Inn in room 14."

"I can help," came through next.

Then came, "This is Roy Calhoun."

How did he get my cell number? He was a reporter; of course he could easily track it down. *Get it together, Marygene.*

"Who is it?" Betsy asked.

"Calhoun. He has some nerve wanting to meet up after that article." Whether I should meet Calhoun or not wasn't an instant decision. I stared at the text, my phone gripped tightly in my hand. "The sheer gall of that man."

Betsy said, "I wouldn't be so quick to tell him off. He could be useful."

She was right. He could. He had somehow weaseled his way into our local paper and was able to get quotes from Bonnie, Tally, and Carl. People talked to him. "Sometimes you surprise me, Betsy Myers."

"Why thank you. I surprise a lot of people by not just being a pretty face."

We both laughed.

My shoulders relaxed and I texted back, "I'll try."

"Listen," I began after she drove around the

square for the third time in search of a parking space. "Just let me out and I'll run over and speak to Bonnie." I wanted to know why she was so interested in selling out all of a sudden. Had Tally tried to intimidate her the same way she had Jena Lynn?

"Okay. I'll pop in and speak to Poppy, and we can meet in the middle."

Betsy let me out in front of The Peach. The building was dark and empty. I rubbed the sore spot that had developed within my chest. *As God is my witness, my sister will have her precious diner back.* I forced my feet to move.

Located on the other side of The Peach was Bonnie's Boutique. I glanced at my watch. If memory served, she was usually styling the mannequin in her front window at this time of day. Bonnie was doing just that now, and she caught me scrutinizing her activity. I smiled, waved, and started toward the store. She returned my wave, but her smile wavered slightly. *Crap.* That didn't bode well. The sign on the front door still read CLOSED, forcing me to knock. The heavy sigh that sent her shoulders up and down made me wonder if she would even talk to me. When she flipped the sign and opened the door, I let out the tentative breath I'd been holding.

With the brightest smile I could manage, I greeted her. "Morning."

The scent of gardenia-blossom candles and cool air-conditioned air encompassed me.

"Morning, Marygene." She returned my greeting with much less vigor. Bonnie was a fashionable woman in her late sixties. She was plump, with a round face and big dyed red hair shaped like a football helmet. Today she was dressed in tan capris and a blue-and-white striped top. Her giant anchor earrings dangled to her jawline. "Can I help you find something in particular? With that figure, you could wear any style you please."

Women the age of my late mother constituted the clientele who kept the establishment afloat. There was absolutely nothing here I would wear. The designs were boxy, heavily floral styles with a large supply of striped patterns strategically designed to hide the imperfections of fifty-plus-aged women.

"That's so nice of you." I tried desperately to find the words to broach the subject. If I led off with an easy question, she might open up about Tally Waters. "I'm terribly sorry to disturb you while you're working, but I was wondering if you happened to notice any unusual activity the day of Mr. Ledbetter's passing?" There, that sounded nice.

Her orangey red–shaded lips pursed. "I have already given my statement to the authorities."

My smile was back in place. "Yes, I'm sure you did. Um, I was just wondering if perhaps something else came to mind since then. The diner being closed is terrible for the business on the square. You know the foot traffic that it brings in daily will suffer."

She nodded. She had benefited from the crowds that frequented our diner for breakfast, lunch, and dinner. Especially during the summer months, when it was just too hot for people to feel like cooking.

"Well, all I can do is tell you what I told Felton Powell yesterday and that detective a week or so ago. It was my busy time of day, and I had a steady stream of customers from the breakfast rush crowd. Avery was trying on the new black-and-white maxi dress." She pointed to the rack over in the corner. "It was perfect for her. She's well above average height and the flow fit lovely around her ankles."

I nodded and forced my face to show interest.

She paused, tapping her long, red acrylic fingernail against her front tooth. "It's probably nothing, but now that I think about it, I overhead Joseph and Felton arguing right outside the diner when you were having your hissy fit." She clucked her tongue. "Mighty unbecoming, my dear." *Great.* Everyone was a critic.

"It wasn't my finest hour."

She nodded her head in agreement.

"Did you hear what they were arguing about?"

"Well, let me think. It was kind of hard to hear over all that commotion."

The front door opened and a couple of ladies walked in. They spotted me and paused. For a second, it was obvious they were second-guessing their shopping trip.

Just terrific. You'd think I have a disease or something.

Their attitude could certainly bring my discovery efforts to a screeching halt.

Bonnie moved past me to greet the new arrivals. "Good morning, ladies." Bonnie had a nervous edge to her tone. "I have a secret sale going on, an additional forty percent off all clearance shoulder bags."

Both women perked up at the potential savings. After she directed them to the appropriate section of the store, she scurried back to me.

"Marygene, I'm going to have to ask you to leave. I loved your mama and you girls are dolls, but this is my livelihood here, and you hanging around is only going to be detrimental to my bottom line." She'd sounded a tad regretful. She huffed. "It was something about Joseph's son, I think. I only got bits and pieces. I think I heard, 'no son of mine' thrown in there." She practically shoved me toward the door.

"One more thing."

She paused, both hands on the door ready to close it on me.

"Tally Waters made you an offer that you considered accepting."

She was quiet.

"Why now? You were always in opposition to the previous developers and their proposals."

"That's really none of your business." She started to close the door.

I kept my shoulder wedged against it, holding it open. Her expression changed. I couldn't discern if it was anger or fear.

"It's my business and you know it! We stick together on this island. No outside development, ever. You were one of the people that stood shoulder to shoulder with Mama touting proudly that we were a

self-sustaining island with our local businesses and
no chain establishments."

"Things change. Get your foot out of my door
before I call the sheriff," she spat.

Startled by her venomous reaction, I didn't protest
when she slammed the door.

Who had gotten to Bonnie? Tally?

Chapter 14

Lost in thought, I meandered my way down the street. Mr. Mason stopped me as I passed his market. "You sure would have made your nanny proud at that meeting, little lady. If we all stick together, we can fight this, just like we always have."

The corners of my lips turned up in a genuine smile.

He took my hand. "You and Jena Lynn have all my support. If you need me to set up a donation jar for her, just say the word."

The lump in my throat forced me silent. I wasn't alone. *We* weren't alone.

Mr. Mason was a smallish man, about five foot seven, give or take, with a hefty midsection. What he didn't have in height, he made up for with heart. Chest hair was always poking up around the collar of his shirt. He reminded me of a cuddly teddy bear.

"Thank you." I forced my voice to cooperate. "My sister will be so grateful for your support." I squeezed his hand before we parted.

I was stopped three more times by others offering their prayers and support for my sister before I reached Betsy, who was standing in front of the Beauty Spot with Yvonne, who had her little white fur baby Izzy tucked against her chest. Yvonne looked tall, standing nearly a half foot taller than Betsy.

"You need to talk to Poppy," Betsy said the second I reached them.

"Okay. I'll be in shortly."

Betsy nodded and went inside the salon.

"Hey, don't you look pretty," I said as Yvonne embraced me.

She was blonder than I was today. Her face had a beautiful healthy glow. She'd obviously spent some time on the beach since returning home.

"Hello, Izzy," I said in my baby voice as I stroked her little white head.

Izzy's tail wagged.

"You look tired." Yvonne's brow crinkled. "I can't believe all this business with Jena Lynn and the closing of your diner. I was as mad as a hornet when I read this morning's paper. How are you holding up?"

I sighed. "My divorce came through."

"It's about time. How did you fare?"

"Not as well as my attorney had hoped. Truthfully, though, I don't care. I'm just glad it's over."

"Well then, I'm glad for you."

We settled into silence as she stroked Izzy's head and focused on her car parked at the curb.

"Well, are you going to tell me about this business with the developers?" It came out more confrontational than I intended. My tone sounded on edge, even to me.

Yvonne blew out a breath, "Please don't start. Mama is set on selling. She's getting up in age, and I'm thinking of moving her into Sunset Hills." Okay, that made sense.

I assumed Yvonne would take over the property like I had with my mama's.

"Okay. I'm sorry. I didn't mean to—"

"I know." She waved her hand. "Jeez Louise, my life is running me ragged the last couple of days. I shouldn't have snapped at you."

"You want to talk about it?"

A flush crept across her cheeks. "My problems can wait. Please tell me what I can do to help?"

I hesitated. "Would it be horrible of me to ask to speak with your mama?" Her face altered and I rushed to add, "Not about the development deal."

"I don't know, Marygene. She's not as strong as she once was, and I don't want you upsetting her."

"I won't. I just want a few minutes, then I'll leave it alone."

"Fine. But not at the house." She sighed. "That place is so cluttered it looks like an episode of *Hoarders*. We can meet for dinner at the Pier Bar and Grill. Say seven?"

That could work. If I decided to swing by the inn and speak with Calhoun, I could do it after. "Sounds good." A public setting wasn't ideal, but I'd take what I could get. "So, we're okay?"

Yvonne smiled. "Of course we are. Neither one of us has asked for the position we've been forced into." She put Izzy down by her side and moved the leash to her other hand. "Betsy's right. You should go talk to Poppy." Yvonne leaned closer as Izzy sniffed around. "I was having lowlights put in this morning, and she got to talking about the meeting and . . ."

An older woman passed us on the street.

"I'll just let her tell you. See you tonight." She hugged me and left.

Poppy was just putting Ms. Maybelle under the dryer when I walked in, and Betsy was spinning around in one of the free chairs.

"Hey, Marygene!" she greeted me. When she noticed her chair spinning, her hands went to her narrow hips, "Betsy! Stop that." She waved and instructed her young assistant to sweep up the hair around her stylist chair. Poppy was the cheeriest, most easygoing person you ever met. Which was why her behavior at the meeting drew my attention. She was a tiny thing, about five foot nothing with a cute bob. Her hair color was continuously changing. She had funky bronze highlights going on today. Her porcelain skin was flawless. "It's just me here until noon, so I can't chat long."

She motioned for us to follow her while she unboxed and shelved hair products.

"Tell her what you told me about Glenda," Betsy said.

Poppy put the box cutter on the floor and lifted out two bottles of conditioner. "Well," she faced me, eyes twinkling, "Glenda was in here yesterday having her roots done. She told me she was over in Savannah visiting her sister, Sally, after that Malcom Investment Corp. made the offer the first time. You know Sally worked for the Ledbetters."

"I knew that," I replied.

"Right, anyway, Glenda went to the office to pick up Sally for their lunch date, and she over-head Joseph Ledbetter chewing Carl out. You know Mr. Ledbetter didn't leave the island unless it was absolutely necessary."

Everyone knew that.

"Well, the twins both had a front-row seat right outside his office. He was shouting at Carl, telling him he'd never agree to sell. Glenda said they almost came to blows. Bet you didn't know that." Poppy's lips were peeled back in a grin, exposing her nearly perfect smile. She was tapping her fingernails against the bottle she held in her hand.

"People confess to you like they would a priest or a bartender," Betsy said, and Poppy nodded excitedly.

"I thought Mr. Ledbetter signed the company and land over for Carl to manage years ago."

"I wouldn't know about that. But," she leaned in as if the information she was giving us was top secret, "Carl fired Sally."

I raised my eyebrows.

"He gave her some excuse about her being re-tirement age. Which she was, of course, but Glenda believes it was because of what they witnessed. She had to move back in with her twin."

"Did they tell Eddie?" I asked.

Poppy lifted both hands. "You can ask her. She moved back in with her sister last week. And Glenda said Sally feared Carl."

I wondered if Sally would know what Mr. Led-better's chicken scratch meant.

"Poppy, my scalp is burning," Ms. Maybelle called.

We thanked Poppy and left.

Chapter 15

Alex was leaning against Betsy's car when we crossed the street. He was out of uniform, wearing a pair of jeans and an Atlanta Braves T-shirt. "Did y'all see the paper this morning?"

"Yeah. Marygene got a text from the reporter too."

Alex's demeanor changed from relaxed to inquisitive. I glared at Betsy disapprovingly.

"Sorry, but maybe he can help," she whispered defensively.

Alex didn't comment on our exchange. His attention darted from Betsy to me. "What did the reporter want?" Alex asked when we reached the Camaro.

"To explain, I guess," I said. "Did Eddie find anything out about what I gave him?"

"He put Felton on it."

I frowned. To say I was disappointed in Eddie would have been an understatement. When I handed that piece of evidence over, I assumed he would handle it personally. There was too much at stake. Did he show it to the detective?

Alex took a step closer to me. He rested both of his hands on my shoulders. I looked up but not that far since he was only four or five inches taller than me. I spied the boy I knew from my childhood, his nose with that little bump that never healed from being broken during a game, his warm, slightly crooked smile. Yes, he still sported his boyish good looks, except for the few new laugh lines. Those, too, were appealing. I was instantly drawn to him, and that alarmed me.

"We're all taking this case seriously." His tone softened.

Can he tell?

"We should talk. I thought we could get a cup of coffee or something. Maybe dinner?"

"W-why dinner? What's wrong with right now?" I'd stammered. I hated when I stammered.

His eyes searched my face. "I've been concerned about you."

A flush crept across my cheeks. "Um, well, um, okay. I . . . uh . . . guess that'll be okay." I really needed to get these residual emotional reactions in check.

His cell chirped, and he dropped his hands. But not before he made a point to convey ocularly that he *really* wanted to see me later. "I'll call you."

I nodded, and he walked off to take his call.

After I slid into the passenger seat of the car, Betsy began snickering. "You still have a thing for him."

"I do not. He just caught me off guard. I can be civil, for Jena Lynn's sake. Besides, it would never work between us."

"See!" Betsy pointed at me. "You were thinking about it."

"Stop acting like a silly schoolgirl and focus on the task at hand," Mama scolded.

I screamed.

"He isn't right for you, never has been," Mama said.

"What?" Betsy shouted and swerved on the road.

I turned around. Mama was sitting in the backseat.

"Where were you?" I shouted. Seeing her with that annoyed expression on her face infuriated me further. "You didn't give me anything I could use to help Jena Lynn."

Betsy pulled over to the side of Back Beach Road. "You're scaring me."

"I told you to close the diner. I warned you that your sister would be charged. I informed you that I didn't have the ability to come back as I pleased, and you're pitching a hissy fit about something I can't change?" Mama shrieked.

"What good are you then?" I threw my hands in the air.

Betsy's mouth gaped, her posture rigid. She kept glancing between me and the backseat.

I sighed, "Mama's back."

Betsy didn't question me, didn't shout that I was insane. Instead she whispered, "What's she saying?" Then Betsy sunk lower in the seat.

"Tell that ridiculous girl I can both hear and see her," Mama folded her arms.

I did.

"Oh, sweet Jesus." Betsy covered her face.

"And tell her that the only thing sage is good for is making cornbread dressing."

I relayed that as well.

"I was thinking about getting and burning sage!" Betsy's face paled.

"Enough of this nonsense. Betsy's meemaw taught her about the island spirits. Tell her to pull herself together."

"She says pull yourself together and that you know about the spirits. Is that true?"

Betsy nodded.

"Why didn't you tell me? Oh, never mind. It doesn't matter."

Betsy wiped her face, took a deep breath, and sat up.

"If she is an island spirit, then that means she's here to atone."

Mama's face flushed as she shifted uncomfortably in the backseat.

I motioned with my hands for Betsy to continue.

"The island spirits are those who have much to atone for before they can cross over. Meemaw has experience."

"Can she harm me?" I asked softly.

"You're being ridiculous," Mama said.

"Said the spirit who *must* atone for bad deeds," I retorted. "Well, can she?"

Betsy was busy staring at her hands, which she was clenching and unclenching.

"She can't curse or hurt anyone in any way. She

can only do good or she'll be stuck roaming for all eternity."

I turned and made eye contact with Mama.

"You can also ignore her and she'll be forced to leave," Betsy added.

"So, it's up to me." An involuntary smile spread across my face. "I'm in charge."

"I'm doing the best I can. I wasn't a perfect mother, but I'm here now doing everything in my power to help you girls." Her lips quivered slightly. She fluffed her hair and sighed, "You're going to talk to the Porter twins, right?"

I nodded as her image began to fade.

"If they're obstinate, tell Glenda you know about Sally's, um, procedure."

My mouth dropped open. I understood what Mama meant by *procedure.*

"She had an ongoing affair with Joseph Ledbetter." She was gone.

I told Betsy everything after she got back on the road.

Glenda and Sally lived in the same house they were born in. A small framed house located in Gulf Port, a county north of the island's city center. Neither of them had ever married, a rarity on the island. There was always speculation surrounding the upbringing of the eccentric sisters. Some said that they were born prematurely and suffered mentally. Others said that they were both different in the sexual orientation department but, with Mama's revelation regarding Sally, that didn't explain it.

Maybe they just never wanted to marry. With my experience with marriage, I commended them. Their lives were their own to live as they saw fit, and I certainly didn't want to bring up what Mama suggested. I wasn't cruel like she was.

Sally had worked for the Ledbetters for years. Years ago, when Carl moved the main office to Savannah, she went too. Glenda stayed behind.

The small house was in immaculate condition. The screened-in front porch, I suspected, was the only addition to the property. The banana and lemon trees were laden with fruit. I really wanted those lemons. They were screaming to be made into lemon bars, shortbread, and coffee cake. Such a comfort.

I inhaled the citrus aroma as I passed by the tree on my way to the front porch, where the two sisters were in rocking chairs. A table stood between them that held a pitcher of iced tea and two glasses. A paper towel was wrapped around each glass to catch the condensation.

"Hello, ladies." I waved. "I hope we aren't disturbing you."

"Afternoon, girls," the twins said in unison. Their usual poufy reddish-brown hair was flat today. The humidity was high. My own hair was a frizzy mess. Both women were made up in their Mary Kay makeup. Some of it had settled within the deep creases in their forehead and laugh lines. Age had dulled their sky blue orbs. They were both wearing a version of the same housedress. Glenda in a pale pink and Sally in a pale blue. I wondered if they used the giant pockets in the front of the dress. Neither of them seemed put out that we came by without calling.

"Afternoon," Betsy said with a smile. "What a lovely day we're having. Your yard looks gorgeous." She pointed to the red calla lilies in full bloom.

"Land sakes alive, Betsy. Your hair is the exact shade mine was at your age." Glenda stood. "You enjoy it while you have it."

"I will, ma'am." Betsy smiled.

"Y'all want to come in and have a glass of tea?" Glenda asked.

"We'd appreciate that." I smiled.

Glenda held the screen door open for us, and Betsy and I moseyed in, settling on the wicker love seat at the end of the porch.

"Let me go in and get two more glasses." Glenda slowly walked inside, the screen door creaking in protest.

Sally gave us a knowing glance. "I suppose you two are here because of what my sister told that little Poppy Davis." Upon my nod, she shook her head. "My sister doesn't know when to keep her trap shut. I retired, plain and simple." She picked up her glass and took a long sip from it.

"So, you didn't see Carl and Joseph Ledbetter arguing?" I certainly didn't want to upset the woman more than my presence obviously had.

Glenda had walked out while I was midquestion. She was watching us with interest as she poured two glasses and then came back and handed them to us one at a time.

"Thank you, ma'am." Betsy began draining her glass.

"Yes, thank you." I took a sip of tea and smiled. "It's going to be a scorcher today."

The sounds of summer were echoing behind us in a chorus of insects, as if they'd cued them to begin.

Glenda settled back in her rocker. The metal creaked. "You might as well tell them, sister. Marygene has had enough trials in her young life. Ain't no sense in them taking away her livelihood too." Glenda clucked her tongue, "A shame is what it is." When Sally didn't speak up, Glenda leaned forward and stilled her rocker, "That snot-nosed brat Carl fired her."

"Sister!" Sally was outraged.

"Well, it's the truth." Glenda met her outrage for outrage.

"I'm seventy. It was high time I retired." She sighed and turned toward me. "I might as well tell you, or Glenda will exaggerate the entire ordeal." Glenda grinned wickedly behind her glass. She seemed to be taking great pleasure in our visit now. "You can't use any of this, and I can't testify to it. I signed a confidentiality agreement."

"I understand," I said sincerely.

"Carl has another office in Atlanta, you know. He goes back and forth between there and the Savannah branch. Well, I worked for his daddy for years before he retired and then, well, Carl just sort of inherited me. Carl was able to hire a new secretary for his Atlanta office, but Joseph, bless his heart, made sure he kept me on in Savannah." She wiped her puffy lids with the Kleenex she kept under her watchband. She had certainly cared for the man.

Glenda patted her hand.

"Anyway," Sally continued, "nobody was aware of this, but Joseph didn't trust Carl to handle everything on his own. All large-figured deals made by the firm required a signature from Joseph. I called him at the end of every month to give him an update on the business and whenever Carl raised my suspicions."

Crafty old Mr. Ledbetter had a snitch on the inside.

"Mr. Ledbetter was still running the business from the sidelines?" Betsy asked.

Glenda nodded.

Sally said, "Not the day-to-day, but he oversaw the bigger-picture kind of stuff."

"Tell the girls about the fight," Glenda said.

"I'm getting there, sister." Sally scowled. "A few weeks back, Glenda and I were at my desk getting ready to go to lunch. Joseph showed up. I never even knew he was coming, and he always notified me when he was in town. Carl wanted to sell off two properties. I'm not sure which ones, but Joseph wouldn't agree to it. Carl was madder than a hornet. He threatened to petition the courts for power of attorney and bypass Joseph altogether."

The twins' faces held shock as their heads nodded in a synchronized fashion.

"Then Joseph hollered, 'You ain't the only son of mine, and the will can still be changed,'" Glenda added.

"That's right," Sally agreed.

"But he is his only son," I said.

"Joseph was a rounder in his younger years." Sally shrugged. "Who knows?"

I couldn't believe Mama wanted me to crush this poor woman. She'd suffered enough, pining away for that man her entire life. At this moment, I really didn't like Mr. Ledbetter.

I pulled out my cell phone and showed Sally the image of what Mr. Ledbetter had given me. "Do you have any idea what this means?"

Sally took the phone and studied the image. It had taken her a moment to focus. She'd moved it closer to her face then farther away. Finally, she'd found a happy medium and squinted. "That's Joseph's handwriting. Could be a file of some sort." She passed the phone back to me. "He kept personal files in his home. Might be one of those, because it isn't a sequence the office uses."

I stood. "Thank you for talking with us. We won't take up any more of your time."

Chapter 16

"Just pull those pictures off the wall, Bets." I pulled the plastic off the giant whiteboard she and I had picked up at the supply store.

She laid the old white frames with pictures of a little girl feeding ducks by a river on my child-hood bed. We'd decided it was time to lay out the evidence. That way we could stand back and see it from a timeline perspective. As a girl, I had witnessed Eddie do this many times. Some of it was for fake cases—training that kept him sharp. Those cases he let me participate in.

I had the giant board up on the wall. Betsy pulled the images off the printer. Together we began building a case. The picture we printed off the paper's website of Mr. Ledbetter went in the middle of the board. Underneath him was one of my favorite pictures of Jena Lynn. It was the one of her at the ribbon-cutting ceremony after the diner had been painted.

She was holding a giant pair of scissors, her grin massive as she cut the peach ribbon.

Then a Facebook image of Carl from Rainey Lane's page was put at the top. To the right went a giant question mark. At the bottom went an awful picture of Tally Waters, caught midsentence, her mouth contorted in an unflattering way. Betsy had laughed her butt off when I printed it. She was laughing again now as I moved it to the left of Carl.

Betsy came to the board with a red dry-erase marker, poised to write.

"So," I began, "Carl threatened his dad."

She drew a line from Carl to Mr. Ledbetter. She put an estimated date of April and May of this year over the line.

Then she drew a line from Tally to Jena Lynn. "She openly threatened to ruin Jena Lynn." Under Jena Lynn, she wrote, "The Peach Diner." Then said, "I'll just scribble Ms. Brooks's name down here at the bottom."

"She didn't do it," I said, "but leave it up there if it makes you feel better."

We couldn't find an image of Charlie, so I wrote his name in blue off to the far left of Carl. "Cause of death could have been a heart attack." I put a blue question mark beside his name. Then, above the question mark to the right, I wrote, "illegitimate son of JL." I drew a line from him to Mr. Ledbetter. "You think he really had another son, or was it typical Mr. Ledbetter, spouting off his mouth?"

Betsy tapped her marker against the board. "Who knows? Mr. Ledbetter was an enigma."

"That he was. For some reason, I believe there must be something to the story. I mean, he was furious with Carl. Perhaps he was aware of his son but the son wasn't aware of him."

Betsy crinkled her nose.

"I'm not projecting my personal issues into the case. I was just pointing out that it happens. That's all."

At the very top of the board I wrote, "AP081587F," and stepped back to see what we had.

Betsy whistled. "We ought to go into the private eye business on the side. Look how professional that looks. It's like something out of one of those police shows."

I folded my arms, not as impressed as Betsy was. From what I could see, we didn't have anything solid to go on. We needed more information. My mind drifted to Calhoun. Gathering evidence was his business too. Without facts, there wasn't a story. He would want the entire story.

I relayed my thought pattern to Betsy and she gave me a thumbs-up.

"But be careful to play him smart. You don't want him to turn the tables and use you for information instead. Now come on, let's go over to Keith's Car Palace. He's got a couple of nice rides for you to test-drive."

"Okay. I'll call Jena Lynn on the ride over." I needed my own means of transportation, and according to Betsy, Keith was happy to oblige even within my budget.

* * *

After I got back from Keith's, I sat down at the dressing table that had been my mama's, and her mama's before her, to apply my lipstick and freshen up. The wind had done a number on my hair. Betsy's influence had landed me in the driver's seat of a sporty little black Mini Cooper convertible. It was an older model than I had been previously driving, but in my price range and with low miles. I'd keep the top up tonight.

I'd decided to pull my hair up for tonight's dinner, allowing a few strands to fall beside my face. It was nearing seven and the temperature was still in the mid-eighties. I stood and examined my appearance in the mirror. The A-line floral sundress was a tad snug, compared to the last time I'd worn it. I sucked in my waist and turned to the side. It didn't change much. Oh well.

My wristlet was on my arm as I padded down the stairs in my white Yellow Box flip-flops, my favorite brand. The conversation I'd had with Zach on the ride over to Keith's weighed heavily on my mind. Jena Lynn was resting, Zach had told me. She was having a really hard time, and Doc Tatum had prescribed something for anxiety. My sister was the last person in the world who deserved to be going through this. Compartmentalizing my rage, I focused on the task at hand. Finding the responsible party. On an island this small, where rumors spread like wildfires in southern California, sifting through to find the actual truth wouldn't be easy but doable.

I was extremely disappointed in the Peach Cove Sheriff's Department. They hadn't been out to have a chat with the twins or they would have mentioned it. A threat was just that—a threat—and they should investigate it. I was beginning to wonder if Eddie had any intention of sharing the evidence I passed along with the detective. If it were me, I'd build a solid case, then take it to Detective Thornton.

The parking lot was almost full when I arrived at the Pier Bar and Grill. I wondered how many of them would have chosen The Peach if it was open. The atmosphere was as different as the cuisine, but our regulars would try new places if our doors were closed.

The Pier was a pastel-colored building. The seating was a mix of wooden tables, chairs, and benches. Low candles were lit on the tables at night, and tiki torches were blazing around the outdoor dining areas.

Yvonne and her mama were seated outside. I bypassed the hostess with the knowledge of Yvonne's preferred spot. After greeting each of them, I sat.

"I ordered you a Bahama Mama," Yvonne said as the waitress delivered our drinks.

"Great." I took a sip from the frosty beverage.

"I just love that dress, Marygene," Ms. Brooks said after we ordered our food. "Doesn't she look pretty, Yvonne?"

"She does. How's Jena Lynn doing? I can't even imagine how she must feel." Yvonne adjusted the spaghetti strap of her coral dress up on her shoulder.

"She's struggling," I said. "I'm hoping all of this

can be resolved soon. The diner has never been closed this long, not even after Hurricane Matthew."

"I miss the peaches and cream bars," Ms. Brooks told me.

Turning to her, I smiled. "I'll make up a batch and bring them to you."

She brightened.

"Um, Ms. Brooks, you were pretty upset at Mr. Ledbetter at the diner that day. Is there—"

"I sure was," she began, cutting me off. "That man played with fire his entire life. It's not surprising someone killed him."

"Mama!" Yvonne said. "We talked about this."

"Well, it's the truth. Like I said before, I'm just surprised it took this long." She snorted in disgust. "He was worse than a tomcat. Evelyn," her head tilted mournfully when referring to his late wife, "bless her soul, was either blind as a bat or just plain stupid. Now, I don't know who killed him. Lord knows, I wish I did. Little Jena Lynn's predicament keeps me up at night."

I gave Ms. Brooks's hand a squeeze.

Our meals arrived, and Yvonne's mama excused herself to wash her hands.

"She doesn't know anything," Yvonne said. "She just never liked the man. That detective asked her a load of questions. She told him that exact same thing about the tomcat."

I sighed and settled back in my seat. The seafood primavera I ordered looked gorgeous and smelled even better, yet I didn't have an appetite. *Yes, me, Ms. Foodie.*

"I know it isn't any of my business," Yvonne said after she swallowed a bite of her filet. "But, getting involved in the investigation doesn't seem wise."

"I'm not exactly involved." I rested my fork against the plate.

"I know you. And sitting on the sidelines isn't your style. You're taking this personally."

"Of course I'm taking this personally. It is personal." My voice rose a little higher than I had intended.

She leaned in, "That's not what I meant. Since we were little, you've felt responsible for everything that's happened to your family. That's one of the reasons you moved away, right?"

"This is different, though."

"Maybe. All I'm saying is you should let the sheriff's department handle it. You'll go poking around and stirring up folks' old wounds. The island is full of people still holding grudges. I'm sure it was a grudge that got Ledbetter killed."

I thought so too.

"Whoever did this, chose your diner. And that was before you even moved back. I care. I don't want anything to happen to you." Concern was etched in her brow.

"I appreciate your concern. I really do. And I'd love to let the authorities handle it. In a perfect world, I could. But it isn't. That detective believes Jena Lynn is guilty. Eddie, to my knowledge, isn't asking the right people the right questions." Then I told her about what Mr. Ledbetter had given me and what Sally had said.

"That's exactly my point. This is a small island. If you start digging, whoever did this will find out and you'll be in danger." She started to say more but her mama came back to the table.

The conversation shifted to chitchat and catching up on each other's lives.

An hour later I was walking up the steps of the gazebo, positioned in front of the pond owned by the Blue Bird Inn. I was feeling down after dinner. It had been ridiculous of me to even think Ms. Brooks had any valuable information. If she had, I probably would have heard all about it years ago. I had almost driven right past Pelican Avenue to seek the comfort of a warm bath and a glass of wine. But, on the off chance I would discover something of value, I turned down the dead-end street. My plan was to gain Calhoun's trust, like he was attempting to do with mine.

The inn was run by my cousin Judy Palmer. She wouldn't be at the front desk now. They would be milling around in the back garden having wine and cheese. That was one of the reasons I decided to wait until this hour to come by. The rumors would fly about the reporter and me if I went up to his room, especially after that nasty article. I had sent a text telling him where to find me if he still wanted to talk.

I stared out over the little pond with the fountain in the middle. It was peaceful tonight. The wind rustled the leaves of the trees as rays of moonlight danced on the subtly moving water.

"I wasn't sure you'd come." Calhoun startled me with his presence.

"Well, here I am." I took a step backward as he entered the gazebo.

"I know you're angry about the article." He appeared as if that fact bothered him. Good. At least he wasn't without a conscience. "Someone was going to write it, and I figured if I did, I would have access to those who wanted to contribute or elaborate further with their information. I don't believe your sister is guilty." He kept a couple of feet between us. Under the brightness of the moon, I could see he was studying my reaction. His tone had me on edge. It was soft. Peter's had always been soft before he struck.

"I don't understand why you care. Once the turtle project has concluded, you'll go back to the city and all of this will be in your rearview mirror."

A gust of wind blew more of my hair loose, and I tucked the few strands behind my ear. He was watching my movement intently. He must have noticed the alarm I was feeling because he put a little more distance between us and shoved his hands into the pockets of his khaki shorts.

"I have a sensitivity to those to whom injustice has befallen. Plus, I have this intense need to get to the truth." His expression appeared sincere.

I wasn't sure if I believed him or not.

"Okay, so have you received any information?" I highly doubted he had any. Perhaps that was what this was—a fishing expedition.

"Not yet. I did overhear a few ladies talking at the market today."

I waited.

"You were the topic of their conversation."

I cocked my head to one side and kept my face as impassive as I could manage. In case he was gauging my reactions, I attempted to appear unfazed. "I hear you spoke with one of the sisters who worked for the Ledbetter family." News traveled fast, by way of Glenda, I was certain. Telephone, telegraph, tellaGlenda.

"So, you're wanting me to contribute information for your next article?" I was unable to hide the annoyance in my tone. I could have run by my sister's house and checked in on her instead of wasting my time with this bozo. He wasn't revealing anything. I turned to leave.

His hand caught my forearm. "I know about the file, or assumption that it's a file number that Joseph Ledbetter gave you."

I jerked my arm free and jutted out my chin and was met with shock.

"Sorry, I didn't mean to . . ."

"Good night, Mr. Calhoun." I walked down the gazebo steps lickety-split. And it wasn't until I had my car door open that I heard him behind me. I whirled around, cautiously, my pulse jittery.

His hands were up in a defensive stance, his posture full of alarm. "I'm sorry. I'm not usually this obtuse. I . . . I like you, Marygene. I want to help."

I kept the car door between us. "You know me about as well as I know you, which is not at all. My sister has been framed for murder, and you're a strange man who happened to be in the diner the day of the incident. You show up at my house uninvited. You wrote a damaging article about my family and my business." He opened his mouth, but I held up my hand. "I came. I take the blame for the lapse in judgment." I lowered my tone. "You may be the nicest man alive. I just don't know you."

He gave a quick nod and began to retreat slowly. "You're right. We don't know each other. There's another reason I've taken an interest in your situation." When I didn't get into the car and slam the door, as I'm assuming he expected, he stopped his retreat. "My brother did time for a murder he didn't commit. It wasn't a situation like this. He was in the wrong place at the wrong time. The police force was pressured to close a case, and he was the perfect patsy. Now, my brother was no saint. But he certainly wasn't a murderer."

"Was he ever exonerated?" I asked after a brief period of silence. From what I could see of his face, there was still raw emotion visible.

"He would have been. He died in prison, exactly three weeks before his retrial."

"I'm sorry." What else did you say to something like that?

"Thank you. Perhaps we can speak again later?"

"Perhaps," I said.

Chapter 17

It shouldn't have surprised me to find Detective Thornton on my front porch when I got home. It had, though. If Calhoun found out about my chat with the sisters, it would have been a breeze for the detective. Thankfully, I'd gotten my berries back in the basket, so to speak.

"What can I do for you, Detective?"

He stepped aside so I could unlock the front door. I left it open as an invitation.

"I have a few more questions I wanted to ask," he said.

"I thought the case was solid against my sister. Why else would you have her indicted for murder?"

He closed the door behind him and followed me through the living room and into the kitchen. I wouldn't allow this man to see he intimidated me.

"Iced tea?" I pulled the pitcher from the fridge.

"No, thank you."

I poured myself a glass.

"I hear you've been conducting your own investigation."

I took a sip as he stared at me.

He was wearing slacks and a blazer on this hot night. He must be burning up. Did he think that made him appear more official? He stared daggers through me. "You could be arrested for obstruction of justice."

"I haven't obstructed anything. Last I checked, having conversations with my neighbors isn't a crime."

"Withholding evidence is." He stepped forward and placed both his hands on the bar, lowering his head to meet mine. "I don't know what game you're playing, missy, but I'm here to tell you to steer clear of my investigation or I'll slap a charge on you so fast it will make your head spin." His tone was lethal.

I swallowed hard. Time to be brave. "Did you investigate the lead I handed over?"

"That isn't your business. If you had handed over that evidence earlier, perhaps it would have led us down another direction before we arrested your sister. Ever think of that?"

I had. On numerous occasions.

"Well, you have it now," I said as firmly as I could manage. "And being the fine detective that you are, you must have figured out the entire Peach Cove Sheriff's Department doesn't believe Jena Lynn is guilty. And much of the island either."

He squinted. "You sure you've got your facts

straight on that?" He pushed off the bar. Satisfaction spread across his face. His finger extended. "This is your one and only warning."

He turned to leave.

Mama appeared behind him. "Well, go after him. Offer to help."

"Detective Thornton."

He turned, pausing.

"Have you ever considered I may be of use to you? People talk freely around me. And even if you believe my sister is guilty, you want to build a solid case that would hold up during a trial. The circumstantial one you've built may have been good enough for an indictment," I paused to gauge his interest. He was still listening. Surely that was a good sign. I squared my shoulders. "We both know it isn't enough for a trial."

Eddie had told me that with a circumstantial case such as this, it could go either way. Detective Thornton didn't strike me as a man happy with those sorts of odds.

"No, Ms. Brown, I haven't. I've worked cases in a lot of small towns. People protect their own. It's human nature. The deeper I dig into this little island, the more it stinks. My job is something I do exceedingly well. Remember that." He left. The door closed softly behind him.

"Well, thanks for that." I turned to Mama. Naturally, she'd left. If she was trying to make amends to cross over, she was doing an extremely poor job of it.

* * *

I was on the phone with Betsy the next morning, filling her in on last night's events while I waited for the coffee to percolate. "I'm really going to have to buy a Keurig. I like instant gratification."

Betsy snickered.

"You know what I mean."

"So, you going to run down the lead on the Ledbetter files today?" Betsy asked.

I put her on speaker as the pot finally finished and poured myself a full mug. "I think I have to. But I'll have to be careful. That detective will be up my ass at his first opportunity." Surreptitiousness wasn't Betsy's strong suit, not that I'd openly hurt her feelings, but, on this one, I'd be going it alone.

"What's his problem anyway? Why doesn't he go home already?"

"I guess he feels he should see it through. I don't know."

"Did you get anything from the reporter?"

"Nothing I can use. I did gain a little knowledge regarding his interest." I relayed what he had told me about his brother.

"Huh. You could use that."

What kind of person would use another man's suffering for gain? A desperate one.

There was a knock at the back screen door. I leaned over the island. "Alex is here."

He was in full uniform today.

"Hear him out. Don't go puttin' a beatdown on him." Betsy snickered.

"Morning, Marygene," Alex said through the screen door. Betsy was on speaker. "Morning, Bets."

"Alex! Guard your nu—" Betsy shouted mid-laugh. I disconnected the call.

I tied my robe around me and tucked a few frizzy locks behind my ears.

He folded his hands in front. "You're not going to knee me or anything, right?"

I laughed. "Not today. Come in." I grinned. "Coffee?"

"Please." He closed the door softly behind him as I poured him a cup. "Sorry to show up unannounced."

"There seems to be a lot of that going around lately." I handed him the cup.

"What do you mean?" His hand closed around the mug. His fingers seemed to deliberately brush mine. Pushing the limits of my comfort zone.

"Never mind." I sighed, "What can I do for you?"

Alex gawked at the baked goods. He sat down on one of the metal barstools. "Feeling stressed out, I see."

"Yeah." I passed the platter toward him. "Help yourself to the peach rolls or turnovers. I made them last night, so they're fresh."

"We okay?"

I nodded.

He didn't hesitate. "God, Marygene," he groaned around a mouthful, an expression of awe on his face. "There is nothing like your baked goods. I mean it. I've eaten pastries in all the best shops in Savannah, and nothing compares to yours."

Well, that was a real nice compliment. There were ample high-end pastry shops in Savannah.

"I'm glad you like them." My mood was marginally improving.

"Listen." His gaze hardened. "I want you to be careful around Detective Thornton."

"He doesn't like me. I know. He came by here last night."

Alex stopped mid-chew. He chased it down with a swig of coffee. "I didn't know that. Eddie would be hopping mad if he knew." That was the truth.

"What's his problem, anyway?"

"He's a serious man and, by his reputation, I'd say a good detective. From what I hear, he doesn't have a family or a life outside the job. He hates small-town politics and feels we let too much slide because of our close relationships with each other. He despises being second-guessed or having any interference on what he views as *his* case."

I snorted. "He isn't that good of a detective if he believes Jena Lynn is guilty."

"I don't think she's guilty either, but the evidence clearly points to her." He cocked his head to one side. "I just don't know what to make of it yet."

I couldn't believe what I was hearing. "Then you're an idiot too! She's been framed. Plain and simple. She had no motive! She gains nothing from Ledbetter's death."

"Now, don't go biting my head off." Alex lowered his tone. "But she hasn't been the most stable person either, the last few years."

I went still. My muscles stiffened. What was he talking about?

"I would have thought Eddie would have told you. Called you when it happened." He shook his head. "Or at least Zach would've."

Was this what Detective Thornton was referring to?

With fingers to my parted lips, I asked, "What?"

"After your mama died, Jena Lynn had a breakdown. Zach closed the diner for a week while she was treated in the hospital. It was all kept hush-hush."

I pulled my hand away. What in the hell was going on with the people on this island? No one called me? Not even Eddie?

"So, it isn't that far of a stretch for Detective Thornton to build a case on that."

I stood staring into the brown orbs of a man I'd grown up with, even thought I'd loved at one point, and he looked like a stranger. Betsy had been with me almost every minute since I'd returned, and she'd not said a word about it either. Did she know? No. Betsy wouldn't be able to sit on information like that. What about Sam? Eddie had had ample opportunities to inform me of something of that importance and he, too, kept his mouth shut. More betrayal.

"I—" I cleared my throat. Twice. "I want you to leave."

"I'm trying to help. I really am." His face was sincere. "I care about you. Always have." I pointed to the door, not attempting to speak again as I feared my vocal cords wouldn't emit a sound.

Alex nodded and stood. "When you calm down, call me."

Chapter 18

My sunglasses, wet with perspiration, slid down my nose as I strode up the staircase of my sister's house. It was going to be a scorcher today. The second Alex had left I'd thrown myself together and flew over here. No wonder she'd been so upset when I had returned home. She had been living in her own hell. It had taken me a few long minutes to get myself under control. I had to get my pain in check before I faced my sister. She deserved better.

I didn't knock, just opened the door and peeked my head inside. "Hello! It's me!"

The house was so quiet. As I crossed the threshold I was startled by Judy Palmer coming out of the kitchen. The little white Camry in the driveway must belong to her. Judy was about an inch taller than me with auburn hair I'd always envied. "Marygene." She sounded as stunned to see me as I had been to see her.

"Hi, Judy." I closed the door behind me. "Where's my sister?" *And what in the world are you doing here?*

"Jena Lynn is upstairs taking a shower. I just came by to drop off a casserole and see how she's holding up." To my surprise, she burst into tears. Poor Judy was an ugly crier. Her face got all blotchy and her body must overproduce mucus. "It's just awful. I still can't believe it." She immediately wiped her nose. "I'm sorry. I'm just a big ole weepy mess."

"That's okay." Had Judy and Jena Lynn become close during the years I had been away? "How are things at the inn?" I might as well do my digging now. After all, she was here.

"We're doing okay. Full lately, with the turtle project, that Tally Waters, and the detective."

"Right . . ."

"You aren't considering selling, are you?" I walked into the kitchen, motioning for Judy to accompany me while I got myself a glass of water.

Judy grabbed a napkin out of the holder on the counter and blew her nose. "No. Well," she seemed to be reconsidering it, "not unless they get a majority. I can't see the inn doing so well when the high-rises start going up."

From her perspective, that made sense. Her inn, not being located on beachfront property, probably wouldn't be the tourists' top choice.

"The family has decided to sell off Big Mama's estate to your friend Yvonne. Though, she's going to have problems with the zoning board if she plans to work out of the house."

"Does she know that?"

Judy's shoulders rose and fell.

I filled two glasses with ice.

"That reporter asked about you."

I handed her a glass of water.

The little rhinestones she had attached to the tips of her French manicure glistened in the light.

I filled my glass and took a few sips. "Did he?"

"Yes. I think he has the hots for you."

More like he was out for retribution. I'd googled him after the detective left. His brother's case had made headlines in Atlanta. From the article, it appeared like a drug deal gone bad. What interested me was that Detective Thornton had been the one who put the reporter's brother away. He would be useful to me. I was just unsure of how to manage a man that full of silent rage. On the outside, he appeared so cool and levelheaded. No doubt he was a brilliant man. I wondered how the detective was handling Calhoun's presence on the island and involvement in his case.

"He seems okay." If we were seen together, I wanted it to get around that it was of a romantic nature, not a calculated partnership.

After a quick sip from the glass, Judy set it on the counter.

"Have you spoken to Rainey Lane?" I kept my tone casual.

"Yes, she and Carl are all tore up. I told her Jena Lynn was innocent, and she thinks so too."

After Carl's display at the meeting the other day, I didn't believe that for a second. It must have shown on my face because she immediately followed with, "You two have always gotten off on the wrong foot. Rainey Lane has her troubles. You know what a tough time she had growing up. Rumors were always flying about how unseemly it was that her sister ran off with their stepdaddy."

Boy did I ever. It was all Mama talked about some days.

"Well, that took a toll on her. She's doing the best she can."

Judy took another step toward me before lowering her tone, "There's something crazy happening on this island. For the first time in my life, I'm locking my doors at night."

Well, I could understand that.

"Just between the two of us . . ."

I nodded. I would keep her confidence.

"Tally has been meeting with Carl on a regular basis." She glanced around as if someone was eavesdropping. She was scared, upset, or both. "She's got no business going after him." She gave a bark of bitter laughter.

Am I detecting jealousy?

"He comes by after midnight when he thinks everyone is asleep. Usually around two a.m., I hear the car drive up." Judy's private quarters at the inn were behind a hidden panel door off the main study. Tally wouldn't know that, but Carl would. "Then it's usually around four a.m. when he brings her back."

"You think they're having an affair?" I wanted to gauge her response.

"What do you think?" she spat, then flushed. She was on the verge of crying again. "Carl better watch himself or some information may get out that he wants buried."

"Judy," I said slowly. "What are you telling me?"

Tearing up, she glanced at her watch, fidgeting, "I've got to go."

I wouldn't push her, not now.

I gave her a genuine smile and gently squeezed her shoulder. "Thank you for coming by and for your support."

She waved my thanks away. "I love you both. We're family. It's what we do."

"You're right. Say, you think I could come by the inn later? We could catch up."

"I-I guess that'll be okay. I don't know anything, not really." She practically ran toward the front door. "Please don't say anything about Carl. He has a temper."

"I wouldn't dream of it."

My sister was sitting on a lounge chair on the top deck. She must have forgotten about Judy, otherwise she would have come down to see her off. The breeze was nice coming in off the ocean as I settled in the lounge next to her, separated only by a small table. For a few long moments, we both tried to just enjoy the breeze. Her hair was still wet from her shower, and her face was covered in moisturizer. She was attempting to decompress from the stress, allowing the salty air to cleanse her soul. She'd once told me that whatever her troubles, the island breeze could always cure them.

Jena Lynn kept her gaze toward the ocean. "Sad about Charlie, wasn't it?"

"Yes. Did he have a heart condition?" I still wasn't convinced his death was natural.

"I don't know. It wouldn't have been the kind of thing he would have discussed with me if he did." That was true. "I didn't place that order for the rat poison." There was a slight hiccup in her tone.

I reached over and squeezed her hand. "I know."

"You need to get out of here, Marygene. Take a vacation somewhere. I'm beginning to believe this island is making people go nuts." My poor sister.

"Why didn't you tell me about your hospital stay?" I asked softly. "You know I would have come home. Maybe I could have helped."

Her expression seemed dazed. "I don't know. At first, I was worried word would spread." She twirled the tie of her robe around her finger. "Then after I got out of the hospital, I just wanted to forget the whole thing."

"We're sisters. Your well-being is important to me." Emotion threatened to spill over.

She faced me. Her face was pale. "I saw Mama. After she died, I saw her." And as if summoned, Mama appeared before us.

A quick glance at my sister told me she didn't see her now. Mama was crying. It was the first time I could ever remember seeing her cry.

"She couldn't cope. I-I just wanted to say how sorry I was for putting her through all that I did. But my poor baby couldn't handle it. It was my fault she was hospitalized. She was never crazy."

I wanted to tell Jena Lynn that, to help her understand it wasn't in her head. But with the knowledge it would only make matters worse, I refrained.

"Listen to me." I moved to sit at the end of her chair. "You're not crazy. You were under great duress. You weren't sleeping. All of us can break if we don't get enough sleep. That's how they torture people in war."

She sniffed and took some comfort in my words. Mama was standing over her, stroking a hand across my sister's hair as the wind blew. "I was a bad mother to you both. I'm sorry. I'm trying to help you, too, Marygene. I wish I had all the answers. I only have bits and pieces. And I'm only allowed to give a little at a time. I'm trying to figure out when to give what. I'm learning."

"How long have you been here?" I asked Mama in a tactical way. My sister would think the question was directed at her.

"About half an hour." Jena Lynn replied and wiped her face.

"Since right before your sister's breakdown. I'm tied to the island. If I could have sought you out then, I would have. I will make amends. I will help you if I can. I will be a better mother to you while I'm here. I'm sorry for . . ." She faded away just as hot tears ran down my cheeks.

"Don't cry." Jena Lynn embraced me. "I'm so sorry you're having to deal with all of this on your own."

"You have nothing to be sorry for. We're going to figure this out. You'll be exonerated and the diner will reopen."

She released me and settled back. I could tell she was medicated.

Her words slurred. "Eddie promised me he'd fix all of this."

"And you know he will."

"If he can't, promise me you'll keep the diner running."

A knot formed in the pit of my stomach as I considered the gravity of her words. "We'll fix this."

"Promise me!"

"I promise," I choked out.

I wanted to ask her about Tally Waters. Wanted to know if they had had any other interactions. But her breathing changed. She was asleep. My questions would have to wait.

Chapter 19

After I left Jena Lynn sleeping, tucked in her bed, I ran through the Finger Lickin' Chicken drive-through for a sandwich and fries. I'd felt weak and knew I needed to eat. The parking lot was only partially full, and I found a nice shady spot in front of a row of palm trees. I had a whole lot to think about as I sat there chewing on a fry. *Betrayal.* That was the word of the day. I'd run from home because of it. Jena Lynn felt I'd abandoned her. Judy had divulged the information she had because she felt betrayed by Carl. Calhoun certainly believed he'd experienced betrayal when his brother was accused and convicted by a broken system and then lost his life. Perhaps Mr. Ledbetter lost his life for the same reason. Yvonne was right, grudges ran deep around here.

A minivan parked beside me and out popped a little family. Mom and Dad smiling with a couple of kids between them. The little girl with pigtails waved at me before skipping ahead toward the restaurant.

Normalcy. That was what I had always pictured it to look like.

When the bite of sandwich I'd been chewing wouldn't go down, I decided now was the time to get my life in order. Before that could ever happen, I had to get my sister out of this mess. Judy knew something, and I was determined to find out what. Hopefully she would be forthcoming. I hated to threaten Judy with exposing her and Carl's relationship. It was low and dirty. Sleeping with your best friend's husband wasn't something that would blow over easily once the news spread. It would ruin her on the island. Unfortunately, this was about my sister's freedom, and I couldn't worry about the consequences of leaking Judy's indiscretions.

I really didn't like Carl. He was a chip off the ole block.

People were milling around in the common areas when I arrived at the inn. Judy had updated it recently. The front desk was the first thing you saw when you entered. It was a large built-in desk made with old-looking whitewashed wood. It was lovely and currently unmanned. Judy should have been there this time of day. The large ornate staircase was off to the side. An elevator was installed twenty years ago, but the staircase was still used frequently. I moved past the desk. The colors were a calming tan and off-white. Large high-backed couches covered with large fluffy pillows, along with two Queen Anne chairs, greeted you in the main sitting room. The walls were adorned with pieces of driftwood, abstract marine life paintings, and seashells.

"Hey, Marygene." Poppy strolled toward me with a basket of cookies.

My gaze drifted to the basket.

"I've been buying these here since the diner's closing. My customers are accustomed to snacking while they're having their hair done." She lifted the basket and inhaled. "Not as good as The Peach's cookies but still good. Any idea when you'll get to reopen?"

"Afraid not."

"Well, that sucks. I guess I'll have to drive all the way over here until it does." She moved closer to me.

People were now moving into the dining room for tapas. The older crowd always ate early.

"Rainey Lane came into the shop yesterday."

I leaned toward her when she lowered her tone.

"She was being all sweet and got Emma Mae talking about the buyout. You know Emma Mae, right? Tall, curly, sandy blond hair with an angled bob."

I nodded. "We refer to her at the diner as 'okra extra brown.'" When Poppy squinted, I supplied, "It's her usual order with her lunch. Whatever sandwich she chooses, she always orders a side of okra extra brown."

"Right, well, I overheard Emma Mae telling her that she didn't think you and your sister would ever sell. And Rainey Lane said something like y'all's vote wasn't relevant."

"What did she mean by that? Of course it's relevant."

"I hate it, but it looks like with all the ruckus

going on with the murder and with it happening in the diner, folks may not be too keen to eat there anymore."

A knot developed in the pit of my stomach.

"You know I will," she rushed to add.

"Marygene, how nice to see you again." Calhoun came into the room, wearing slacks and a deep green Hawaiian shirt with white flowers. He had his leather bag attached to his side, which, I assumed, held his laptop and notes. Perhaps even recording devices, if he didn't use his phone for that sort of thing.

"Afternoon, Mr. Calhoun." I bit the inside of my cheek.

"I've got to get back to the shop. Forget what I said. I'm sure business will boom at the reopening. Rainey Lane and Emma Mae are idiots. See ya." Poppy bopped through the front door.

"How's your sister holding up?" Calhoun asked.

"She's fine. Is there something you wanted?"

"No. I was looking for Ms. Palmer. There's a small leak in my shower. It drips all night."

"Ah, well, I'm sure she'll get it taken care of." Like I cared.

"I was going to wait to inform her, seeing how upset she was before."

"What do you mean, upset?" He motioned for me to follow him out onto the porch. "I was having coffee out here when she came flying into the parking lot. Her car ran up on the curb," he pointed, "there."

Judy's car was parked haphazardly, with two wheels wedged into the azaleas.

"Huh."

Our conversation must have torn her up.

"I should go and check on her." Guilt set in when I thought about my earlier idea to use her feelings for Carl. It wasn't fair to push her with that. I'd have to convince her to aid me in another way.

"Of course. I also wanted to apologize to you for the way I came across the other night. Maybe if you have some time later, I thought perhaps we could talk."

"Maybe," I said noncommittally. "I really should go and check on Judy."

He followed me through the door into the main sitting room.

Normally I would have waited until he left the room to go into Judy's private rooms, but the wall panel door was ajar. She must be upset. She never liked guests to have access to her personal space. If they knew where she was, they'd be banging on the door at all hours of the night when they needed something. After I asked Calhoun to wait in the sitting room, I slipped through the opening and ventured into her tiny living area.

"Judy, it's me," I called out softly. "You all right?" When there was no response, I ducked my head into her bedroom. It was small, and the masculine furniture that had belonged to her mama and daddy remained. Everything looked in order, and it was empty. The French doors leading to the master bath were slightly ajar as well. Maybe she was soaking in the tub. "Judy, hon, it's Marygene. Are you okay?"

Still no response. My skin tingled.

"I'm coming in." Using my elbow, I nudged the door the rest of the way open and stepped inside. "Oh my God! No!" I shrieked. My head spun and spots blurred my vision. I propped myself against the wall.

"What is it?" Calhoun peeked his head inside the room.

Gasping for air, I tried to speak but couldn't. I pointed to the tub. The blood visibly drained from his face.

He turned abruptly. The two of us scampered from the room. I took a seat on the cedar chest in front of Judy's bed. It had been impossible not to glance back at the lifeless body of my second cousin. She'd been partially submersed in a full tub. The water red. Her left arm slung over the side. A puddle of crimson on the yellow ceramic tile. A single rhinestone laid at the edge.

I was sitting on the front porch wrapped in a blanket, shivering, despite the warm temps. Calhoun was sitting next to me, so close that our shoulders were touching. His face drained of color. I didn't resist when he reached out and took my hand. His hand was warm, dry, and comforting. The mere connection to another human being was welcome. And like it or not, we were now connected. It had been Calhoun with me on the floor with Mr. Ledbetter, and it was Calhoun and me that found Judy. All the guests were being held inside.

"Don't give them any information other than the basic," Calhoun whispered. His words hardly registered.

"She wouldn't have killed herself," I told Calhoun just as two more cars arrived on the scene.

Alex got out of his car. Eddie and Detective Thornton emerged from Eddie's beige pickup with SHERIFF written down each side. Calhoun released my hand.

"You okay?" Alex put his hands on my shoulders.

"No," I said.

He caressed my cheek.

I nestled my face in his palm, willing myself not to cry. I didn't want him to move.

"It's going to be okay." Alex glared at Calhoun suspiciously.

Alex helped me shift the blanket higher on my shoulders. I used this as an excuse to reposition myself farther away from Calhoun. The shock Calhoun had shown in the bathroom was the reaction of an innocent man. At least I had thought so. But then, I was so worked up, I could have missed something. He had been the one to bring up Judy. Though his reasons were believable. I needed to get upstairs and check his shower.

Dread swept over me when Eddie instructed Alex to go inside. I was going to have to speak with that detective again.

"Pumpkin, do you need to see a doctor?" Eddie asked from the detective's side.

"No, sir," I said weakly.

His glare toward Calhoun matched Alex's. "I'm surprised to see you're still on the island, Mr. Calhoun. According to your editor in chief, the turtle project concluded three days ago."

"I'm working on another piece now."

"Not for your paper you're not," Eddie countered. "Nor for the *Gazette*. I have it on good authority they will no longer be acquiring articles from reporters not on staff."

If I had been feeling better, I would have praised Eddie for shutting Calhoun out. That article would prove to be damaging on multiple fronts.

"It's a freelance project," Calhoun replied smoothly.

"Uh-huh," Eddie grunted. "I look forward to hearing about it."

Eddie and the detective disappeared inside. But not before the detective growled at us, "Don't move a muscle."

"You think I did this to Judy?" Calhoun whispered.

"I don't know what to think. You did write that disgusting article. Freelance project?"

Calhoun had the decency to appear abashed. "I explained that. My intentions were pure. But I lied about the freelance project. I'm not actively working on one at present."

"That wasn't wise."

"It's easily remedied. I sell freelance pieces all the time. Not all of them get published." He leaned closer to me, and I couldn't help myself: I flinched. "I didn't do this." His tone sounded urgent. "Why would I? I hardly knew the woman. And before you go down that rabbit hole, I didn't know the old man either."

Was he capable of murder? Who knew? And motive? Serial killers didn't exactly have motive. They were just plain nuts. Calhoun pushed his frames back up on his nose. Honestly, I didn't believe he was psychotic. But what did I know? You see those interviews with neighbors on the news who always say, "He was the nicest guy. Friendly and quiet. Always had a smile on his face. I'm just shocked by it all." Exhaustion took hold.

The rumblings of guests inside grew louder by the second. Many of them wanted to check out. Not that I blamed them. Judy's younger sister would probably take over managing the inn, or maybe her brother, Nate. The second my lids closed, the tears fell.

"I'm sorry," he said softly.

Not thinking, I said, "We weren't all that close, but she was family and not a bad person."

"We're going to be questioned again, even if this does appear to be a suicide. Detective Thornton doesn't particularly care for either of us." His expression appeared fixed. "Plus, I think he's dirty."

Chapter 20

"Either you have the worst luck on the planet or you didn't heed my warning, Ms. Brown," Detective Thornton said.

"Providence has not been in my favor lately," I said.

The detective had elicited all the facts regarding what transpired before his arrival from me in a series of concise questions that led to further questions. I answered all of them as simply and directly as possible. Now, seated in the front seat of Eddie's truck, I was worn slap out. My second cousin was being taken out in a body bag. I sniffed and glanced away from the gurney.

"You said it appears to be a suicide," I whispered with effort. "I don't know how I could have had anything to do with that." Eddie paced in front of the truck.

"*Appears* is the key word there." His tone was

razor sharp. "What were you doing here in the first place?"

"I saw Judy at my sister's a little while ago. She was really upset about this whole business with Jena Lynn being falsely accused. I came to check on her after I left there." I wiped my nose with the Kleenex someone had given me. For the life of me, I couldn't recall who it had been.

"And you and Mr. Calhoun just happened to go in and find her together?"

I blew out a breath. "I was talking to Poppy in the front entryway. Mr. Calhoun came down and told me Judy had appeared really upset. I went to check on her in her room. He heard me cry out, I guess."

"Was it his suggestion to check on Ms. Palmer?"

Alex handed me a bottle of water. He didn't make eye contact with the detective. He was silently cautioning me to be exceedingly careful. I shouldn't poke the bear. *Tell him the truth,* his stern expression shouted. Did he believe I wouldn't?

I took a sip from the bottle. "Not to check on her, but he mentioned he wanted to complain that the showerhead in his bathroom was leaking."

"You were willing to take a perfect stranger into your cousin's private quarters to complain about the showerhead in his room?" His tone said that was an outlandish allegation that no one was buying.

Well, piss on him. My face heated. "No. I wasn't. I told you I was worried about her. I went into her rooms without Calhoun. Then when I found her, I guess I screamed."

"And that's when Calhoun joined you?"

"Yes." There was an edge to my tone.

The detective smiled. He seemed to enjoy rattling me. Sadistic bastard.

I took another sip from the bottle and attempted to calm myself.

"What did you and your cousin talk about at your sister's house?" the detective asked as Alex moved toward Eddie.

Felton had just put something in a little plastic bag. I tried to lean around and see, but the detective moved to block my view.

"I'd advise you to answer my question."

"I have been answering your questions," I huffed. "She told me how absurd she found the notion that my sister was guilty. She said Rainey Lane agreed with her." I rubbed the back of my neck. "They talk. Rainey Lane is . . . was her best friend." I wiped off the condensation from the bottle with my fingers. "Then she told me Tally Waters was meeting Carl some nights. She heard his car pull up at around two in the morning and then he brought her back around four." I didn't say anything about her raging jealousy. "She was upset."

"Why?"

"It seemed to bother her that Carl was seeing Tally." I didn't have proof that Judy and Carl were having an affair. And I wouldn't speak ill of the dead.

"How would she know they were meeting?"

"Her bedroom window is there." I pointed to the large window at the front of the inn. "The lights woke her, I guess."

"Why were they meeting?"

"She thought they were having an affair."

"Why is that?"

The tediousness of the questioning agitated me. "What else could they be doing in the middle of the night, Detective?" My tone became shrill. "I'm sorry." Recollection of the horrific sight caused the tears to freely flow. "This is just a little too much to cope with."

Eddie abruptly intervened. "Detective Thornton, I'm taking my daughter home now. She's had a shock. You can speak to her again tomorrow if you feel it necessary. Although, we both know it won't be."

The two men stood less than a foot from each other, locking horns in a battle of wills.

In the end, the detective relented, his boots crunching hard against the gravel as he retreated.

I learned two things on the ride home. One, Eddie's struggle with emotional ties to me and the critical detecting his job required drained him. Two, he hated that I kept witnessing violent crime scenes. He desperately wanted to protect his only daughter from the gruesome side of his job.

The warmth of the mug in my hands was my only comfort as I stared from the couch toward Eddie. He'd been debating how to approach me. I could tell from the way he kept furrowing his brow.

He finally blurted, "What's going on with you and that reporter?"

"Nothing."

His tone upset me.

His lids nearly closed to slits. "He was sitting

mighty close to you and holding your hand when I first arrived."

"I was distraught. He was just being nice."

Eddie sat on the couch next to me. Apparently, he wasn't moving until he got answers. "I don't want to upset you further, pumpkin, but I need to know what's going on here."

He probably already knew about the issue Calhoun had with the detective.

"He has a beef with the detective. He believes his brother was falsely charged and was on the path to proving it when his brother was murdered in prison. He also believes the detective is crooked." I sighed. "He has no motive that I can see."

"Other than to complicate life for the detective."

There was that. "I can think of a hundred other ways to hurt the detective. Killing Judy isn't one of them." I sniffed.

"I can't see that either." Eddie almost sounded regretful. "But stranger things have happened."

"If he wants to hurt Detective Thornton, getting arrested for murder isn't going to fit that bill."

"Most murderers don't have plans to get caught. But you're right. There are more effective ways of inflicting pain. That doesn't mean you can trust him." Eddie also appeared relieved that I had confided in him.

My mind went back to the whole reason I'd gone to my sister's in the first place. "Obviously I can't trust you either. You didn't tell me about Jena Lynn spending a week in the hospital!" My heart ached with the rawness of the wounds I carried deep within.

Eddie shoved both his hands through his hair, his face weary. "She made me promise not to. She didn't want you to worry. I thought it was in your best interest not to know."

"Like not telling me you were my father was in my best interest?"

He blew out a breath. "How many times do I need to apologize for that mistake?"

"Okay, I'm sorry. I need to let that one go. But this situation was completely different. She's *my* sister!"

"No one knew but Zach and me."

"And Alex!"

"Alex was told weeks later, after the diner re-opened. He overhead my conversation with Zach when he came by my office. I certainly didn't go into specifics. It was a rough time for your sister, but, in the end, it was her decision. I had to respect that." He sounded agitated.

"I'm tired." I was done with this conversation.

He stood. "I'll go."

We were both irritated.

"It's been a long day. I have an island in turmoil. I don't need you on my case about something I have apologized for profusely or for keeping confidences."

As the door closed, I rolled onto my side and cried myself to sleep.

Chapter 21

My brother was there when I woke. He was in the kitchen, wearing one of my aprons over his jeans and a Metallica T-shirt, frying diner-style hamburgers as I stumbled in.

"What time is it?"

"Eight thirty. The sun is about to go down. Have a seat. These are almost ready."

There was a pack of buns on the table, along with ketchup and mustard, cheese, and two bags of chips. And a pitcher of iced tea. "Betsy called about a dozen times."

"I didn't hear the phone."

He plated the burgers and brought them over to the table. "I took your phone. I thought you needed to sleep." He pulled my cell from his pocket and slid it on the table next to me. I had fifteen missed calls. Two from Alex, one from Jena Lynn, two from Yvonne, and the rest from Betsy.

Sam made me a plate and put it in front of me.

"Thank you." I gazed into his eyes.

"It was pretty awful, huh?"

"Yeah, it was." I poured myself some tea.

He sat down and filled his plate with two bacon cheeseburgers and a mound of chips. "She left a note," Sam said around a giant bite of burger.

"She did?" That had to be what Felton had in that little bag.

"Felton told me."

He better be careful telling Sam police business.

"The good news is the note exonerates Jena Lynn."

"What?" I couldn't believe my ears.

"She wrote something like, she was the one responsible for old man Ledbetter's murder. She switched out the sugar."

"Why would Judy do that?" That made no sense whatsoever.

"She was in love with Carl. Obsessed. When he wouldn't have anything to do with her, she lashed out. She wanted to hurt him. I don't think she thought about what might happen to the diner or Jena Lynn."

"She put all that in the note?"

"That's what Felton said. That and 'I'm sorry' to Jena Lynn. The guilt ate her up, I guess." Sam polished off his burger, while I tried to process all of this.

Judy had been upset about Tally and Carl, but I didn't think anyone saw her around the diner that day.

"Are they sure *she* wrote the letter?" I asked and Sam stopped mid-chew.

"They have ways of validating that. This is a good thing, Marygene. Judy was always an odd bird. I know it must have been terrible finding her. But at least she did the right thing by confessing before she checked out. The case against Jena Lynn will be dropped, and we can all finally get back to work. Which is a good thing, 'cause I'm about slap broke." Sam refilled his tea glass. "You should really try and eat."

Not wanting to seem like an ingrate, I dutifully picked up the burger and took a small bite. How long would it be before the charges were dropped? Would Detective Thornton buy this unfathomable coincidence? A letter admitting to the crime was mighty convenient. Plus, I just didn't see Judy killing Joseph Ledbetter. If she was so enraged, wouldn't that be a crime of passion? And that crime would have been enacted on Carl, not his dad.

"Are you listening to me?" Sam interrupted my thoughts.

"Sorry. What were you saying?" I focused on my brother's face.

"I was saying that now all we have to do is concentrate on getting those investors off our island."

I put the chip that I held between my fingers back on the plate. "That reminds me." I wiped my hands on the paper napkin. "You and that Tally Waters?"

He avoided eye contact. "It was dumb."

"She thought you had a stake in The Peach, right? That you could convince Jena Lynn to sell?"

He gave a quick nod of admission.

"You weren't using your head, or not the right one, anyway."

"I know." He got up and went to the fridge. He popped his head inside. "You don't have any beer." He grunted before closing the door.

"She's kind of scary looking, if you ask me. Plus, she threatened Jena Lynn."

"I thought she had an exotic look. She's not so bad." He leaned against the counter. "I think she was just trying to stand her ground with Jena Lynn. Show-no-fear kind of thing."

"I don't trust her. Judy told me she was seeing Carl."

Sam whistled. "Rainey Lane is going to be pissed." He glanced at his watch. "You all right here on your own? I mean, I'll stay if you want me to. Sleep on the couch or in your old room."

I stood and began clearing the table. "No. You go on. I appreciate you coming by and checking on me." I was sure Eddie put him up to it.

Sam deserved thanks anyway.

He took off the apron and gave me a swift kiss on the cheek. "Call if you need anything."

After Sam left, I added Judy to the evidence board and referenced the suicide. I also erased Ms. Brooks. Then I returned Betsy's call. According to her, news had spread all over the island about Judy's suicide. The note had as well. I bet the detective was bursting a blood vessel. He already hated small towns. If it got back to the department that

Felton had been running his mouth, Eddie might take his badge.

"Seriously, though," Betsy went on, "this might be just the bad publicity the investors need to clear out. Who's going to vacation on an island that had a murder and suicide so close together? Hey, maybe we should leak about ghosts lurking too. You get your mama to destroy some houses. Oh, we could make a list of our enemies. Scare the crap out of them in the process." She laughed. "That would be so fun!"

Only Betsy would say something like that.

"Bets, I'm not so sure Judy killed herself." I'd been mulling this over in my head since Eddie left. "And I certainly don't believe she killed Mr. Ledbetter."

"Why?" That's what I loved about Betsy. She never judged me. Never shouted what a nut I was for questioning the status quo.

"Well, for one thing, her fingernails were broken. When I saw her at Jena Lynn's, she had a beautiful manicure. But when I saw her in the—" I couldn't bring myself to say it. "Her index fingernail and pinky nail were jagged."

"You think someone killed her and made it look like a suicide? Maybe the same killer that took out Ledbetter? She was a snooper and ran her mouth a lot." Betsy went silent for a minute. "You shouldn't say anything about her nails."

"Because that would be bad for Jena Lynn." I finished her thought. "But surely they will take note of the state of the nails in the autopsy report. That should give them pause in ruling the death a suicide."

"Maybe, maybe not." I hated to think the killer was still out there. That none of us were safe.

We both settled into a worried silence. It appeared neither of us could come up with what to say next.

"I'll call you in the morning," I said.

"Okay, bye."

After my shower, the creaking of the old porch swing chains comforted me. The insects were loud tonight, but the breeze was nice. Sleep had eluded me and my mind was overloaded. How did Calhoun handle his questioning? I glanced at my phone. Did he come to the same conclusion I had? Would he leave the island if the case was closed? Surely, he would. His vendetta was against Detective Thornton. Understandably so. The detective would be assigned to another case, and Calhoun would probably follow. He definitely wasn't the one I should be discussing my theories with. Still, I debated calling him.

It was late. Too late. I called Alex instead.

He answered on the second ring. "What's wrong?" Alex sounded both alarmed and groggy.

"Oh, you were asleep. I'll let you go."

"No." There was a rustling of bedsheets. Was he alone? I regretted the call now. "It's okay. How are you?"

I let out an exaggerated sigh. "I can't even bake."

"That bad?"

"Yeah."

"Not to sound mean or anything, but you and Judy didn't exactly get along so well."

"She was still my second cousin. There was so

much blood. Gruesome is what it was." I'd nearly shrieked when I uttered the last word.

"I'm sorry. I didn't mean to sound callous. I know it was traumatic for you."

We settled into an awkward silence.

Then I asked, "Who interviewed Calhoun?"

"Detective Thornton." Silence. "You got a thing for that guy?" He sounded jealous.

"No."

"You sure were cozied up next to him."

"I was upset. Is it being ruled a suicide?" I was met with more silence. "Still under investigation then, huh? It's all over the island. Betsy called and knew about everything except the note. That I got from Sam."

"Detective Thornton is pissed about it too." Confirmation. "I heard him and Eddie going at each other in Eddie's office. I'll be so glad when this case is closed and things get back to normal."

"Me too. Detective Thornton said something to me the other day that I haven't been able to get out of my head."

"What was it?" He sounded interested.

"He seemed to believe that not everyone in the department thought Jena Lynn was innocent."

"He was probably just antagonizing you. It's a tactic to see what you'll divulge when you're angry. People get careless when they're riled."

I supposed that was true. "Sorry I woke you. Night."

"Night. I'm glad I'm the one you called."

Chapter 22

The charges against my sister were dismissed. The lawyer Eddie had hired was on the ball, filing a motion with the court. The new evidence was sufficient for the judge to rule. The state could still pursue the case; however, they would need new evidence to present. Jena Lynn's lawyer said he wasn't concerned. A huge relief for all of us, especially for my sister.

The detective had been waiting for me outside the diner last week with an unpleasant gleam in his eye. "Something is off about you," he'd said when I asked what I could do for him. "I can't put my finger on it." The way he'd studied me as if I was some exotic caged animal had made my skin crawl.

I'd scrounged up all the bravado within me. "People in glass houses shouldn't throw stones. Isn't that what they say?" I'd left him to chew on that.

He'd called after me, "You haven't seen the last of me, Ms. Brown."

I didn't even acknowledge it. Dissatisfied with my reaction, he'd peeled away from the curb.

The diner was scheduled to open again early next week. We needed time to place our orders with vendors. Almost everything that the forensic team didn't take had to be thrown out. It would be good for people to see us cleaning house, so to speak.

Charlie's son, Levi, applied for the new janitorial position. Jena Lynn hired him on the spot, despite my reservations.

"You sure that's such a good idea?" I asked after he left.

Jena Lynn continued wiping down the long counter. "Why would I penalize Levi because his dad died of a heart attack at an inopportune time?" She sighed. "Listen. I just want to put this whole ordeal behind me. The Peach Cove Sheriff's Department made a formal statement to the local paper citing my innocence. Let's just leave it at that."

They hadn't exactly cited her innocence. Eddie had simply stated the charges were dropped. Then he followed with how devastated the community was by the loss of a lifelong resident, who had tragically taken her own life, he added.

I hadn't mentioned the nails. It wasn't that Judy didn't deserve justice. She could have broken them some other way than a struggle for her life.

"Okay. We'll leave it at that," I said.

Jena Lynn smiled and dropped the rag into the bucket of bleach solution. "I saw you and Alex coming out of the movies the other night."

I smiled. "We're just friends. You know, hanging out."

"Whatever you say. Hey, I've got a doctor's appointment." She glanced over at all the menus that needed washing and sugar packets that needed to be unboxed.

"Everything okay?"

"Yeah. Just a checkup with Doc Tatum." Guess she was still on the meds.

"You go on. I can finish up here."

"You sure?" She began untying her apron.

"Of course. I can refill all the salt and pepper shakers and unbox the condiments too." We usually married all the condiments at the end of the night. Since we were starting over, we'd need to stock the shelves under the counter with what we'd need for the week. The rest of them would remain in cases back in the stockroom.

"Thanks. We'll need to be back in on Friday to receive the shipments and then again on Sunday to start making dough. Other than that," she glanced around the lit diner, "we're ready." She smiled and waved bye on her way out the front door. "Oh, one more thing," she paused. "I couldn't get ahold of Heather about her work schedule. I left messages, leaving your cell number as a backup if she couldn't get me."

"She was at Judy's funeral last week. You haven't heard from her since?"

"No. That's what concerns me."

"Are you worried she'll be a no-call-no-show?" People not calling and not showing up for work was common in the food service industry.

"That would be completely out of character for her. Finding work in Peach Cove can be arduous. That was one of the points Tally Waters used in her attempts to persuade residents."

"You think she'll be back?"

"Tally Waters?"

"Yeah."

"Maybe. She was close to having a majority."

"We'll be ready for her when and if she does. She'll be in for the fight of her life."

Jena Lynn agreed.

"Back to Heather," I said. "I'll try her again in a few and I'll let you know when I hear from her."

"Thanks. Lock the door," she yelled through the closed door, tapping on the glass.

It astounded me how she had readjusted. I was thankful. Jena Lynn walked to her car with a spring in her step after I secured the lock. Mama hadn't made another appearance. Maybe she was gone. Crossed over or whatever.

I had just finished stacking the last of the ketchup when there was a tap at the door. Rising from the floor, I stretched. Calhoun was waiting patiently for me to mosey on over.

I opened the door. "We're still closed."

"You alone?"

"Yes." I moved aside to allow him to enter and re-locked the door behind him.

"You wouldn't return my calls."

I lifted my hands, palms upward. "What's to say? Besides, I thought you would be long gone by now."

"Why?"

I moved over toward the pot of coffee I'd brewed earlier. I placed another mug next to mine and filled both. "There's no story. Jena Lynn's free. The detective's gone. It's over."

He took a sip from the mug. "You don't believe it's over." More sips.

"My back is tired." I moved around the counter in favor of a booth. "Let's sit back here." I slid onto peach vinyl. "So, tell me what you're still doing here. Eddie told me Detective Thornton has been reassigned. Why aren't you wherever he is?" I rubbed my neck.

"I can't get this case out of my mind. The suicide doesn't feel right. You don't suspect me anymore, do you?"

I shook my head.

"Good. It kept me up nights."

"Why?"

"You know why."

"I'm afraid I don't," I said.

Behind his lenses, he pierced me with his green gaze. His pupils were visibly dilated. *Uh-oh.* My pulse sped up, slightly. "Fate, or whatever you want to call it, brought us together."

"Fate, huh? I thought it was a cold-blooded killer."

"And that cold-blooded killer is still on this island. How can I go knowing that?"

I didn't respond.

"I went by Joseph Ledbetter's residence. It had been ransacked."

I leaned forward. "His villa or his house?"

"The villa." Intensity seeped from him. "I bet that's

where he kept those extra file copies. The house, not the villa."

"We really should leave this alone," I said half-heartedly.

"I can't. And, quite frankly, I'm surprised your father has."

Neither one of us knew for sure if he had. I, for one, didn't believe for a second Eddie would just let a case like this go. Let the public believe he had, perhaps. Not that I would let Calhoun in on my suspicions.

I wrapped my hands around the warm mug and debated how to broach the subject of his brother. The more information I had, the better I would understand this man sitting across from me. "How old are you? Thirty-seven, thirty-eight?"

"I'm forty-one." He pushed his mug around on the table. "You're wondering why a man of my age is still in the field chasing stories?" He read me well. "I love the field. Sitting in the office managing writers isn't for me."

"So, it's the chase that has you hooked?"

"That and exposing the truth to the world. Too many writers are in the pockets of those in power. They're more interested in lining their own pockets than embracing our First Amendment rights. If we stop utilizing the freedom of the press, then we're no longer the country we were intended to be. My brother's story was shut down." He gripped the handle of his mug so tightly, I feared it might break. "The other man found at the scene who was arrested the very same night as Timothy had his arrest expunged. There's no record of his involvement whatsoever."

He had my full undivided attention. From my searches, I saw no record of another man being at the scene who had also been charged with his brother, Timothy.

"Someone with clout had it erased?"

He nodded. "He was the son of a state senator."

"You believe Detective Thornton led the investigation deliberately away from the senator's son and falsely toward your brother? That's why you said he was dirty?"

"I do."

That detective had some nerve criticizing any of us.

"So, why not go after him instead of concerning yourself with what's going on in Peach Cove?" I got up and retrieved the coffeepot.

"Like I said, I can't stand by and allow the truth to be swept under the rug. And you're here."

I warmed up his coffee but didn't meet his intense gaze.

"Forget about my interest in you for a second. That doesn't mean anything to you, yet."

I looked up.

"Don't you want to know the truth? Expose whoever is behind this?" He was already aware that I did. Otherwise, he wouldn't be sitting here.

"If someone else dies because we sat on this information, I don't think I could live with myself."

I chewed on my bottom lip. "Neither could I. On

the other hand, I'm also afraid of what I might find. Or perhaps stir up." I sat the pot on the table.

"You don't strike me as a person who sticks her head in the sand. Why isn't the sheriff's department uncovering anything about this file Joseph Ledbetter had?"

"We don't know what the department is doing. And we have no evidence it's even a file we're looking for." But it had been weeks.

Alex hadn't had any new information on that front. I certainly didn't believe it was because Eddie was incompetent. My thoughts drifted back to Calhoun's story. Was it possible we had our own sort of corruption in the department? Could it be that Eddie was blind to what might be happening? Could Felton or even Alex be bought? No. Alex couldn't. Felton had grown up scrounging for anything and everything he possessed. His father had been cruel when his mother left, no longer able to handle her husband's abuse. I recalled Felton not having lunch on many occasions, and teachers bought it for him. He also had a mean streak if you crossed him. Maybe Carl bought him off.

"Tell me what you're thinking."

Did I trust this man before me? If I divulged my thoughts, could it hurt anyone or anything? Trust didn't come easily for me. But letting him in on my train of thought certainly wouldn't cause harm. That I could see, anyway. I relayed my thoughts.

"Do you think Felton would purposely derail the investigation? Is he capable of that?"

I drummed my nails on the table. "Maybe. Felton

was always so sweet on the outside. But you never felt like you really knew him. Heather would be a better judge of the man he now is." I leaned against the booth. "You know, I haven't seen much of Heather since the diner closed. And Jena Lynn said she left messages on her voice mail about the shift schedule."

"Would it be odd for you to drop by her house and check on her? Ask some questions while you're there?"

"I don't think so."

He had me. I wanted to find out the truth. Not just for myself. Also, to expose who had put my family through such an ordeal and for Judy. Then there was Mr. Ledbetter. As much of a cad as he was, no one deserved to be murdered.

Calhoun slid out of the booth. "Think on it." He glanced at his watch. "I have to drive back into the city. My editor in chief isn't happy with me at the moment."

"Thanks to Eddie," I added.

"I should be back the day after tomorrow."

Now that Calhoun was leaving, I second-guessed my decision to tell him anything. It must have shown on my face.

"Make no mistake that I'm invested in this. And my feelings for you are real." I opened my mouth to refute his claim but he cut me off. "I know, it's fast. Too fast."

Then, to my surprise, he leaned in and kissed me gently on the lips. His lips were soft and tender at first. Then he pulled me tighter and kissed me with more urgency.

I was breathless when he released me.

"I've been dying to do that since the first moment I saw you."

"Calhoun, I—"

"You don't have to say anything. I have no expectations. Hopes but not expectations." He pushed his glasses up on his nose. "See you in two days, three at the most."

Chapter 23

The old Ledbetter place was a large beach house sitting on the west side of the island. An elevated two-story, low-country-style cottage with a large wraparound porch. It was painted a pale blue with gray storm shutters. It had been glorious in its day, but time and salty air had taken a toll on the old place. A couple years before I was born, to preserve wildlife, the area around the Ledbetter home was zoned and protected by conservation efforts. In school, we were brought here on a field trip to watch sea turtles hatch and migrate back to the ocean. It was a real private place, and the more I considered what Sally had told me, the more I was convinced I needed to see for myself that what Mr. Ledbetter had given me was nothing. Or at least I'd convinced myself that even if Calhoun hadn't sparked my curiosity, I would be checking this out anyway. I'd gone by Heather's place. She hadn't been home. Her niece was there babysitting the kids.

The weathered wooden staircase creaked under my weight. I took a moment to take in the ocean view. The breeze coming off the ocean was glorious, and the moonlight dancing on the wave peaks was a sight to behold. How had I ever left the island of my birth? I was a Georgia coastal girl through and through.

The front door opened with the barest of touches from my fingertips. My heart was beating in my ears. I fought to keep my legs from shaking. It wouldn't be like the Ledbetters to leave the place unsecured, especially since he was interested in selling. What was I doing coming here at this time of night?

Three schools of thought ran through my mind— one, I could call Eddie and he could send a patrol car over here and investigate the scene. Two, if Carl was involved in the death of his father or Judy and I sounded the alarm by making the call, I'd be in hot water for trespassing on private property. And three, if I waited to decide, and someone snuck up on me standing here, I could end up like Mr. Ledbetter. I listened at the door for about thirty seconds. No rustling sounds. No noise was detectable whatsoever, except for the waves and the chorus of insects.

Still, part of me wanted to turn back. The other encouraged me to continue. That latter part won out. I clicked on the flashlight icon on my cell phone. It had been years since I had been inside this old place. But, from the way the contents of cabinets and drawers were strewn all over the floor of the large living-dining room combo, I was certain that, like the villa, this place had also been ransacked by evidence seekers. Perhaps those searching didn't know exactly what they were after. I did.

It could have been the sheriff's department. Alex and Felton probably weren't accustomed to cleaning a place up after searching for evidence. I stepped around the piles on the floor and shined the light on them. It just appeared to be a bunch of old bills and receipts. I moved around the large white leather couch to a door that led to the basement. Sally had said that was where Mr. Ledbetter kept his files.

After a deep breath and a cross of my chest for good luck, I opened the door. "Do you honestly believe—"

I let out a scream that would have rattled the rafters, if there had been rafters to rattle.

"Good Lord, Marygene!" Mama huffed. "Get ahold of yourself."

I put my hand on my chest. "Are you trying to give me a heart attack?" I panted. "I thought you were gone. It's been weeks."

"Obviously, I'm not gone. I told you I can't appear at will. I'm here *now* to try and talk some sense into you." Mama frowned. "It shouldn't be possible, but sometimes, child, you surprise me with your sense of logic." Mama glanced around, turning her nose up at the mess. "You never were able to let sleeping dogs lie."

I snorted.

"Maybe you should call Edward and have him come investigate this place." Mama never addressed him as Eddie, like everyone else did. To her, he was always Edward.

"Because, Mama, he can't legally search the premises. That would be unethical. I don't have the constraints the sheriff's department does, so I'm the one who should be doing the snooping."

"I'm not a fan of that tone." She gave me *the* look. You know, that *you should know better* glare.

"Sorry," I grumbled.

"What you're looking for isn't here, anyway," Mama said. "So, you might as well run along home now."

"And you know this how?"

"I know this, child, because I have knowledge of who has possession of the file." Finally, she was going to use her ghostly handicap to assist me.

"I'm waiting."

"I can't tell you."

I let me head fall backward. "Then why are you even here?" I ground out between clenched teeth. "You show up at the most inopportune times with useless information. What the hell is the point?"

"Don't you use that tone and language with me, young lady."

Ugh, I refocused the light and went down the basement steps anyway. Despite her urging that the evidence was no longer in the house.

"I honestly believe you're actually here to hinder me." The basement smelled damp and full of mold. My light reflected off several large spiderwebs.

This place was majorly packed with old boxes and furniture. The minimal amount of light that came through the small square windows at the top of the wall wasn't enough to illuminate my path.

"I'm doing the best I can," Mama insisted. "My predicament is far more complicated than you realize. It isn't as if I can just pop in and solve your problems for you. They want me to work for this. To earn my place." Mama kept prattling on about the difficulty in completing her task of making amends. Clearly, in her mind, this was all about her.

"Cry me a bucketful." I shoved a couple of boxes aside.

"If you're going to be snippy, I won't tell you where the file cabinet is. Not that it will do you any good."

I put a hand on my hip and shined the light directly on her reflection. "There's nothing in there I can use? That's what you're telling me?"

"I didn't say that. On the back wall." She pointed to the opposite side of the room. "There."

"Gee, thanks." I gave her an exaggerated eye roll.

My shin hit something extremely hard, and I yelped. My yoga pants weren't much protection from whatever had left an imprint on my leg. I rubbed the sore spot and shoved a large metal umbrella stand aside. Against the back wall stood six metal filing cabinets. I started with the first one.

It took me nearly an hour to get through all the files. Mr. Ledbetter obviously didn't believe in filing things in alphabetical order. It contained mostly copies of billing receipts and business documents. Then, in the last cabinet, there were loads of documents about Carl, Carl's mother, and several other women in the community who were no longer with us. All were labeled with letter and number combinations similar to what Mr. Ledbetter had given me. It *was* a file he had led me to.

I came to one on Miss Sally.

"What's in there?" Mama asked over my shoulder the second I pulled the file. She obviously wasn't privy to everything.

"It appears to be medical records." I flipped through several documents. "Here's a record of Sally's hospital stay and what she was treated for. Complications after a D&C procedure." Poor Miss Sally.

"How could Mr. Ledbetter get his hands on her medical records? Those are sealed to everyone except the patient." I considered having a word with Doc Tatum. Her uncle preceded her as the practicing physician in the family practice.

"It hasn't always been that way. Plus, Sally could have signed a document allowing him access."

"Why on earth would she have consented to that?"

Mama gave her head a sad shake. "Sally loved that man, and for the life of me, I have no idea why. He warmed her bed when Evelyn had enough of his shenanigans and threw him out for a few weeks. And, from the rumors, Sally wasn't the only one," Mama said.

I flipped through a stack of pictures, some of which should never see the light of day. "She should have never allowed him to take these of her." I put the pictures back.

Mama agreed. For her protection, I considered taking them with me and burning them. But, that would be unwise.

In the back of the folder, I found a death certificate. According to this, five years after her procedure, Sally had given birth to a girl. She had been stillborn.

"Did you know about this?" I asked Mama.

"No. Poor Sally."

Miss Sally sure had her own crosses to bear.

"Well, this doesn't explain what the twins overhead about another son. Mr. Ledbetter said Carl wasn't his only son, not his only child," I told Mama. "And this particular child didn't survive."

Respectfully, I placed the file back into the cabinet. That was when I spotted a torn document lying at the bottom of the drawer. I reached in and extracted the remnant. It must have been torn on the jagged edge, perhaps taken out in haste.

"It's part of a birth certificate," I turned to Mama.

Her mouth was moving, but I heard nothing. Her hair appeared to sizzle with electricity. "Get down!" she shouted.

A force slammed me to the hard floor. A loud popping echoed. Flashes of light lit up the basement. Shards of glass exploded from the old lamps and framed images. I laid there, in the darkness, waiting to feel the penetration of a bullet.

"Run!" Mama shouted in my ear. With my phone

and the torn piece of certificate clutched in my hand, I shot up the stairs, the small light from my phone my only guide. More shots whizzed past me. I felt the air disturbances as the bullets sliced through dead space.

My legs were jelly. My arms and face tingled. I slipped on the papers on the floor of the living room and went down hard. The side of my head hit the tile with a thud. Stars exploded across my vision.

"Get up!" Mama shouted. "Marygene! Get yourself up!"

With as much force as I could muster, I pushed myself upright and scrambled to my feet. When I reached the front porch steps, I didn't take precautions and survey the area for the shooter. Mama was at my ear shouting for me to go, go, go! I raced down the stairs.

The car door flung open just before I reached it. I felt no relief as I peeled out of the driveway, driving faster than was safe.

"Oh God, Mama," I said, but the car was empty. "What on earth have I stumbled onto?"

My vision was a bit blurry as I drove. I kept blinking to clear the spots. I'd be okay if I could just get home. I *would* be okay.

I talked to Mama the whole way. It didn't matter if she could hear me or not. I told her everything. All about my life, about how horrible Peter had been. All my theories on the investigation.

Relief hit when the old place came into view.

Once home, I barricaded myself inside. I checked

all the windows to make sure they were locked. In the darkness of my living room, a thought occurred to me.

Thank God Mama had been there or I might not be here.
"Thank you, Mama," I whispered in the darkness.

Chapter 24

That night I slept with Mama's old revolver on my bedside table, not that I had managed more than a few interrupted hours of slumber. I had considered calling Calhoun, since it was his influence that spurred me on, but then I decided against it. He would feel obligated to rush back here, and I wasn't sure how I felt about that. Sure, he would be willing to help me dig, but his feelings for me complicated matters. If I told Alex, he would tell Eddie. Not to mention how angry he would be about Calhoun. Another complication. I called Betsy instead.

"What in God's name were you thinking, Marygene?" Betsy shouted at me. "You could have been killed. At least your spook mama is good for somethin'."

Betsy was the only person on the planet I would confide in with that tidbit about Mama. Betsy had huffed and puffed but, in the end, she was curious about what I had found. I had to insist she wait until morning to come over and promised to add the incident to our board.

I was worn out and needed to try and get some sleep. It had been her urging that sent me rummaging through the closet to find the revolver. It certainly wasn't a surprise to hear a car pull up as I moved a sheet pan of biscuits from the oven to the counter the next morning. I had taken solace in rolling out the buttermilk dough and making a giant skillet of sausage gravy.

The melted butter sat next to the pan, my pastry brush poised and ready to apply it. There was a knock at the back door.

"Coming!" I placed the brush in the dish. With the hand towel slung over my shoulder, I swung the door open.

Betsy was standing there with a guilty expression on her face. Before I could inquire, I spied Alex, dressed in his uniform, stalking up on the porch, fuming mad. I swear I could almost see the steam emitting from his ears.

"Betsy!" I could have pummeled her with my fists.

In response, Betsy slammed her plus-sized figure against me and squeezed me for all she was worth. "Don't be mad. I was scared to death for you." A couple of seconds later, she said, "Oh, biscuits and gravy," and released me.

"I haven't buttered them yet." I tried to avoid Alex's gaze. Those eyes piercing me the way they were now always forced my heart into dangerous arrhythmic patterns.

"I'll help. That's what I'm here for." Betsy went toward the stove.

Alex wasn't much taller than me, but since he outweighed me by a hundred pounds, he was slightly imposing. Especially with all the rage rolling off him.

"What were you doing at the Ledbetter place?" His tone was low. "Other than breaking and entering, that is."

"I didn't break in. The door was open." I moved aside to let him enter. "You didn't tell Eddie, did you?"

"No. Not yet." This wasn't a side of him I enjoyed.

My eyes stung with fatigue. God, I was *so* tired. "Listen, I just needed to see for myself if there was anything to what Mr. Ledbetter gave me. And," I paused as he closed the screen door, "it turns out there was." I informed him of everything I found in the basement. The files with numerical sequences, like what the old man had shoved into my hand. How the place had been tossed and, from his expression, I was certain it hadn't been the handiwork of the Peach Cove Sheriff's Department.

He gripped my shoulders with both hands, his fingers digging in. "You still shouldn't have gone there." He gave my shoulders a little shake. "You aren't authorized to investigate anything. You could have been killed!"

"Get off me!" I shoved against his chest. "What's wrong with you?"

He dropped his hands and stepped back, his chest heaving with emotion. "There's nothing wrong with me. I am an officer of the law. If the incident was reported, I could be forced to arrest you."

"I doubt the person firing at me will report anything. They'd have way too much to explain."

"She has a point there," Betsy said around a giant mouthful of biscuit and gravy. "And Alex cares about you, Marygene. He's just too stubborn to admit his feelings for you."

Alex and I both whirled on her.

"Marygene has the hots for you too. But she's just as bullheaded as you are."

If looks could kill, she would be dead.

"Don't mind me." She refilled her plate. "Just pretend I'm not even here. You two have got a lot to work out."

"Betsy, give us a minute," Alex said.

"No, you don't have to. We're through," I said.

"Betsy, go," he said and she started toward the living room, plate in hand.

"Betsy, stay," I said and she stopped mid-stride. I had no intention of complicating my life further.

Alex felt he had the right to impose his will on me. Sure, there were unresolved feelings between us. That was obvious to both of us. It just wasn't the time. I moved to the hutch, where Mama's knick-knacks were kept, opened the drawer, and extracted the partial certificate.

"Since you're both here, you might as well have a look at this." I placed it on the table.

The three of us crowded around, trying to make out what we were seeing.

"That's a birth certificate all right," Betsy said.

I pointed to the mother's name. We could only make out the first two letters. An H and what appeared to be either an e or o.

"This is all you have?" Alex asked incredulously. "It could belong to anyone."

"If you ask me, it is puzzlin' that old man Ledbetter had those records," Betsy said, her mouth slap full.

"I thought so too. I figured we could go down to the courthouse and see if we can match it with a birth certificate on file. It shouldn't be that difficult to narrow down the mother on the certificate and find out if Ledbetter was named as the father," I said.

"That's a good idea, Marygene." Betsy patted my shoulder. "If we can find out if the old codger had another son, we'll finally be gettin' somewhere."

"Oh, yeah, great idea," Alex folded his arms. "There's only a few problems with that."

Betsy and I waited.

"For one, birth certificates aren't public records, and we would need a warrant to access the records. We have absolutely no cause to gain one nor do we have an idea who this belongs to. Two, say we we're able to obtain a warrant, this piece of so-called evidence would be inadmissible because it was obtained by illegal means. Three, not everyone claims paternity of their offspring. And four, say we got lucky and he had signed off on said kid, you would have to go on record, admitting to a crime. They might even call the detective back to investigate further."

"Calhoun believes Detective Thornton is dirty," I said thinking out loud. "Perhaps he took the file."

Alex shouted, "You've been keeping in touch with the reporter?"

"He came by the diner the other day. And that reminds me, you told me he was a by-the-book detective. Calhoun has evidence to the contrary."

He squared his shoulders and faced me head-on. Betsy was pushed out of the middle.

"What are you implying?" he spat.

"Hey, y'all," Betsy interjected.

"I'm not implying anything. I just want to know if you still think Detective Thornton is a pristine detective."

"Do you always believe everything people tell you?" Alex's jaw clenched.

"No." I bared my teeth.

If he wanted a fight, he'd certainly get one!

He took a step closer to me. "You believe the reporter?"

I jerked my head.

His neck was corded and his arms tensed. Boy, was he angry. "Some asshole floats into town with tall tales, dangling bait in front of your pretty little face, and you just bite? You've known him for two seconds. Me, you've known your whole damn life."

"Um . . . y'all," Betsy said louder.

"Where is all this anger coming from?" I shrieked. "Somebody is going around murdering people.

And since the department had to march to the tune of a crooked cop, I felt I had to do something."

That was a grave allegation I honestly didn't believe. He had ruffled my feathers and I was lashing out.

"And your keen investigative skills led you to believe I was dirty? Perhaps you think I'm the one going around killing people?" His voice teetered on unhinged.

"Don't be stupid," I said, more calmly.

He felt patronized, that was beyond obvious. Guilt washed over me like a tidal wave and I was searching for the appropriate words to apologize effectively, when he said, "What's with you and older men? Daddy issues?"

I gasped. "How dare you?"

That was the ugliest thing he could have ever said in this moment. And *he'd said it.*

His facial expression changed, and he took a step forward. I took one backward.

Eddie's commanding voice boomed, "Enough."

"I tried to warn y'all," Betsy said softly.

Chapter 25

Eddie wasn't happy with any of us. Alex had to start his shift, so he got off easy. He'd been dismissed with a deep growl and a sharp glare that promised a major chewing-out was in his future. His "daddy issues" comment would cost him. Betsy had tried to leave with him, but I had a vise grip on her arm. She'd reluctantly sat down at the kitchen table next to me.

The clicking sound my nails made against my blush nail polish bottle drew Eddie's attention.

He closed his large fist over my hands as he sat. "Tell me in detail what happened and what you saw at the Ledbetter place."

What I hadn't realized until this moment was that he wasn't angry because I had made an impulsive decision that could have ended my life. He was terrified that I had.

My knees wouldn't stay still as I rested my hands in my lap. "It all happened so fast. I was in the basement searching through the filing cabinet. One minute I was reading a file and the next shots were being fired. I hit the floor and waited. When the firing ceased, I took off up the stairs." I took in a shaky breath. "I felt a bullet slice through the air beside my head."

His jaw tightened and he glanced away, his hands clenching and releasing as if he was having a one-man battle. The next words he uttered came out softer and more controlled. "When you were on the floor, did you hear anything. Footsteps, a window creaking open?"

"Actually," I thought, "I heard glass breaking. Like, with a hard object."

"Like with a butt of a gun?" he asked.

"Could be. It was to my left, so it had to be one of the windows below the wraparound porch."

He nodded.

"You're going to go and see if you can find a footprint?" The ground might be soft enough after the rain to grab on to a boot or shoe.

"So, you ran up the stairs . . ." Eddie encouraged me to continue.

"I did, then tripped on a pile of paper in the living room." My hand went to the evidence on my forehead. "It had been tossed before I got there."

"What happened next?" Eddie asked.

"I scrambled to my feet and—"

Betsy interjected, "She ran for her life."

"Right. I didn't see anyone, but I wasn't looking either. No one shot at me when I was outside." Hearing the words aloud, puzzled me. *Wouldn't they have had a clear shot?* I was a panicked woman, running haphazardly out in the open. Could Mama have protected me?

Eddie's brow was wrinkled as he rested his hands on the table.

I could almost see the wheels turning within his skull. "You're thinking the person didn't want to kill me. They were just trying to scare me away?"

"That's exactly what I'm thinking," Eddie said.

"Wow, you guys have got like ESP or somethin'." Betsy stood. "Y'all don't need me here, so I'll just mosey on home."

"Wait," Eddie said and Betsy slowly sat back down. "I take it when Marygene got home, she called you, then you called your cousin?"

"Um, yeah." Betsy hesitated, unable to meet Eddie's gaze, "That's, um, right." She turned to me. "Sorry about that again. I just didn't know what else to do."

"It's okay," I said. "I probably wouldn't have listened to you either if roles were reversed."

Betsy's face relaxed marginally.

"What else do I need to know?" Eddie asked. Did he think I would withhold information? Clearly, he did.

Betsy fidgeted in her seat, readjusted her sage-colored flounce top, and then pretended to dust something off her white capris.

"Betsy," Eddie said more sternly. "Look at me."

I willed her to be strong. It would be easier if it came from me. Slowly, Betsy's chin lifted.

The second she made eye contact with him, she cracked. "Nothin' much." She held her breath for a whole two seconds. "Only that Marygene noticed that Judy's fingernails were broken when she found her and they hadn't been earlier that day when they spoke. She must have been in a struggle. But if she said anything, it would look bad for Jena Lynn, so she kept her trap shut."

"Betsy!" I cried. That was news I planned on telling Eddie. The way Betsy phrased it made it sound awful.

"And?" Eddie said calmly as he held her gaze.

Betsy squeezed her eyes shut. "And she has a timeline and witness list upstairs in her old bedroom."

I gaped and sat back. The wood creaked in protest.

"It's real professional, though. I might've helped a tad."

Eddie spared a glance in my direction. I couldn't tell if he was amused or surprised. "Is that all?"

"Yes," I said.

"Betsy?"

She cringed. "She and that reporter have been secretly meetin'." She mouthed sorry to me. "Oh," she took a breath.

Please don't mention Ma—

"And her mama has been hauntin' her. She's stuck here trying to make amends."

I did a double take on Betsy's face. Her mouth was still moving. She was merciless in her account.

"She saved Marygene's life last night, though, so I guess it's going okay." She slowly rose from the table and took a step back. "I'm sorry! He was interrogatin' me like a common criminal. Anyone would crack under that sort of pressure." She snatched her purse off the chair opposite her. "Don't be mad."

Betsy bolted toward the door. The screen door slammed behind her.

Eddie folded his arms across his uniformed chest and zeroed in on me with his eyes. His spine was as straight as a board as he studied me. There was no use trying to get out of this. He would drag me downtown officially if he had to.

"Do you want some breakfast?" I stood. "I made some biscuits and gravy. Coffee too."

He didn't respond.

"Well, I need some coffee." I marched to the pot and poured myself a full cup. I took my time doctoring it with sugar and cream.

Eddie stayed silent during my seven-stir ritual. I poured him a cup, too, with two sugars and no cream. When I got back to the table, he was still seated in the exact same position. Not even his facial expression had changed.

After I sat his mug in front of him, I retook my seat. A few sips later, I rubbed my upper arms and sighed. "Judy was at Jena Lynn's when I went by to check on her. We chatted in the kitchen for a bit. That's when I noticed her new manicure. She had lovely little rhinestones glued to the tips. She acted skittish." I slowly sipped from the mug and thought back to that day. It wasn't difficult. This whole island mystery consumed my thoughts every waking minute. Not to mention the ordeal with Mama. I was not going to bring that up. Eddie would lock me away in the looney bin for sure.

"You didn't mention the nails to the detective due to a lack of trust?"

My head nodded in a jerking fashion. This wasn't going as well as I planned. "You investigated Carl, didn't you? I mean, he would have motive to end his dad's life. And maybe Judy found out . . ." I paused, considering the possibilities, while I cradled my mug close. "Or what if she knew all along and couldn't live with it. That would explain the suicide, if it was indeed a suicide. And if not, Carl could have staged it to appear as one. He would have access to her quarters, especially if they were having an affair."

Eddie scooted his chair closer. "Did you tell the truth about why Calhoun was with you when you found the body?" he asked when I had hoped he would divulge information on his investigation.

"Yes." I shouldn't have felt insulted, yet, on some level, I did.

"How many times have you met with the man and what was the topic of discussion when you were together?"

"He and I had only met on a couple other occasions."

No surprise showed, despite his emotional fatherly tie to me. He was good at this. I had to give him credit. I recounted every single detail I could think of that Calhoun had shared with me. And his concern that someone in the Peach Cove Sheriff's Department might be taking bribes to throw off the investigation. Had I been foolish to trust the man? Mr. Ledbetter had said not to trust anyone. But surely that was just the ramblings of a dying old man who had burned every bridge he had ever crossed. A young woman in my position had to confide in someone. Sometimes it was easier to unburden to a stranger. And dangerous. Time to come completely clean.

After I told him of my visit to the twins, I slid over the partial birth certificate. In my assessment, I had pretty much covered it all. "That's everything."

Silence seemed to stretch out for days. "You didn't feel that you could come to me? Your own father?" His tone was low, his face set to stone.

I sighed. "I didn't want to cause you any trouble with that detective in town. He obviously hated me." Then I told him of the detective's visit and his jaw clenched. "I mean, I suppose, from his perspective, I was at the scene of both crimes. I was the daughter of the sheriff, and if he was accustomed to being pulled by his strings like a puppet by people in power to protect their own kids, he would naturally assume you'd protect me."

He and I both knew that he would. "He never should have come here in the middle of the night like that. He owed me the professional courtesy of coming to me first." The vein in Eddie's forehead made an appearance.

The scrap of paper I had given him was between his fingers. I don't think he even saw it. His mind was obviously elsewhere. In Atlanta. With Detective Thornton.

"Do you think Felton could be swayed to derail the investigation?"

He whipped upright.

"I know he's one of your guys, but is it possible?"

He rubbed the nape of his neck several times in

succession, while he appeared to be contemplating his word choices. "If I've learned anything on this job, it's that anything is possible."

"Don't be too tough on Alex. He felt I insulted his integrity."

"That boy has a hot temper, but he's solid and trustworthy," Eddie said grimly. "We will have words."

"With the risk of becoming redundant, I sincerely believe we may have a clue here," I said in an attempt to redirect his attention to the more important matter.

"All the unlawful reasons Alex listed preventing us from gaining access to this document, plus establishing paternity, are accurate, pumpkin."

I sighed, scrambling my thoughts in hopes of discovering a brilliant solution to the problem.

"That reporter, Roy Calhoun," Eddie broke into my thoughts. "Where is he now?"

"He told me he had a meeting with his editor in chief and would be back in a few days."

Eddie wasted no time. He pulled his cell phone from the holster on his hip and he tapped the screen.

I got up while he was making the call, nervous Calhoun had deceived me. Still, I hung around and listened while he asked for the editor by name. Cringing, I placed the mug into the sink when Eddie inquired about Calhoun and froze when Eddie said, "I see. Thank you for your time." I wouldn't lie to myself. It would hurt if he hadn't been honest with me. Using me to get information would be an unforgivable offense.

"He's there, or at least his editor says he is. And

I see no reason why he would lie. It would be easy to confirm if he was," Eddie said.

"Phew, that would have been a pisser," Betsy said. Her face appeared and pressed against the screen door. "I need a ride home. I forgot I rode over here with Alex."

Chapter 26

Doc Tatum's waiting room was painted a cool pale blue. Green plants were strategically placed throughout to give her patients a pleasant room to sit in while they waited for an exam room for ages. I'd called first thing this morning and was able to get Mrs. Gentry, the receptionist/office manager, to squeeze me in. Mrs. Gentry had been on staff at this practice way before Doc Tatum took over.

"Marygene," Mrs. Gentry called from the little patient window at the front of the room.

"Yes, ma'am." I propped my elbows on the open window.

Mrs. Gentry's hair always reminded me of a dandelion. One blow and her roots would fly all over the room. She had a puckered mouth, from her former years of smoking, I presumed, and large hazel eyes. "How's Mayor Bill and Junior doing?"

Mrs. Gentry smiled warmly, "You know the mayor. Always up to his eyeballs in work. And my son is doing quite well. He's working the docks this summer, training with the old fishermen. Thanks for asking about him. I'll tell him you said hi."

I nodded as she turned back to the computer screen. I'd always wondered about Junior. He was a few years younger than me and hadn't gone to our schools. He's been sent away to a boarding school in Savannah. His mother was so protective of him.

"Hon," Mrs. Gentry brought me back into the present. "You haven't been seen since we updated our record system, so I'm going to need you to fill out the new patient forms." She handed me a clipboard with several forms attached, along with a pen.

"What happened to all the old records?" I had been hoping they wouldn't have me on file. A perfect excuse to ask questions.

"Oh, we have them, most of them, anyway. But we only added active patients to the computer." I wanted to ask where they kept the old records. Unfortunately, for me, another few coughing patients were behind me, waiting for their turn to sign in.

I held my breath as I took the forms and settled in a seat in the corner of the room. This would be a horrible time to come down with a cold.

To say I was surprised to see Ms. Brooks and Yvonne would have been an understatement. Yvonne settled next to me after she signed her mama in. "What are you doing here? You sick?"

"Headache," I lied and rubbed my forehead.

"Oh, that's a nasty bruise," Yvonne whispered. "What happened?"

"I ran into the door," I lied.

"Uh-huh." Her brow wrinkled.

"No." I put the clipboard aside. "This is not like before. I swear. We're through, and I haven't seen him since I moved back."

Her brows relaxed and she squeezed my hand. "I'm sorry. It's just . . ."

"No, I know. Never again." Perspiration soaked my neck. I'd made that promise to myself on so many occasions. But the day it all came pouring out to Yvonne at lunch was the day it solidified within my heart. Since Yvonne still lived close to me, she had been the one I confided in first. It had taken me far too long to seek help, and if I was being honest, I hadn't even intended to tell her. Shame is an awful damaging emotion and one I never should have owned. I'd been at my wit's end the day we had lunch and it all just came out. She'd urged me to move back home to the island with her, and moving back together had been the moral support I needed to get me through. I loved her for it.

"How's the house buying coming? You got a contract on it yet?" Need for a subject change was dire.

"Yeah, but with what happened to Judy, things have slowed to a snail's pace."

"Marygene Brown." My name was called, and I stood.

"I'll catch up with you later, okay?"

Doc Tatum examined my forehead, had me follow the light with my eyes, and checked all my vitals while I sat on the paper-lined table in the small examining room.

"Say," I said casually, "what happened to all the

old records you used to keep? I mean, I didn't see any filing cabinets in the hallway. That's where they used to be."

Doc Tatum was an elegant woman in her late fifties. She was tall, slim and had the appearance of a woman ten years her junior. She regarded me with curiosity as she rolled the chair away from the laptop. "If you're concerned about your file, we still have it. Inputting all inactive patients would be incredibly time-consuming. That's why we made the decision to only include active patients."

"What about deceased patients? Do you still have those records?"

"We always retain patient records. Why do you ask?"

"Like all the way back to your uncle's practice?"

"I suppose so. Unless some of those files were destroyed when Hurricane Matthew struck."

Oh, I'd forgotten about that.

She stood. "Well, you don't seem to have a concussion. You do have a good-sized contusion, but the knot came out, so I wouldn't worry. I'd just take ibuprofen for the pain. I can write you a prescription for eight hundred milligrams if you'd like."

I hopped off the table. "No. That's okay. I would like to ask you one more question, if that's all right."

Her head cocked to one side.

I took that as a yes. "Around the time I was born, or perhaps fifteen years before that, were all the island babies delivered in Savannah?"

"Some of them. My uncle assisted at some home births during his practice. And I've delivered a few babies right here in this office. Why do you ask?"

I glanced at my feet. "Losing Judy, I just got to thinking about the past. Our history and how something like this shouldn't have ever happened here." I raised my head. "The island has always been such a close-knit community. I remember Mama and Nanny packaging up meals for families after a new birth."

She smiled. "Marygene," her tone was gentle. Too gentle. "I noticed you have several healed fractures on your X-rays."

I flinched. How had she gotten ahold of my X-rays?

She pointed to the computer. "With the new software, we're able to share records and test results with other practices and hospitals."

I bit down on my bottom lip. Hard. "I didn't say you could gain access to those."

She reached out and gently touched my shoulder. "You did. You signed the waiver in the new patient packet. It's pulled when your name and social security number are entered into the system."

My throat was dry. That meant that Mrs. Gentry would know. God, if she told anyone, I'd be mortified. "Well, erase it." My tone rose. "Erase it all!" I wasn't ready for this. A tremor ran through my body. I didn't want my past to define me. Looks of pity from neighbors and friends would be excruciating.

"Honey, it's confidential."

"Nothing is confidential on this island." I jerked open the door and bolted from the room. My chest constricted. I couldn't breathe. Disoriented, I went the wrong way, knocking over a potted plant near the restroom. I plowed through the emergency exit, and the alarm went off.

"It's okay." Doc Tatum was at my side. She had calmed the staff down and had the alarm disabled. "Head between your legs and take long, deep breaths. In through your nose and out through your mouth."

I did the exercise. I had done it many times before.

Her hand stroked my back. Tears blurred my vision. "No one will know. This is your cross. You can unburden when and if you decide to. But honey, there is an excellent support group for women that is run by a colleague of mine. It would help. You have absolutely nothing to be ashamed of." The sobs grew and she held me to her. "I know it doesn't feel like it now, but you will heal. And you have lots of family and friends who will support and love you through this. It is not your fault."

The air blew full blast against my cheeks as I stared out the windshield across the street toward the diner. Lovebugs speckled across my line of sight as I continued my deep-breathing exercises. I had allowed Doc Tatum to phone me in a prescription. Panic attacks were something I'd like to avoid in the future. My chest still felt tight and my hands tingled. Doc Tatum had offered to meet me later, be a listening ear. She was one of the good ones. She genuinely cared about her patients. I wasn't ready but promised that I'd consider the support group, and I would. Especially now that I understood that this sort of trauma proved more difficult to put behind me than I anticipated. This needed to be dealt with, faced head-on, and then, like Doc Tatum had said, I would heal. Being a perfectionist, I never wanted to admit that I wasn't special enough to fix Peter and my marriage. Too full of pride, my nanny would have said. And I had been too prideful to seek help. And maybe on some level I felt as if I was partly to blame. Whether factual or not, I had to flush these feelings out.

One last deep breath and I began to calm. My hands were steadier now, a good sign. When a large Suburban pulled out of the space next to me, I noticed Betsy's car parked on the far left side of the lot. I needed some normalcy and a friend. Without a moment's hesitation I hurried across the street and into the diner.

"You still mad at me?" Betsy asked as we were wiping down tables and booths.

I'd taken solace in the mundane tasks. It was amazing how comforting menial tasks were.

"No," I said. "Eddie wouldn't have let you leave until you were completely forthcoming with any information you had."

"He didn't ask you about your mama. That was a relief." She tossed her rag into the bucket of bleach solution.

"Why would he? I'm sure he thought it was your superstitious nature talking." I tossed my rag in with hers.

"Guess so." She scooped some ice in a glass and pressed it to the Diet Coke dispenser. It came out clear. "Yuck! It's out of syrup." She dumped the contents out in the sink.

"The truck's coming first thing tomorrow," I said.

It had been a long day but a good one. Betsy had relieved Jena Lynn, who had a meeting with the director at Sunset Hills. The contract we had with them for the delivery service was up for renewal, and my sister believed, after all the bad publicity, a face-to-face meeting was in order. Doc Tatum's uncle, Doctor George, was a resident of Sunset Hills. Perhaps, I should pay him a visit later.

I leaned against the counter and examined the dining room, pleased to see it was ready to go.

"So, we're backing off the case?" Betsy poured herself a cup of coffee.

"I think I have to," I lied. "Eddie will be watching me like a hawk. Besides, I really wasn't keen on getting shot at." I picked at my cuticles.

"Eddie will be investigatin' that, I'm sure. And with him in charge, you know Jena Lynn will be in the clear."

Yeah. That was true. He'd spent a few minutes reading over what I had in my childhood bedroom. He didn't ask me to take it down, either.

Even though when he left, we'd been on good terms, I could feel the tension thrumming through his body when he hugged me goodbye. Unfinished business and Eddie didn't mesh well.

"They reopening the case?" Betsy wanted to know.

I shrugged. "If they do, I hope it stays hush-hush.

It would really upset Jena Lynn. But, I don't know for sure."

"What about that detective? Think he'll come back?"

"I don't see a reason why he would. Especially if Eddie handles the shooting as a separate crime altogether. But I'm not in the loop."

From her facial expression, I surmised neither was she. She hadn't mentioned Alex, either, and I hadn't heard from him.

"You ready?" I started cutting off the lights.

Morning would come early, and I was opening with my sister. So was Betsy.

"What about Calhoun?" Betsy asked as I closed the door behind us and locked up.

Poppy waved at us from down the block. She was walking to her car.

We waved back.

I sighed. "Haven't heard from him. He was supposed to be back yesterday."

We walked toward our cars, which were parked side by side across the street.

"You didn't really like him, did you?"

"He's okay," I said. "I'm not romantically interested in him, if that's what you're asking. I just ended my marriage. I need time."

"He was kinda old, anyway."

"He's older, not old."

"I really think Alex loves you." She opened her car door. "See you tomorrow."

Alex had been my first love, and Betsy had never

held back on her approval of the two of us together. He would always hold that special place in my heart. But I'd be a fool not to be suspicious of Betsy's matchmaking agenda. Besides, loving again would require a risk that I wasn't certain I could handle yet.

Chapter 27

A black Chevy truck was parked next to Rust
Bucket, under my nanny's favorite oak tree when
I got home. I gave the truck a once-over and recognized it as Alex's. When I reached the back porch,
Alex was sipping a glass of tea languidly and rocking
on the porch swing. His face altered when he saw
me, and he abruptly stood. The swing slammed into
the porch railing.

"You left your door unlocked," he said by way of
explanation. "I, uh, I should apologize about the
other day." He set the glass of tea on the railing.
Aware that he would be anticipating me jumping in
and helping him out with the wording of his apology, I climbed the steps and said nothing, leaving
him to tread water alone. He shoved both hands
into his unruly hair and tugged. Did he believe he
could extract information that way? "I don't know
what came over me. I say things in anger I don't
mean. You know that I—"

"We're okay." I cut him off. It was painful watching him flounder the way he was.

He blew out a breath. "Good. I hate being on the outs with you." He held the door open for me. "Oh, I'm your protective detail."

"What?" I shouldn't have been surprised. Eddie was overprotective.

"The sheriff is worried, and when the sheriff worries, we all worry."

"Something smells good." I tossed my bag on the table. Two boxes from Tony's Pizza were sitting on the counter, along with a six-pack of beer.

"Did Eddie find anything at the Ledbetters'?" I was keenly interested now. Had he been able to cast a footprint? Or perhaps find prints he could run through the system? Did he contact Carl to ask permission to dust the place? Then a thought occurred to me. My prints would be everywhere. What would Eddie be forced to do then?

"Can't discuss it with you. But, I brought dinner. If it's cold, I'll microwave it. I can cook too."

I smiled and shook myself out of the funk I'd fallen into.

"Think of it as a peace offering. I was an ass."

"We were both angry." I moved to the counter. "Pizza and beer works for me."

Since we were going to be spending so much time together, it was good to be back on decent terms. He cracked open two beers while I retrieved plates and napkins.

"You know, it isn't like I get any company out

here. And I would hear if anyone drove up. I don't really need someone babysitting me."

He put two slices of the works on my plate.

"Not that I don't appreciate it," I rushed to add.

"Eddie says shadow you, I shadow you. It'll only be until we make sure this trigger-happy nut is behind bars. Personally, I think it's a completely unrelated incident. It could have been a teenager looking for drugs." He took his plate and beer into the living room. "You got ESPN?"

It was possible, I guess. "I don't know. I bought the extended package." I sat my beer on the end table then looked at the plastic-covered furniture. "Help me." I put my plate on the coffee table.

Alex did the same and the two of us ripped the plastic off all the furniture. Satisfied with my task, I sat down and picked up my plate, propping my feet on the coffee table. Something I had never been allowed to do growing up. He flipped on the TV and found a replay of this afternoon's Braves game. We settled into silence, eating our pizza and drinking beer. I occasionally threw a glance in his direction. His thick mass of hair needed a trim. The Mötley Crüe T-shirt he wore was stretched out and appeared to be at least ten years old. His shorts were new. Would this have been a typical evening if I had married him instead of Peter? Age had filled him out some. He obviously still had a fondness for weightlifting.

Stop it! I chided inwardly and instantly pushed that thought out of my mind.

The crunching of tires out front caused Alex to go on alert and mute the game. He pulled his gun from the back of his shorts and went to the window. "It's Yvonne." He sat back down, unmuting the game.

I went to meet her at her car.

Yvonne emerged from her vehicle and waved. "Hey, I'm in a hurry, but I wanted to stop by and see you in person." She placed her sunglasses on top of her head. She was wearing white capris and a pink tank top. Her wrists were adorned with pink and white bangles. She was obviously on her way somewhere. She gave me a hug when I reached her car, the bangles making a clinking sound on her wrists. "You have company?"

"It's just Alex. What's going on? Not that I'm not happy to see you."

"Just Alex." She grinned.

"It's not like that. So, what's up?"

She let out a sigh. "Issues with my partner regarding the business. I've got to drive back into the city."

I nodded. "Everything okay?"

She threw her hands up. "God only knows. And now I find out Mama has more financial problems I was unaware of. She's mortgaged to the hilt, and with the investors stepping back, there's no way I can sell the place for what she owes."

"I'm sorry."

She raised her eyebrows.

"Well, obviously, I was against the buyout, but I hate that your mama is having problems and you're feeling the effects of it."

"Yeah, me too. But I'll get over it. I'm thankful my investments have done well and I can catch the payments up. Hopefully I can find some work here. That's one of the reasons the buyout appealed to me. Designers historically don't do well on this island." Her shoulders rose and fell.

"Times are a-changing. Maybe you can get some work from some of the more well-to-do families on the island."

The beginnings of a sheepish smile appeared. "Please don't think me insensitive." Yvonne's tone was placating.

"No, I won't."

"It's about the Palmer house. My agent informed me that Nate Palmer is moving his mama into Sunset Hills. She had a mild stroke."

I had hated to hear that. Sam had left me a voice mail about that too.

"Well, I was wondering if you could call Nate and see if we could get this ball rolling. I wouldn't ask if it wasn't vital. I have to have a place to showcase my designs."

"Give me a day or two, but I'll call Nate and see what he says. The family probably could use the extra money. Especially after moving his mother into the retirement community. Plus, it should give her peace of mind that the property will be in the possession of another Peach Cove family."

She smiled before glancing back to the car, where Izzy was happily wagging her tail in the front seat. "I have one other favor to ask."

"Shoot!"

"Well, Mama isn't really able to take care of Izzy while I'm away, and with all the moving preparations that will be going on—"

"Say no more." I cut her off and smiled. "I'll gladly watch Izzy for you." I moved around to the passenger side of the car. "Izzy and I are old pals, aren't we, Izz?" I stroked her little head.

Yvonne thanked me profusely before handing off all the little dog's supplies in a giant diaper bag–style tote. "It'll only be a couple of days." She kissed the white furred head in my arms.

"We'll be fine."

I waved goodbye from the porch as she drove away. It would be great to have her back home again, and I was more than excited to have Izzy with me for a few days.

As I turned to go back inside, hefting the bag onto my shoulder, a shadow to my left caught my eye. Izzy began barking.

"What is it, girl?"

The sun was close to setting and that made hard shadows across the yard. I could have sworn there had been a man in a baseball cap standing between Mama's pink rhododendrons. Izzy had thought so too. Huh.

Izzy settled down, so I chalked it up to hard shadows. Surely, if there was someone there, Izzy would still be going nuts. The little dog was a Chihuahua, poodle, and terrier mix. Terriers and Chihuahuas were good watchdogs by nature. At least I thought so.

"What did Yvonne want?" Alex eyed the dog.

I told him of her plans and that I was watching after Izzy until she got back.

"Nate should hurry up and unload that place before she changes her mind."

I let a squirming Izzy down on the floor to investigate. "Exactly. It isn't like he's going to have buyers beating his door down."

He got up. "Want another beer?"

"Sure." My phone rang. It was my sister.

"Hey," I greeted her and began unpacking Izzy's bag. "I forgot to ask you. How'd the meeting go?"

"Not well. The retirement community has decided to cancel the delivery service." She sounded completely deflated.

I took the beer from Alex when he came back into the room. "Thanks."

"Who's there?"

"Alex. We're having pizza." I knew she would have us back together in her mind. Not that I could tell her otherwise.

"Hey, did the diner ever make any deliveries to Doctor George? He's a Sunset Hills resident now, correct?" I asked.

"Mm-hmm. He was partial to peaches-and-cream bars. They're soft enough for him to chew without pain."

I filed that tidbit away for later.

"I wouldn't worry about the contract. In a few months, they'll get over their concerns and hire us back." I tried to sound casual.

"Maybe. When did you and Alex become a thing?" Her voice lifted slightly.

"We're just hanging out."

Alex raised his eyebrows.

"Right." I could hear the smile on Jena Lynn's face. "Oh, I went by Heather's."

"How is she?" With all that had gone on, it had completely slipped my mind to ask about her.

"She's been under the weather. I took her off the

schedule this week and called Betsy. She was more than willing to work a few double shifts."

I bet she was.

Betsy had been out of work for a lot longer than she could afford. I felt bad for not asking her if she needed help.

The crunching of tires had Alex at the window again, and Izzy leaped up on the couch. Her paws scratched on the windowsill as she sounded the alarm. I liked having a warning bark, and the idea of having a pet around permanently was appealing. Maybe even healing. Someone to love unconditionally. Perhaps even provide a bit of security. I'd give that some thought when the tumultuous climate calmed.

"Well, that's good, and I can work out front if needed. Listen, I've got to run."

Alex's back was straight, his chest puffed. I knew I had a problem when he charged out the front door.

"Did you get a dog?"

"No, it's Izzy, Yvonne's fur baby. I'm looking after her while she gets her affairs in order. Long story. I'll fill you in later."

"Sorry. I'm being rude. You have company." She was grinning again.

"See you in the morning." I disconnected the call.

After calming Izzy, I tossed her a chew toy from the bag onto the floor. She occupied herself with that while I went to investigate.

"You can just get right back in that car and drive back to wherever you're from," I heard Alex say when I reached the front porch.

Calhoun was standing beside his car; the door was still open. Alex had his gun in his hand. Quite intentionally, I was sure.

"I'll go if Marygene tells me to go." Calhoun's tone was much calmer than mine would have been if I was facing a snarling Alex armed with a loaded gun.

"Alex, back off. Please." I raced down the steps and over to where the two men stood. Both sizing the other up.

Alex didn't budge, his stance wide, chest poked out. He slowly and deliberately folded his arms across his chest, resting the gun against his left bicep.

Calhoun focused on me, seemingly unaffected.

"There was an incident. Alex is here at my father's behest," I explained.

Concern flashed across his face. He closed the distance between us. "What happened?" His tone was low.

I was instantly uncomfortable.

"She was shot at," Alex answered for me. "Know anything about that?"

Calhoun didn't spare Alex a glance when he growled, "I certainly do not. And your sheriff is aware of that fact. He called and checked up on me." Calhoun didn't sound upset that Eddie had questioned his whereabouts. A good sign in my book.

Alex took my arm and pulled me back from Calhoun. "We need to get you inside. You're too exposed out here." Not that he'd been worried about that when Yvonne was here.

"He's right." Calhoun didn't sound happy about it.

I could clearly read that he wanted to question me regarding every single detail of the incident.

"I'm back in town. I'm staying at the inn. Judy's brother is running the place now. But I guess you already knew that. Anyway, that's where I'll be." There were probably a load of vacancies.

"Okay." I attempted to understand his message. Was he wanting me to come by? Did he have information?

He lifted his hand, and I did the same before he got into his car.

Alex had me back inside and the door shut before I could watch Calhoun drive away. I was about to tell him that Calhoun and I were just friends.

Before I could speak, he said, "I thought you didn't get any visitors. This is Grand Freaking Central."

Chapter 28

After I took Izzy out and made sure her automatic feeder and waterer were working properly, I was on my way to work and decided to check in with Eddie.

"Morning, pumpkin." Eddie answered on the first ring. "You calling to bless me out about Alex?"

"No. I'm on my way to the diner and just wanted an update." I turned onto the square.

Alex was behind me in his truck. He was escorting me to work and then again when I got off to go home. Thankfully he wouldn't be sitting in the diner all day long.

"On?"

"On what you found at the Ledbetters'," I huffed. "I deserve some sort of explanation. You're practically pimping out your only daughter." I grinned when I heard the choking sound on the other end of the line. He'd been having his morning coffee . . . perfect timing.

"He was supposed to sleep on the couch." Eddie didn't sound happy.

"Was he? He said otherwise." I parked and hid my snickers by pressing the mute button.

"You better be riling me up for the heck of it."

I let the line go dead silent.

"All you need to know is I'm conducting a thorough investigation. If you'd rather have me stay over until someone is apprehended—"

"No! I mean, that isn't necessary. I'm at work now. Speak later." I disconnected the call. I honestly didn't think anyone was coming after me.

The more I considered it, the more I believed the person had been trying to scare me off. Eddie was just being overprotective.

I checked all those thoughts at the door as it tinkled upon opening. Sam was already sitting at the counter eating his pound of bacon and a dozen eggs breakfast. How he wasn't as big as a house, I'll never know.

"Didn't make me any?" I flicked him on the ear.

He swatted my hand away but laughed. "I heard you and Alex were getting hot and heavy." He wagged his eyebrows at me.

"Not hardly." I poured myself a cup of steamy hot goodness.

"Morning." Jena Lynn came out from the kitchen with a massive smile. She waggled her finger in front of me. A gorgeous diamond twinkled on a very important finger.

"Oh my God!" I squealed and we jumped around and hugged for a few minutes. "I'm so happy for you and Zach."

"Thanks." She was happier than I had ever seen

her. "We're going to get married in the fall on the beach."

"The weather will be perfect then." I was grinning so hard I thought my cheeks might crack. If anyone deserved happiness, it was my sister.

"Yeah, we'll have to figure out the work schedule for the honeymoon. We're talking about taking a few weeks in Europe."

"That's fantastic. Don't you worry about the work schedule. I'll be here day and night if I have to be."

She hugged me again.

Sam was waiting to hug her next. He picked her up and spun her around while she giggled.

When Betsy arrived, the squealing began all over again until the sign was flipped and the first few customers arrived for our reopening.

Calhoun came in around two. He'd apparently familiarized himself with the slow time of day. With Heather out sick, I had waited tables with Betsy for the lunch shift.

Jena Lynn had a fill-in girl taking a shift for the dinner rush.

He pushed his glasses up on his nose as he settled at the counter. I put a menu, napkin, knife, fork, and spoon before him.

"What can I get for you?" I asked quietly.

The few stragglers we had seemed mighty interested in why the reporter was back in town. And I think some of them were uneasy when they found out that there was a town hall meeting this evening.

Maybe they thought the meeting's topic would be another wave of murders or sudden deaths. I didn't know what the meeting was about, which is why I planned on attending.

"Peach tea and a diner burger," he said.

"How do you want that cooked? And which side?"

"Medium and fried pickles."

"You want that burger all the way?" I wrote down his order.

He waited until I glanced up. "All the way sounds great to me."

Oh dear, more complications. "I'll get your order right in."

Betsy had been watching the exchange with interest. She quite happily devoured her lunch, California BLT and fries.

After I hung his ticket, I poured his tea and set it in front of him.

His fingers purposely brushed mine. "You didn't call."

"I had an early morning and, with everything going on, I was beat." I honestly just didn't want to deal with telling him I wasn't interested in him that way. Plus, Alex was waiting for a reason to haul Calhoun in and interrogate him again.

"Have they made an arrest yet?"

"No." I lowered my voice. "Eddie isn't exactly keeping me up to speed. He may have a suspect."

"Did this happen at your house?"

I shook my head and began wiping the counter to lower myself inconspicuously while I decided how much I wanted to share. "I was at the Ledbetter house."

His face showed surprise.

"Marygene, girl, this is the best lime cheesecake I ever put in my mouth," Mr. Collins said from the back booth.

I stood up straight and smiled. "Thank you, Mr. Collins. That's so nice of you to say."

"Is it a new recipe?" his wife, Nita, asked.

"Not really. I tweaked it a tad. I added a bit of cream at the end that I folded in by hand. It makes the batter bake off light and airy."

"It does. So good." Nita took another bite. "Every time you tweak another recipe, you bring me a slice for dessert."

"Yes, ma'am," I said.

"I'm going to need me a slice of that cheesecake." Betsy dropped her plate in the buss tub. "I'll go top off everyone's drink first."

"Thank you, Bets."

I turned back to Calhoun, whose face was hard. "What?"

"You never should have gone there alone. When we discussed the idea, I thought it was understood you would wait for me."

"No, it wasn't."

He directed a condescending glint toward me over the top of his glasses. It was the first time he'd ever given me such a glare, which let me know how immature he thought I was. He'd never talked down to me before—it was what I liked about him when we first met—but apparently now he thought he could. I'd had enough of men with superiority complexes. They could all stuff it.

"I'll go see if your order is ready." I spun on my sneakered heels toward the kitchen.

Chapter 29

The main hall was packed at the courthouse that night. I was smiling and trying to act natural when community members turned in my direction. Someone in this very hall could have been the one who had taken shots at me.

Now I had to pretend like everything was peachy keen. Just me and my shadow buddy Alex, who was sitting uncomfortably close, with his arm resting on the top of the bench seat behind me. There was no getting around the rumors now. It was a tad too hot in here. I had made time to run home, let Izzy out, shower, and change into a maxi dress. Izzy had wanted me to stay and play. The sadness in her little doggy eyes when I left made me promise her hours of playtime when I got back, plus a treat. Yvonne had checked in on her twice since leaving. We had to FaceTime so she could see that Izzy was adjusting just fine. Yvonne was thrilled to announce that my phone call to Nate had indeed paid off. She would be closing on the property at the end of the month.

Olivia waltzed past us, arm in arm with Mr. Mason's grandson. She tossed a casual glance in our direction. Alex sat up straight, taking in her long, slender frame. She was taller and thinner than me. Her auburn hair hung down past her shoulders. Until now, I hadn't been sure how close the two of them had been. The sullen look on Alex's face made me want to hurl. I put a few more inches between us.

My sister and Zach slid onto the bench in front of us. She turned around and waved. Happiness was simply oozing out of her ears. Alex removed his sour expression long enough to shake Zach's hand. Eddie was at the front of the room, standing next to the mayor.

The natives were restless, as they say, waiting for someone to say something. A few murmurs to my left drew my attention. What in the world was Carl Ledbetter doing here? He wasn't accompanied by Rainey Lane tonight. No, whose hand was he holding? I leaned over the edge of the bench, glad I'd chosen an aisle seat. OMG, if it wasn't Tally Waters.

I gave a deadpan stare across the row where Sam was seated. He lifted his hands, showing me he had no idea why she was here. He better be telling the truth. He had a bad habit of hiding valuable information if he feared it would make him appear less than stellar.

Eddie's face, from what I could tell five rows back, didn't show surprise either.

I turned to Alex. "Did you know about this? Did Eddie?"

"I didn't. If he did, he sure as hell didn't tell me." Alex was adamant against outside investors. It was one topic we saw eye to eye on.

"I thought this was done. Over with, for the time being," I said to Alex.

Jena Lynn turned around to give me the same outraged expression I had. "What is going on?"

I shook my head.

"I guess we're about to find out," Alex said.

Mrs. Gentry arrived and I could have sworn she gave me a look of pity when she passed by our pew. My face flushed. Pulse raced. I fought for control, cradling my stomach.

"You okay?" Alex whispered.

"Fine," I croaked.

"Folks!" The mayor's voice boomed over the sound system. "If I can have your attention, please. The Malcom Investment Corp. has asked to make a final pitch to our residents."

I focused on his words and slowed my breathing.

"What's wrong?" Alex asked.

"Something I ate," I lied. "I'm okay now."

"This is outrageous!" Poppy shouted.

"I'm not staying around here all night to listen to that woman yammer on," Mr. Collins stood.

His wife, Nita, followed suit, giving her head a disgusted shake.

"Now, Gerald," the mayor began. "If you'll just simmer down a minute and hear Miss Waters out."

"We vote no!" Mr. Collins said as his wife started for the back door. Several others followed, with the same sentiment. More than three quarters stayed behind.

Despite the rumblings from the mayor, who seemed as exasperated as the majority, he gave Tally and Carl the floor.

Carl stepped up to the mic. "I know, I know. This is getting old. And even after all the trauma this island has suffered, I felt I owed it to all of you and my daddy to bring you this final offer." Oh, he was so generous. Always thinking of the island's best interest.

Alex leaned forward and listened.

"What the Malcom Investment Corp. is offering is a onetime lump sum for the properties located on the west side of the island. They are no longer interested in purchasing business fronts or inland properties." The protected land his father owned was on the west side of the island. "Since the turtle project was a bust, the land is well on its way to being rezoned."

More murmuring. It didn't take a rocket scientist to understand that now that the corporation wasn't interested in majority island ownership, this decision would no longer be up to those of us who fought tooth and nail to keep this type of business out. If the land owners agreed to sell, there would be absolutely nothing we could do to stop it. And the one with the most ownership of that side of the island was standing in front of us encouraging them to sell.

The doors closed loudly as a late attendee arrived. Felton Powell took a place along the back wall. That was when I noticed Calhoun sitting on the far-left bench.

Carl and Felton locked in an ungentlemanly glare, then he gave the floor to Tally, who simply reiterated the exact same spiel. Just highlighting what she saw as positives for those of us who would still reside and conduct business here.

Jena Lynn and I got up at the exact same time. We were closely followed by Poppy, who appeared as outraged as we were. We made a point to take our time leaving, ensuring everyone present understood our feelings.

"At least they aren't going to be putting up highrises," Alex said as we rode home together.

"I guess. It's not that I mind some tourism on the island. It's having developers that couldn't care less about preserving the beauty and natural aspects of the island that bothers me."

"Hey, what if it was Carl Ledbetter firing at me? I would love for you to lock him up." There was nothing about Carl that I liked. He was a cheater and double-crosser. There was no honor in that man.

"I highly doubt it was Carl. But even if I'm wrong, you would be the one locked up for trespassing, not him." Alex sounded amused.

"Oh, right." I grumbled. "Well he sure ruined what was a great day for Jena Lynn."

The two of us walked into the house like an old married couple. Scratch that . . . I had to stop thinking that way. Alex and I weren't a couple. I was just lonely and he was here. Besides, he appeared to have some unresolved feelings for his ex.

"I'm going to bed. Can you take Izzy out for me?"

He gave me an annoyed glance, the remote in his hand.

"She takes like a minute to go. The game will be there when you get back."

"Okay. When does Yvonne get back?"

"Oh, puh-lease, don't even begin to act like she's a lot of work for you. She's the best houseguest I've ever had." I scrunched up my face.

He reluctantly agreed. Hey, this was like a marriage, after all.

Before going to my room, I spent a few long moments going over the board in my old room. It made a lot more sense now to suspect Carl because he had the most to lose, and it was completely possible he either had his own place tossed, or— the voice of the Braves announcer blared loudly from the flat screen in the living room. And Izzy was now at my feet. I picked her up and baby-talked her a bit while I noodled the info.

"Hey, Alex," I called over the banister.

"Yeah?" He was now at the base of the stairs.

"Did Carl report the break-in at the villa?"

"He did. Some of the old man's drugs were stolen. And his neighbor at Sunset Hills spotted a group of kids running from the scene. No arrests yet."

"Okay. Night." Back in my room, I put Izzy down, pulled my dress over my head, and tossed it on the floor, lost in thought.

"Marygene Brown," Mama scolded the second I closed the door.

I screamed. Izzy was growling and running around Mama, barking.

Alex bolted through the door, gun in hand, scanning the room for an intruder. "What is it?"

I held my hand over my heart, a familiar response for me now, and scooped Izzy up. Mama was giving me a chastising glare, her arms folded across her chest. She didn't seem to like the idea of Alex sleeping in the house. She was such a hypocrite. That was when I recalled I was standing in nothing but my bra and panties. Alex devoured me with the intensity of his gape. I snatched the dress off the floor, using it to cover myself.

"Um . . . I thought I saw a mouse. Sorry I alarmed you," I stammered.

"Mouse, my derriere," Mama said. "That boy doesn't need to be in this house. You have a blind spot when it comes to him." She had never been fond of Alex.

He was subpar in her eyes. He didn't own his own business, like Zach did, nor did he come from an aristocratic family. He was a common boy who grew into a common man, who earned a deputy's salary. Like Eddie.

Alex had a lopsided grin. "If I didn't know better, I'd think you were using that as an excuse to get me up here. A little jealous tonight, were we?"

"You watch yourself, young man!" Mama scolded, her finger in his face. Not that he saw her.

"Shh," I said to Mama.

"What are you shushing me for? Any man would think the same," Alex said.

"I thought I heard it," I held my hand to my ear, "the mouse, listen."

He put his gun back into his holster. "Right. If you want me to stay," he waggled his eyebrows at me, "all you have to do is ask."

"I mean it. You're about to get it, young man," Mama was waving her arms around like a lunatic, and I wasn't certain she could do no harm. She had slammed me to the floor the other night.

"No. I swear it was a mouse." I shoved him out the door. "I'll be fine. Good night, Alex."

"Good night, Marygene." He grinned again as I closed the door. "If you *need* me, just holler." He put extra emphasis on the word *need*.

Chapter 30

"Mama, you've got to stop popping up like that. I swear you're going to kill me," I said the second I heard Alex make his way back down the stairs.

Izzy was now settled at the foot of the bed. She adjusted to Mama's presence faster than I originally had.

"What is that boy doing in this house?" Mama asked as I dropped the dress and began searching for something to sleep in.

"Eddie asked him to keep an eye on me while they hunt down whoever shot at me the other night." I pulled on a nightshirt. "He's worried for my safety." I walked into the en suite, flipped on the light, and began rummaging through the drawer that held my hair ties.

Mama didn't comment on the messy state of the drawer, although it was a major pet peeve of hers. She never could understand that we creative types didn't concern ourselves with such things.

"I thought the nonsense between you and that Myers boy was over years ago," Mama said.

I made a face. "Stop projecting your issues on me. Eddie wasn't good enough for you, so Alex isn't good enough for me. Not that it matters. He's here because Eddie wants me kept safe."

She waited until I began my facial cleansing ritual before speaking. "This has nothing to do with Edward and me."

"Right." I had a good lather going with my facial brush as I stared at her reflection in the mirror.

"You aren't in danger, not at this moment, anyway." She left the Eddie discussion alone.

"And you're aware of that fact how?"

Her shoulders rose and fell, a very atypical Mama gesture. That worried me. She was either uncomfortable with the question or something else was going on here.

After a few splashes of water to my face, I patted it dry with a towel. "Explain how you're privy to certain facts surrounding this situation and not to others."

"All I can say is if your life was in danger, I would be notified." Pretty vague.

I leaned against the sink. "So, that's why you were at the Ledbetter house, then?"

She inclined her head.

I took it as a yes. "And the reason you were able to stay visible for as long as you did?"

Another incline.

"Right. And you're here now because?"

"To spend time with you."

Oh, that was rich. Laughter bubbled up in an uncontrollable fashion.

"I'm serious."

"I'm sorry." I held my hand over my face as I continued to laugh. "But I find this notion completely absurd." I sobered. "That is just so out of character for you."

"What is that supposed to mean?" Mama folded her arms, and I decided I needed to lie down for this.

I flipped off the lights and crawled into bed. The bedside lamp immediately came on.

Propping up two pillows, I leaned against them. "From what I can surmise from your cryptic info dumps, you're in limbo here. You're forced to make amends with those you wronged to cross over to where, Heaven?"

She didn't respond.

I supposed that was also some big secret. Moving on. "You presented yourself to Jena Lynn first, and her mind fractured, or was close to it, landing her in the psych ward for a week. When I came back home, your only option left was to appear to me." I gave her an irritated grin when she opened her mouth and held up my hand. "Now, I'm exceedingly grateful to you for the other night."

She sat on the bed at my feet, next to a snoring Izzy. Izzy cracked one eye open then went back to sleep.

"But let's be honest with each other, shall we?"

"Okay."

"If Jena Lynn had been able to cope with your

ghost or spirit, whatever you are, I would have never seen you."

"Actually, I was presenting myself to your sister to discuss you. And before you go shouting I'm a liar and you'd be a fool to trust me, know this, I can't lie."

Was that true? My face must have shown my doubts.

"It is. It's an impossibility for me now."

"May I ask you anything and you have to tell me the truth?" I studied her, gauging for any change to clue me in on her level of truthfulness.

"I suppose. Yes or no answers only."

Oh, I had to test this out.

"Then give me this. The next question I ask you, you must answer. No head nods or shrugs allowed. Deal?"

She sighed and chewed on her bottom lip. A mannerism I had inherited and never realized until this exact moment. "I'll answer if I am allowed. Some information is off-limits."

"Okay. So, deal?"

"I agree. Deal." She smiled.

What to ask? "Why didn't you tell me Eddie was my father?"

She sighed. "Because it would have disgraced you. I know you think we live in a day and age where things like that no longer matter. But you must understand. Here, in Peach Cove, they mattered. At least they did when you were growing up. I honestly believed I was protecting you."

"You mean it would have disgraced you?" I accused.

"Yes. It would have disgraced me too. Honey," she scooted closer, "I said some horrible things to you. One thing has haunted me. I was having a bad day when you came home carrying on about culinary school. Eddie and I had, well, he had given me an ultimatum, and I didn't handle it well." No, Mama never did well when she was backed into a corner. "Then you wanted to leave me, too, and I reacted badly."

I flinched. Badly didn't cover it.

"Horribly, I behaved horribly." She started to fade but not before my tears had caused hers to stream down her cheeks.

There was a knock at my bedroom door. I was too upset to speak. Slowly, it creaked open.

"You okay? I heard you talking and—" Alex's brows narrowed.

"I was just talking to Izzy. I'm having . . ." The words wouldn't come. There was no good way to explain this.

"Can I come in?" He stood in the doorway and waited for permission. Once granted, he came over to the bed. "Scooch over."

I should have pondered why I did so without question or reservation, but I didn't.

When he crawled in bed with me a second later, I was glad. Glad to not be alone. Glad someone cared how I was feeling. And if I was being honest with myself, I was glad that the someone was him.

He opened his arms to me and I went. "I can listen," he said.

Everything I had been holding in for the last four years came out in between sobs and hiccups. Doc Tatum had been right. Holding it in was eating me alive. I fell asleep with Alex stroking my hair.

My last thought was, *Mama was wrong about Alex.*

Chapter 31

"Marygene, can you pull and box up three more of the lime cheesecakes before you leave?" my sister called into the kitchen as I was cutting the last tray of berry crumb bars.

"No problem." After I wrapped the tray in plastic, I slid it onto the appropriate shelf in the walk-in. Then I began assembling three logoed peach boxes.

Alex and I hadn't discussed the night before. When I woke up, he was already showered and dressed. He gave me a cup of coffee before telling me I needed to hurry or I'd be late for work.

When I was dressed, he was already in his truck, waiting to escort me to the diner. At first, I was mortified I'd confided in him about the abuse. But it had come so freely and felt so healing and right. Boy, had I needed to unburden. The weight I'd been carrying alone for so long had lifted somewhat, and elation took over. I wouldn't focus on risks or anything else for that matter. I deserved a little good emotion.

He followed me to work, then told me to check in before I left the diner. When he hugged me goodbye, I'd felt better. It was as if he was telling me it was okay and we didn't have to speak of it again.

Mama and I were on better terms as well. That would make my sister happy, if I could tell her about it.

Sam was frying up three Surf and Turf Burgers, and I thought this might be the appropriate time to sneak in my thoughts on his recipe.

"What can I do you for?" Sam always got folksy when he was in a chipper mood.

I grinned as I stopped by the grill line. "I had this idea."

"About?"

"Your Surf and Turf Burger."

"I told you I overcooked yours just a tad," Sam explained about the one I'd ordered for lunch earlier today. "Don't go judging the recipe based on one bad experience."

"Just listen and stop getting so defensive." I patted his shoulder. "Your burgers are good."

His face looked grim.

"Great, they're great."

Jena Lynn came by with the stacked boxes I had just filled. She paused to see what we were talking about.

"I'm not suggesting we change the recipe."

"Good. It's the only item I have on the menu. Do you have any idea how long I worked on the crab filling?" He wasn't a happy camper.

I grabbed a white towel from the line and began

waving it. He laughed and Jena Lynn went to ring up the cheesecakes, leaving us alone.

"My idea won't change the recipe. Your burger and filling are divine."

He gave me a cocky grin. "Damn right they are."

"I just agreed. What I'm suggesting is we can offer my idea as an add-on. You know, for an upcharge."

"Just tell me. You're going to anyway." He didn't seem upset anymore.

"What if we added blue cheese to the burger or crabmeat?"

He scooped the burgers up and put them on a warm bun. He was listening.

"Maybe call it Surf and Turf Black and Blue. Or something."

"That's the best idea I ever heard." Betsy hung a ticket on the wheel. "I wish I hadn't had lunch already. I'd be the guinea pig for that!"

The fryer alarm went off, and Sam pulled the basket of chicken fried chicken and hooked it to drain. "We should definitely try it. We could experiment with a couple of cheeses."

That was fine by me, as long as blue cheese was one of them.

"You know," Betsy said before picking up her order. "I'll just take one for the team. I can make room." Betsy patted her stomach and grabbed her order from under the heat lamp.

It had been a good day. I walked out the door at four. That morning, Jena Lynn and I had worked out the schedule for her wedding and honeymoon. We were going to shut the diner down for the rehearsal and day of the wedding. I was making the cake, and the diner would be catering the food. Eddie would be giving her away, and I would be the maid of honor. Betsy and Heather would serve after the wedding.

Just then, I had another good idea. I paused at my car, turned around, and went back inside the diner.

Jena Lynn raised her eyebrows at me.

"I was thinking, why don't I box up some food for Heather and her family? With her feeling so poorly and all."

Jena Lynn smiled, "Sam," she called through the service window, "drop a half dozen chicken fried chickens."

"Sure thing!" Sam called back. "Want a quart of white gravy with those?"

"Yes, that should be enough," my sister replied.

"I'll put another turkey meat loaf into the oven and take one out of the warmer. With a few sides and dessert, she should be set for a few days," I told Jena Lynn.

"You sound just like Nanny." Jena Lynn gave me a hug. "I'm so glad things are getting back to normal. You and Alex are making a go of it . . ."

Betsy's eyes went wide and her face split in a grin. She loved the idea.

"I approve, of course." Jena Lynn went on. "And even if we lose the west side of the island, I believe things are looking up for us."

"When we lose the west side," I said when she released me.

"It's funny. Today, I'm not too bothered about it

either. It might be nice to try out some of our recipes on fresh palates."

I pinched her nose like Nanny used to, and she roared in laughter. It was great to hear.

While I was at it, I decided to box up a few peaches-and-cream bars. A quick stop at Sunset Hills seemed in order.

"Hey, Bets?" I paused on my way toward the door when the order was ready.

She was serving a table of road crew workers.

"When your shift ends, would you mind running by the house and letting Izzy out for me?"

"No problem."

I untied my apron and threw it into the backseat. I was going to have to treat it with stain remover before I put it in the wash. I had an accident with the ketchup while topping the turkey meat loaves.

The air-conditioned lobby of Sunset Hills was bright and cheery, decorated in reds and yellows, with cream accents. The tile floor was covered with large colorful rugs accented with palm trees and exotic birds. The receptionist gave me no trouble when I asked to see Doctor George.

I found him sitting in a wheelchair by the koi pond. I announced myself several times, but he never acknowledged me. Until I presented the cream bars, that was.

"Who did you say you were again?" he asked around a mouthful of cream cheese. It wasn't a pleasant sight. Some of the cream dribbled down his chin.

"Marygene Brown. My sister and I own The Peach Diner." I sat down on the cement bench next to him.

The old man was much smaller in stature than I recalled. He was shriveled up like an old prune. He had to be pushing a hundred. There was something kind about his countenance, though, and I could see he still retained some of his wit.

"Why do you want to know about Joseph Ledbetter's offspring?"

"Just curious. He had two sons, didn't he?"

The old man's shaky hand moved over the box and retrieved his second bar.

"I can't keep up with all the kids I delivered over the years. But Joseph, I remember. He called me up any hour of the day or night when he had some pretty little thing in trouble."

I glanced around to make sure no one was close enough to hear our conversation.

"Pain in the ass, he was." The old man shook his head. "Those poor girls. All of them thought he hung the moon." More chewing.

Lord, he said *girls*. How many women did Mr. Ledbetter impregnate? "Do you remember if he had more than one son?"

The old man became mesmerized with a large koi fish swimming back and forth.

"Doctor George?"

"What, who did you say you were again?" After I explained who I was for the third time, I tried my question again. He mumbled on about the one, meaning Carl, and another that came out into the world fisted and ready for a fight.

"Do you remember the mother's name? The one that had Joseph's illegitimate son? What about this?" I showed him the image on my phone. "Does this look familiar? A file number perhaps?"

He'd fallen asleep after that. A nurse arrived and scolded me for allowing him to consume that much sugar in one sitting. Apparently, he was a diabetic. I felt awful and assured her I hadn't known.

With the thermal bag placed back inside the trunk, I closed it. Calhoun was standing there.

I jumped. "God, you scared me! What are you doing here?"

He laughed, "Sorry. I called your name. Guess you didn't hear me."

"Was it that obvious?" I gave an exaggerated eye roll and scooted past him.

"I came by to speak with the administrator about the diner's loss of the contract. I wanted to make sure my article hadn't cost the diner the business. I saw your car parked out here and waited for you. Guess you were here visiting someone?"

"Oh, and?" Who I was visiting was none of his business.

"Sorry."

I gave a derisive snort.

"I can't do anything about that now. I wish I'd never written it. And I wanted to apologize for upsetting you yesterday." He pushed his glasses up on his nose then shoved his hands into the pockets of his khakis. "It wasn't my place to pass judgment on your choices. I hope you understand I was simply concerned."

"It's okay." I decided to leave it at that. "I'm on my way to deliver some food to Heather. Guess I'll see you around." I unlocked the car door.

"I'm on my way to meet with a source in Savannah. I wanted to run by here first and then I was going to come by your house. Unfortunately, I just got the call that the meeting time was moved up."

"Source?" I was intrigued.

He gave me a distasteful face.

"Off-limits," I said, laconically and slid into the driver's seat.

"I do have some news I wanted to share with you about Carl Ledbetter. If you're interested, of course." The smirk on his face was a tad annoying. There was no doubt in his mind I'd be interested. "You going to be in the car long?"

"A bit."

"I'll call while we're both in transit."

"Okay." I started the engine. While the convertible top lowered, I twisted my hair into a messy bun. It would be a twenty-minute drive out to Heather's house. And I intended to allow the salty air and sun to soothe my soul while en route.

"You're a beautiful woman." He watched me with great interest.

I glanced at him.

"I just had to say it."

I readjusted my sunglasses. "Thank you but—" I was about to tell him this relationship wasn't going in the direction he desired.

"I know. You don't feel the same way about me that I do about you." He saved me the trouble. "I'm a patient man."

What was that supposed to mean? That he'd wait until I did? Before I could respond, he had gone to his vehicle.

As I pulled onto the expressway, my phone rang through the speakers

"Go on and tell me." I didn't want to get side-tracked with other discussions.

He didn't seem to mind. "While I was in the city, I did some digging. It seems Carl Ledbetter filed paperwork with the court to declare his father inca-pable of handling his affairs. There was an appoint-ment scheduled for Joseph with a mental wellness facility in Atlanta."

"You're thinking that maybe Carl was worried his dad might pass the test or whatever? Maybe he got desperate?"

"Could be. I also noticed there was a piece of property on the island that was put up for sale a year before the Malcom Investment Corp. showed inter-est. It was the," he paused, "Bayside Marina."

"You better not be looking at your phone while driving," I scolded.

"I was at a red light."

"That's no excuse. It's dangerous."

"You're right. I won't do it again."

"Good. That marina was destroyed when the hur-ricane came through. The cost to reopen it was as-tronomical. Last I heard," I pulled off onto my exit, "Mr. Ledbetter was waiting until he could negotiate a better deal with the fishermen's association. The fees were stuck in the Stone Age, and he needed to raise the rent and dock fees to make up the loss. It was a big hullabaloo."

"If Joseph was out of the decision-making picture, Carl could do what he wished with the property," Calhoun said.

"Yep. That must have been one of the properties Miss Sally mentioned. What else did you find?"

"Oh. Another interesting thing I dug up was that a year ago in Savannah, a police report was filed against one of Peach Cove's finest."

"What? Who?"

He had my attention and he seemed to enjoy it. I could tell by his tone.

"From what I got off a buddy of mine at the station, Carl pressed charges against Felton Powell."

"No. For what?" I pulled onto Heather's street.

A white heating and air van came barreling down the street. "Oh my God!" I shouted and swerved, to avoid being sideswiped, then laid on the horn.

"What happened?"

"Some idiot nearly hit me. What a jerk!" I shouted. It wasn't like the driver could hear me. It just made me feel better. "There are kids living on this street."

"Well, at least you're okay," Calhoun said as I pulled back onto the road.

"Back to what you were saying."

"Right, well, most of the report was redacted. But, from what I could dig up, Felton and Carl got into an argument that came to blows at one of the finer dining establishments in Savannah. Carl had to have a few stitches above his left eye. A few hours later, and I mean hours, the charges were dropped and Felton was released. You wouldn't even know there was a report filed, if you weren't good at sifting through the muck."

Twenty-seven Castaway, that was it. I pulled into the little driveway. "But you are *that* good?" I put the car in park next to Heather's minivan.

"I am." There was a grin in his tone.

"Well, want me to tell you what I found at the Ledbetter house?"

"I'm all ears."

I supposed this was a tit-for-tat dialogue. It was only fair. I told him of the birth certificate and what had transpired after.

He was silent for a good few minutes. "And no one came after you again?"

I told him no.

"Did they find anything that would lead them to the shooter? The department, I mean."

"Not that I know of. But, I plan on pestering." I shut off the engine. "And at Sunset Hills, I spoke to our old doc." I left out his name. Calhoun would be able to dig it up if he wanted to. I just didn't see the need to mention it. "He recalls that Joseph Ledbetter did have another son. Now, granted, the man is a hundred and can't hold a train of thought longer than a few minutes, but I believe him."

"Did you get a name? Mother? Child?"

"Afraid not."

"Well, it could be something. A little digging

might uncover some skeletons that the Ledbetter family wants buried."

I let out a sigh. "Still, even with all of this, we have nothing. All circumstantial evidence that won't hold up in court. So, Felton hates Carl. Who doesn't? Maybe we could use that anger to get him to dig deeper. Payback." I blew out a breath. "I don't know. I still don't see any solid evidence we can take to Eddie. I'll talk to Alex tonight and see what he has to say."

"Where is your bodyguard?" he asked.

I cringed. "He's going to be so pissed off. I was supposed to call him when my shift ended. I never know when I'm actually going to leave."

"You two got something going?"

"We're old friends. We care about each other, but, no, we're not together."

We technically weren't. And I still hadn't worked through what last night meant.

"Will you call me if you get anything from your source?"

"Yes," he said.

"Speak to you then." I disconnected the call, got out of the car, and popped the trunk.

Chapter 32

Heather lived in a little brick house. I was surprised to find the yard in such disarray. There were rusty folding chairs sitting around an inflatable pool. The yard needed a mow. It was surprising Felton wasn't handling the yard work for her. I would offer to send my and Jena Lynn's yard guy over.

The front door was open and a box fan was placed in front of the screen door. I tapped on the aluminum. "Heather, it's Marygene." The handles of the heavy bags were starting to dig into my arm.

Slowly, the door creaked open. I'd managed to give it a good pull with my free pinky. I stepped around the roaring old fan, being careful not to knock it over.

The cream ceramic-tiled living room was littered with Legos. "Heather, hon, I'm putting some meals in your fridge," I called out, in case she was in the bath or something. Maybe she was taking a nap. I navigated through the maze on the floor into the kitchen.

I had started unzipping the bags when I overhead Heather's cries. She was sobbing. My hands froze. A flashback of my own sobs flashed before my eyes. More sobbing and a thud.

My pulse echoed in my ears. Without another thought, I shoved the past aside and hurried down the hall. I ducked my heads into the boys' room and the little hall bath. Messy but empty. I overheard whimpering. The sound of a defeated creature. I hated that sound. The master bedroom was located at the end of the hallway. Heather was on the floor in nothing but her robe. Her left eye was swollen shut and her lip was bleeding. A giant bruise was already forming on her left cheekbone.

"Oh, nonono!" I was on my knees next to her a second later.

She shrieked and recoiled, shielding her battered face. I knew what it was like to feel broken—for the realization I was no longer in control to strike a blow. To suddenly become aware of how fragile your security bubble actually was. Sitting in a hospital room with a broken finger and fractured wrist trying desperately to come to terms with what had happened to me. All the while hoping it was just some bad dream I'd wake up from and everything would be all right again. I didn't want that for Heather.

"It's okay," I whispered. "It's just me."

"M-Marygene, I'm so glad you're here." She inched marginally closer. It took effort.

"What happened? Who did this to you?" I hated to think Felton, but I did.

"Is . . . is he gone?"

"Is who gone?" My heart hissed in my ears as I glanced around to ensure we were alone like I'd believed. "Do you mean Felton?"

Her good eye widened. "It wasn't Felton. Somebody in a mask came through the back door while I was doing the wash. He," she cleared her throat, "grabbed me by the hair and dragged me down the hall and into the bedroom. I-I tried to get away," she stammered. "He hit me over and over." She held on to my thighs.

"It's okay. You're going to be okay." I stroked her hair with one hand and whipped out my phone with the other. I called for an ambulance first, then Alex.

"You leaving?" he asked.

"Listen, I'm at Heather's. She had an intruder and is hurt bad. An ambulance in on the way. You've got to get ahold of Felton." My tone was as steady as I could make it. Heather didn't need me blubbering along with her.

"Got it," he said tersely.

I slid the phone back into my pocket and continued to stroke Heather's hair while she cried for a few minutes.

"I should have locked the doors. Felton told me to keep them locked," she choked out.

"This isn't your fault," I told her firmly. "We shouldn't have to be afraid to open our doors and windows."

"Everything is so messed up." She wiped her nose

with the back of her hand. "Peach Cove used to be such a safe place to live and raise a family." It had. "I thought he was going to kill me. My kids would have had to grow up without their mother."

Had I just missed the intruder? I hadn't seen anyone running away. Nor had I passed . . . oh shit . . . the van.

"I've got to get some clothes on." She tried to stand but stumbled.

"Here." I tied her robe for her. "Don't worry about it. You're decent. Where are the kids?"

"At my brother's. He and Mindy just put a pool in," she said with a hiccup. "Thank God they weren't here." More tears fell down her cheeks.

Sirens were audible now, and the next face we saw was Felton's. He filled the doorway, his eyes full of fury.

"Felton," Heather cried, and I moved aside for him to take my place beside her.

"What the hell happened?" He looked her over.

I relayed what she told me as she bawled her eyes out on his shoulder. "I'll give y'all a minute."

"Thank you," Heather said. "I'm so glad you came by."

Felton grabbed my hand. "Thank you for looking after her until I got here."

I nodded and rose to my feet. "I'll be outside."

The ambulance arrived next. I directed the crew to the room on my way out the door.

Alex was right behind them. He swung open his car door and was shouting the second he saw me. "You didn't call me!"

"I forgot," I said wearily. "I decided to bring food by for Heather and her family since she was ill. Calhoun was by my car when I went out and he had found some information he wanted to share with me, so I was on the phone with him the entire ride over. When I got inside, I heard Heather. Someone beat her up bad, Alex." A tear leaked down my cheek. I'd managed to hold it together for Heather. Now, my fissures were separating.

"Come here." He pulled me into his arms. "You've got to shake that reporter loose. Something feels off about that guy."

"I think he's just trying to help."

"What did he tell you?" Alex asked.

"I'll tell you everything he told me, I promise. I just can't right now." I pulled away and wiped my face. "There was a van."

"What van?" Alex asked.

Felton was making his way over to us. "Yeah, what van?" His eyes were close to slits, his jaw clenched tight.

"How's Heather?" I asked and wiped the tear from my cheek.

"She's been given a sedative. They're taking her in for X-rays." Felton told Alex and me.

"She was so shaken up." I took in a shuddering breath.

Alex's hand rested on my lower back. Felton seemed to notice.

"Tell me about the van," Felton said more calmly. I did.

"Do you remember the name of the company?"

I thought hard.

"Comfort Zone, Cozy Comfort, something like that. I wish I could remember. It was swerving all over the road. Out of control–like. Scared the living daylights out of me."

"Did you see who was driving?"

I shook my head. "I wish I had. I was trying not to wreck."

"Okay," he said.

"Marygene, give me a minute with Felton. I'll drive you home."

"Should I go in and put the food away? She might want it when they release her." I felt like I had to do something to help.

"That's a good idea." Felton said, and I walked back toward the house.

On autopilot, I unpacked the food. I set the meals together on each refrigerator shelf to make it easy for her. When I had collected the bags, and was on my way out the door, I considered tidying up the house but stopped myself. This was a crime scene. I shouldn't be touching anything. They probably shouldn't have allowed me to come back inside, period.

I was glad Detective Thornton was no longer involved with the sheriff's department. At this point, I would be questioning me too. Three violent crimes, and I had been present either before or immediately after each of them.

Chapter 33

When I walked back outside, Alex said, "We have to wait until the sheriff arrives. He's contacting forensics. They'll need to dust for prints."

"We still have access to that team?"

"They're available to the department through the end of next month. Eddie is in talks with the mayor about electing our own coroner and putting together a team." That was a good idea.

I hoped that having a team in place on the island would prevent Detective Thornton from being called back in. I had my concerns that, with this incident, he may be recalled. Not an ounce of me wanted to cross paths with that man again.

"Before we can go, Eddie will want you to show him where you were run off the road."

He wrapped an arm around my shoulders, and I squeezed his midsection in response. He groaned.

"What is it?" I asked, as he winced.

He favored his left side. "It's nothing." He dropped his arm.

Before I could question Alex further, Eddie drove up. His brow was furrowed and his face weary.

I met him at his truck. "I'm sorry," I said penitently the instant he opened the door.

"What do you have to be sorry for?" He rose to his full height and I had to step back to meet his gaze.

"I'm the first on the scene at yet another crime. I swear I'm not doing this on purpose."

The weariness of his face made me want to go back and erase this day and the weeks prior.

He gave my arm a squeeze. "What do we have here?" he asked Alex, staring over my head.

Alex ran down what he knew.

"Where were you all day? You were supposed to be shadowing my daughter." Eddie's tone was intense.

"It isn't his fault. I forgot to call him when my shift ended. I was concerned about Heather and brought her food from the diner." Where had he been all day? That Eddie didn't know concerned me.

"I had an errand off island," Alex explained. "I left word with dispatch. I planned to be back before she ever got off her shift."

"But she came by to check on Heather?"

Alex and I nodded.

"Which was exactly what her nanny and mama would have done if they'd been in her shoes."

Shocked by the gruffness and irritation in his tone, I kept my trap shut. I would wait to speak until spoken to. Forgive me for caring about my Peach family. I just wanted to get into my car and drive home. Some distance between us was what I needed.

"Don't you walk away from me, young lady."

"You want some distance from me right about now, trust me on that!" The door slammed shut after I slid into the driver's seat. It was hotter than Hades and I would pass out from heatstroke if I didn't get some airflow. With the top now closed, I blasted the air on high. The cool air on my face was bliss for a couple of seconds.

Then Mama was in the seat next to me. "I'm sorry. I know this is a trying time in your life. And it's my fault."

"What do you mean, your fault?" I asked, not following.

She let out a huge sigh. "When one of us is forced to remain, it creates an energy around the person we're communicating with. An aura, if you will. The deceased will be drawn to you."

I stared at her, unblinking, "You mean to tell me that since you're having to make amends, all the dead will want to die near me?"

"Not exactly." She rubbed her forehead with her index finger. "It's more like they will try to alter space and time to have your path intersect with their bodies."

"Why?"

"To help put them to rest. Solve their crimes. Or at least be their voices, since they no longer have one. They can't speak to you or interact with you. They can only direct energy toward your aura."

"Heather's alive," I said.

"Yes, well, that I have no reasoning for. Other than wrong place, wrong time."

I considered what she had said. "You're telling me that more dead bodies are in my future?"

"I don't know. If someone dies by way of a crime, perhaps. It depends on the deceased. At least that's how I understand it." She sounded remorseful that needing me was costly.

My limbs quaked. The last thing I wanted to encounter was another dead body. She might be able to control things from that side, but I controlled the reality of this side. At least as much as I could. "I could ignore you. Make you go away. All my problems would be over then."

"You're bitter. I get it."

I slammed my hands on the steering wheel. "You don't get it! You've never gotten it! That's why I left in the first place. And now that I'm back, you're once again making my life a living hell."

"Calm down. You're making a scene. They're going to think you're a lunatic," Mama hissed as her image vanished. Of course, bail out while I deal with the aftermath.

Nanny used to say things such as "Everything happens for a reason." And, "What doesn't kill us makes us stronger." I wasn't a believer in that school of thought. How could everything happen for a reason? That didn't make a lick of sense. Sometimes stuff just happened. And we were forced to deal. I was wading through a boatload of it today.

Eddie came over to the car, and I lowered the window.

"You okay?" His face was full of concern.

"Not really," I said.

"It's been a long day and you've had a real shock."
He paused when his name was called, turning.

He was managing me. It wasn't his words, although
they were generic. It was his tone that gave it away.
I had witnessed Eddie firsthand when he interro-
gated a petty thief. He played the soft sympathetic
friend to get the perp to confess. Later he taught
me that that was a well-known approach. And far
more effective at getting confessions and other information. I didn't believe for one second he thought I
had anything do with this. He was simply doing what
he did best. It hurt. He had no idea what I was dealing with here. *I have no idea what he's dealing with on
his end.*

"Sorry about that," he said.

Time to pull my big girl panties up. "Okay. Sorry
I lost it for a minute." I made direct eye contact with
him. "You want me to show you where I was run off
the road?"

He gave me a nod.

"Let's go."

He opened the car door for me and I got out.
The adrenaline that had been thrumming through
my veins made my joints ache. Nevertheless, I
showed no weakness. My shoulders were straight
and squared. I climbed into the truck smoothly and
placed my hands in my lap. I had practice pretend-
ing everything was okay, and I was good at it.

"Can you recall any distinctive markings on the
van that could help us locate it?" Eddie pulled out
of the driveway.

I thought hard. Yes, I did recall something.

"There was a large dent in the driver's-side door. I remember thinking this wasn't the first time he had driven so haphazardly and that there should be a number on the back of the van. You know, like those 'How's my driving?' signs you see on the back of tractor trailers and commercial work trucks."

"Anything else?"

"There." I pointed to the side of the road, where there were obvious tire marks from my skidding.

Eddie pulled over and we got out. He took several pictures with his phone and then sent a text to his team, I supposed. His phone rang. I walked over to the opposite side of the road and squatted down. There, I found the dirt stirred up and a cigarette butt. Had there been another person in the van?

"Eddie," I called and he came over. I pointed to the tire imprint and the butt. "If, and I don't recall clearly, but if there was another person in the van, this could be his butt. The van was swerving on both sides of the road. We could have a getaway driver freaking out."

Eddie regarded me with interest before he stalked around the back of the truck. He came back wearing gloves and holding a ziplock bag.

"You might want to check for tire marks and butts in Heather's yard. If the guy was nervous and, from what I could see, he was shaken up, he may have been chain-smoking and carelessly dropping butts on the ground," I said.

"Astute observations."

"I have a brain. Imagine that." I stalked toward the truck.

"No one said that you didn't, Marygene." Eddie sounded cross.

His team arrived, and I climbed back into the truck to wait. My cell phone rang. It was Calhoun. I wondered what he got from his source. I sent him to voice mail.

"Alex is going to come and take you home. We'll need to go over your statement again later tonight. I'll come by the house after I wrap things up here and find out about Heather's condition and get her statement."

"Sure." My tone sounded flat, even to my own ears.

"No one is blaming you. You don't have to be all defensive."

I cut my eyes in his direction.

"What have I done to make you distrust me? And don't say—"

"Please," I cut him off.

"Listen," Eddie began, his tone stern, "I'm sorry, little girl, but—"

I pierced him with my gaze. "I'm sorry too." My teeth were on edge. "I'm sorry Mr. Ledbetter and Judy died, I'm sorry someone took it upon themselves to try and kill me, I'm sorry Heather got beaten up and I had to find her, I'm sorry all of this puts you in a precarious predicament, and I absolutely hate the fact there is nothing I can do to stop all of this."

Eddie ran a hand through his hair before he placed his hand on my shoulder. "I forget," he grumbled. "Sometimes I forget that you're just as fragile as Heather and Jena Lynn, and, God, I don't mean that in a condescending way, just that this is affecting you the same way it is them."

His acknowledgment made me feel ridiculous, well, cared about and ridiculous.

I wasn't the victim here. "I'm okay, really. This isn't about me. I just hate this. Please, come to the house to take my formal statement and bring Felton, because this has to end."

Chapter 34

When I emerged from the shower, I pulled out a pair of blue cotton sleep shorts and a T-shirt. I was exhausted after retelling the events as I recalled them backward and forward a dozen times or more.

I felt heartbroken for Felton, who'd said he felt helpless about Heather. She had a broken collarbone, a concussion, a bruised cheekbone, and, worse, emotional scars that would take much longer to heal. Alex told me they hadn't found any cigarette butts at Heather's. They did find a partial tire print they could match to the one on the road. And, if they got lucky, the butt I found would be a DNA match for someone in the system.

They were also running with the theory, after I was shot at, that this criminal might just be targeting young women. A thief who had graduated to assault and battery. I wasn't so sure I bought all of that. What happened to me didn't quite fit the profile. All the other victims incurred injury or were dead. Not me. Then I had to recount what I recalled about

Heather. The department was going to have to canvass the island without respect to persons. Not that that information would be made public.

It was late when I finally listened to Calhoun's voice mail. I had several missed calls from him.

"Marygene, this is my fourth call. Why aren't you picking up your phone? I don't want to share this on your voice mail. Let's just say my source was a wealth of information, and there's something not kosher about the Peach Cove Sheriff's Department. I'll drive to your house tonight. It may be late, but I need to talk to you."

I softly padded down the stairs at 2 a.m. Alex was asleep on the couch as the slow crunching of tires was audible. When I gently nudged his shoulder, he jumped. "Sorry," I whispered. "Calhoun is outside with information and I think you need to hear it."

Alex rubbed his face and sat up. "What?"

I eyed his gun on the end table. This meeting had to be civil. That he didn't like the man shouldn't matter.

"Calhoun is outside. He went to speak to a source and has information."

There was a soft knock on the front door.

Alex was on his feet now. Shirtless and in boxers, visible by the moonlight streaming through the blinds.

"Um, you might want to put some pants on."

"What is he doing here at," he checked his watch before shoving a leg into a pair of cargo shorts thrown over the back of the couch, "two in the morning?"

"He'll tell us. Listen," I placed both palms on his

chest to make a connection, for him to hear me. "I won't hide anything from you anymore. I see the error in my judgment now. We need to put our heads together to get to the bottom of the crime wreaking havoc on our island."

Another soft knock.

"You have your suspicions of Calhoun. Fine. Hear him out, and if you find cause to investigate him, so be it."

Alex took one of my hands and squeezed. His gaze bored holes through my eyes. "He means nothing to you?"

"He's a friend."

"You think."

"Yes, I think."

"Let's go see what he has to say." Alex held my hand tightly as we both walked toward the front door. He flipped on the porch light and opened the door. The foyer and living room were still dark.

"Mr. Calhoun," Alex greeted. "Marygene tells me you have information for me."

"I have information." His gaze was intent on me.

"It's time we all shared info, Calhoun. People are still getting hurt. *My people.* If you're willing to work with us, please come in." I stepped aside.

A couple of beats later, Calhoun crossed the threshold. Alex turned on the lights and shut the door behind him. The second the room was illuminated in light, I noticed the bruising around his midsection that ran down his left side.

"That's a nasty bruise," Calhoun said.

Alex waved it away. "It's nothing." There was

something almost gloating about the way Alex glowered at Calhoun, I realized as he grabbed his shirt off the back of the couch and pulled it over his head.

It was an odd combination. Izzy barked twice then, after a quick sniff of Calhoun's shoes, decided he wasn't worth her time. She curled up on the little dog bed in the living room.

"You got a dog?" Calhoun turned his attention to me.

"She belongs to a friend. I'll go start a pot of coffee." I left the two men alone. It wasn't my place to play referee and I was tired of feeling as if it was. There was far more at stake here than the size of their, um, egos.

When I came back with three cups of coffee on a tray, Alex was seated in the recliner and Calhoun on the couch. Alex was leaning forward as he was brought up to speed on what Calhoun had already told me earlier today.

Alex stood. "Before you continue, I should get the sheriff on the phone. This needs to come directly from you."

Calhoun nodded. "Of course."

Alex stepped outside, closing the door behind him.

"Cream and two sugars." I placed a warm mug on the coffee table.

"What happened today?" he asked softly and I sunk into the recliner.

"Heather was attacked." I wrapped my hands around the warm mug.

"Marygene, I'm sorry. Is she going to be all right?"

I nodded and took a sip, swallowing slowly. "She was beaten up both physically and emotionally. She'll heal."

"Thank goodness for that." He leaned forward. "I found out that—"

I held up my hand. "Better wait for Eddie."

He closed his mouth.

"All this secret keeping might have cost Heather. I don't want it to cost anyone else I love."

He sat back, his eyes understanding. "Of course."

"Listen, I don't want you to be angry with me." The sympathy in his gaze immediately made me uncomfortable. "I never intended to pry, just gather information that could prove useful."

Oh God. My face heated up. The hair on my neck stood and so did I. "You had no right!" I stepped away.

"Please don't be upset." He didn't advance when he stood. "Your confidence is safe with me. I swear it. But, Marygene, you have nothing to be ashamed of."

"Shut up! Just shut up!" My whole world was crashing down on me. I'd run from that disastrous life, that man. I needed the clean slate that Peach Cove would provide me. It wasn't that I was hiding from what I'd gone through so much anymore. Or that I felt shame in this moment. Being blindsided with my own story before I'd even confided in my close family members stirred up anxiety. I didn't exactly blame Calhoun. He harbored no ill will toward me. He'd simply been doing his job. Despite that fact, it felt like an invasion of privacy.

"What the hell is going on in here?" Alex rushed back into the room.

Panting, I bolted through the kitchen and out onto the back porch. *Get yourself together, Marygene. It's over. You divorced him and he's out of your life forever. Inhale, hold for eight seconds, exhale. Good. Again.*

Once I got myself together, I overheard the low rumble from the living room. Alex hadn't followed me out here, and I was majorly appreciative.

"Eddie will be here in ten," Alex said when I came back in the room. He held out my mug to me and I took it.

Calhoun was standing by the window. When he turned around, he opened his mouth, I assumed to apologize, but I gave my head a little shake. He let it drop. Thankfully, it seemed they both had.

"How's his mood?" I tested my voice before taking a sip from the mug.

"Quiet."

I sighed.

"He'll be fine once all of this is out in the open. He'll be mad, though, that you didn't mention any of this today."

"I know. It will be better if it comes from Calhoun," I told Alex. "He's the one who gathered the information. It should come from him."

"I'll explain it to him," Calhoun said.

"Calhoun, were you using Marygene for a story?" I jerked my head toward Alex.

"With all the chaos on the island, it would make for a riveting piece. No?"

Could I have possibly been so stupid that I hadn't realized what Calhoun was doing? He had gone digging into my past. Was I the focus of the story? Calhoun had the decency to appear appalled by the notion.

"Nothing Marygene has discussed with me has been on the record. Nor is any information I came across during my investigation." The sincerity in both his eyes and tone gave me some peace of mind. He pushed up his glasses and pierced Alex with a glare. "Despite how you view me, Deputy Myers, I am a man of honor."

"Sure you are," Alex said with an edge of sarcasm.

"I lived through a terrible ordeal, Deputy. One I wouldn't wish on my worst enemy. Yes, what initially piqued my interest was the fact Detective Thornton, a crooked cop, had been called in for the case. Someone involved obviously believed he possessed deep enough pockets to keep Thornton in line. Later, I saw a similar pain in Marygene. I didn't want her light to be snuffed out because of some asshole's agenda." Calhoun was irritated.

Alex was irritated. I had no idea how to describe my emotions. *Overwhelmed* would be the term I would use if I was forced to choose.

Eddie was at my house in under eight minutes. He didn't knock, as Calhoun had. He was dressed in uniform. A statement, I was guessing. I got up to get him a mug of coffee, but he motioned for me to sit back down. I did as commanded.

"Mr. Calhoun. It seems you have information for me." Direct and to the point. That was Eddie.

I listened as Calhoun explained what he had found out about Carl. I cringed when he got to the part about Felton. "This is the part that your deputy isn't yet privy to."

I stared into my mug. He didn't say I wasn't privy to the information. I could feel the eyes on me for a few long seconds.

"Marygene has nothing to do with this." Calhoun came to my defense.

"Don't you concern yourself with my daughter, Mr. Calhoun. You best get to your point."

And he did. He told them about Felton and Carl having it out. The report and arrest that had been erased from the record. I could almost see the steam emanating from both the men standing.

"And your source would be?" Eddie said when the quiet stretched out far too long for my taste.

"Sheriff, you are aware of the sanctity of protecting one's sources." Calhoun had been firm when he made the statement.

"Uh-huh," Eddie said. It wasn't an "I understand" uh-huh.

"That brings me to what I came here to discuss with Marygene." Calhoun was a lot stronger in countenance than I gave him credit for. He wasn't rattled under Eddie's scrutinizing gaze, as most would be. His experience in his field was evident. He had obviously been in the hot seat more than a few times. And protect his source he would.

"I need more coffee." I stood and went to retrieve the pot. I was back and pouring hot mugs full before Calhoun had gotten more than a sentence in. I even brought a mug for Eddie and, this time, he accepted. It was clear I hadn't been involved in Calhoun's information gathering. All I had been was a sounding board.

Calhoun opened his phone and placed it on the table. On it was the image of a man dressed in black, a cigarette hanging out of his mouth, appearing to burn boxes of documents in a large barrel. I leaned forward as Calhoun flipped through a series of pictures. There had to be six or seven large boxes. The man was tossing file after file into the barrel.

"Where were these taken?" Alex asked.

"Behind the warehouse owned by Carl Ledbetter," Eddie answered Alex's question before Calhoun could.

Calhoun confirmed with a nod of his head.

"See here," Eddie picked up the phone and zoomed in with his index finger and thumb.

I couldn't see it but Alex could and he seemed to agree.

"They were taken the night Marygene was shot at," Calhoun said. "I didn't take them. They were sent to me anonymously. I had the source traced, with no luck. And my guy is good."

"We're going to need these," Eddie told Calhoun. And then he paused. His eyes squinted as he zoomed in more.

"What?" I wanted to know and Alex met my gaze.

Impatient, I got up and leaned over Alex to see the image. A burned file lay in the bottom of the barrel. Blurry and faded was the captured image of SP062379. The *S* had been partially burned away. The exact same type sequence that had been scribbled on the paper Mr. Ledbetter had given me. Then it hit me, "I know whose file this is." I had everyone's attention.

Chapter 35

I woke to the ringing and vibrating of my phone against the bedside table. My first thought was, *I'm so glad today is my day off.* It had been a long night. I hadn't even crawled between the sheets until after four.

My hand fumbled around on the table until I found the phone and checked the caller ID. I didn't recognize it. To voice mail it went. After a quick peek at a still-snoozing Izzy, I rolled onto my side and pulled the covers over my head to block out the sunlight. The phone began buzzing again.

Throwing the covers back, I snatched the phone. "Hello," I croaked.

Izzy's ears perked and I swore she gave me an *ah, come on* glare through her cracked eyelids. I completely agreed.

"Marygene. This is Tally Waters," the voice on the other end informed me.

"How did you get this number?" I asked rather coldly.

"Rainey Lane gave it to me." Okay, that was weird. Why Rainey Lane would even be speaking to the woman sleeping with her husband was beyond me. But not my business. "I apologize for the abrupt phone call, but I must see you."

I sat up to clear the cobwebs. "I thought your business was concluded. As I'm sure you're aware, neither my sister nor I own property on the west side."

"It isn't about that. Carl is missing." She sounded a bit breathless, and the pace of her speech had increased. She was scared.

"Wait a minute, let's back up." I got out of bed and stood. "What do you mean missing?"

"I mean missing. Deputy Myers came by the apartment early this morning around six."

Alex must have left after I went to bed.

"He had questions for Carl."

"The apartment in Savannah?"

"That's correct. I insisted Carl refuse to answer any questions without an attorney present."

They had something to hide.

"He ignored my warnings and I left. I was angry." Sure, angry she would be compromising the sale she promised to retain for her corporation.

My brain was firing slower than usual. That happened without my morning cup of joe. I slogged down the stairs toward the kitchen.

"When I came back a couple of hours later, the

apartment was in disarray. Furniture was overturned, and I found blood on the floor. I couldn't stay there."

The pot was already made from last night. I poured a mug and popped it into the microwave. "Did you call the police?"

"I can't."

"You believe Carl was abducted. You found evidence of a struggle and you didn't call the police? You're an intelligent woman, Miss Waters. Surely you see how unwise that decision was."

"Yes. But Carl instructed me that if anything happened to him, not to alert the authorities. Especially the Peach Cove Sheriff's Department. I was to come directly to you. He said you would know why." A loud honking was heard in the background. "Shit!" she shouted. "Sorry. I'm driving. Even if I went against his wishes and called them, the police won't do anything for twenty-four hours and, by that time, it might be too late."

Too late? Did she believe Carl was going to add to the body count? My blood ran cold. Carl was definitely mixed up in something dangerous.

"May I come out to your house? I'm close."

How could I trust Tally Waters? My silence stretched out for several seconds longer than she was comfortable with. "I'm not a bad person. A shrewd businesswoman, but I'm not a monster. This is real, Marygene. Indulge me this once, and I swear you'll never see my face again."

When I finally agreed to her terms, she let out a sigh of relief before she disconnected the call.

I stood in my kitchen in front of the microwave as

I pondered the information I had just received. Perhaps Carl had double-crossed the hit man he used. Or maybe he withheld the money he promised him. The sisters hadn't been fond of Carl. His character was in question by most who were close to him. He didn't retain any friendships with islanders. That was incredibly suspect in my mind.

As I walked to the fridge and got out the creamer, I kept replaying the conversation in my mind. It hadn't been earth-shattering news that Carl didn't trust the Peach Cove Sheriff's Department.

Before Eddie left last night, I swore to him I would step back. If information fell in my lap, as I insisted had happened at times—Mr. Ledbetter was the proof—I was to turn over whatever I had. I poured cream into my mug and sat it on the table. Izzy was up now and barking at the back door.

As I took her out to do her business, I called Eddie.

It went straight to voice mail. "Eddie, it's me. Tally Waters phoned me with disturbing info about Carl. Call me."

Alex was next on my list. He answered on the second ring. "Hey, I'm sort of tied up right now. Did you need something important?"

"Alex, did you have a conversation with Carl Ledbetter this morning?"

"How did you know that?" He sounded tired.

"Does Eddie know you were there? Was he with you?" I sure hoped he accompanied Alex.

"Yes, to the first. No, to the second question." I heard his blinker in the background. "I take it you're still at the house?"

"I am. It's my day off. I told you that last night."

"Oh, right."

I jumped right into it. "Tally Waters called me. I tried calling Eddie but couldn't get him."

"Yeah, he's out of pocket for the day. New information has come to light."

"What new information?"

Silence.

"Fine, don't tell me. I'm keeping my word to Eddie by calling. Tally said Carl is missing. When she went back to the apartment, there were signs of a struggle and she found blood."

More silence.

"I hope you have witnesses seeing you leave and someone else arriving."

"He was perfectly fine when I left him." Somehow, I doubted that.

"As in not broken or bruised?" Alex's temper got the best of him sometimes.

"He was alive. The place was in order, and I didn't draw any blood."

"It's not me you're going to need to convince. You better get ahold of Eddie. Things are about to get dicey again."

The line went dead.

Chapter 36

Tally Waters pulled up into my driveway ten minutes later. I was standing on the front porch dressed in cutoff jean shorts and a tank top when she emerged from the Lincoln she left running. This was the first time since her arrival to the island that I hadn't seen her pressed and together. She was in a pair of jeans and a T-shirt. Her hair was up in a messy bun. No makeup.

"I brought everything Carl instructed me to." She reached the front porch. She set a leather briefcase down in front of me.

"What's in the briefcase?" I didn't pick it up.

She made direct eye contact with me. "I honestly have no idea. Carl didn't offer an explanation, and I didn't ask. He and I had a common goal. That was the only thing I saw in that man. This sale was going to do wonders for my career. Now, I can say with absolute clarity that I'm sorry I ever met the man, took him up on his offer to pitch the development to my firm, and I ever set one foot on this island," she said with sincerity.

"Then why come back? Why not just ignore Carl's instructions and leave?" I took a sip from my mug.

"Because I'm not a heartless monster, that's why." She was clearly insulted. "He *is* a human being. A man I spent time with. He matters."

"He matters to his wife."

She flinched. "I deserve that. Look, I'm following through with what I committed to. And lest you think I'm here to protect my own hide and that I had something to do with Carl's disappearance, I have a rock-solid alibi. There are at least a dozen credible witnesses to attest to the fact I was sitting in the coffee shop across the street from the apartment. The doorman saw me leave after he admitted Alex into the building. Carl was with me in the lobby when Alex showed up. They both watched me cross the street." Okay, that did sound solid.

She started down the stairs.

"Miss Waters."

She turned.

"I don't think you're a monster." For some reason, I felt the need to tell her that.

"Thank you for that." She gave me a half-smile that didn't reach her eyes. Suddenly, I felt sorry for Tally Waters. She had an emptiness about her that I now detected, not that I had much time to dwell on it. Nanny always used to say, "Child, don't judge anyone till you've walked a mile in their shoes."

There was nothing in me that wanted to slip into that woman's sneakers.

After she left, I picked up the briefcase and went back inside. I sat at the kitchen table, staring at it for a few minutes as I luxuriated over my breakfast. A slice of cheesecake and another cup of coffee. There was no one around to judge my choice, and, honestly, I wouldn't have cared if there had been.

Eddie's cell still went to voice mail, and Alex didn't pick up either. Betsy came to mind next, but she would be working her shift right now. Calhoun was out of the question. The last thing he needed was having something else to explain.

With my plate pushed aside, I opened the case and dumped the contents onto the table. Three manila envelopes dropped onto the table. I opened the first. It was all the paperwork that had been filed with the courts for Carl's power-of-attorney petition. Mr. Ledbetter's blood and urine test results were inside. He had also had an MRI and CT scan. Even after a quick Internet search, I had no idea how to read either of those images. Luckily, there was a physician's summary on the last page.

While the patient cannot be diagnosed with the condition of dementia, he does exhibit symptoms of amnestic mild cognitive impairment, or amnestic MCI. According to this report, Mr. Ledbetter had trouble remembering things and was losing things often, forgetting to go to important events and appointments, and having trouble coming up with desired words. He appeared to be in the early stages.

If the judge presiding over the case had had a chance to review the material or not before Mr. Ledbetter passed, I didn't know. Who knew if this would be enough to rule him incompetent, especially if Mr. Ledbetter had retained his own attorney and probably his own specialists to offer a different diagnosis completely refuting this doctor's.

The next envelope contained land and deed titles. The marina was the one that stood out.

There was a dispute filed on the property claim, citing Mr. Ledbetter's will. The will wasn't in the folder, which I found peculiar. A letter that had Carl contesting the amendment to the will that was also referred to as section 6a. Carl had testified during his deposition about the medical records and claimed his father hadn't been in his right mind when the will had been changed. That document I scanned meticulously. There was no mention of who the property was willed to. I shoved the paperwork aside and tore open the final envelope, stunned to find it contained blank sheets of printer paper. Someone had gotten to these files without Carl's knowledge or Tally had removed the contents. I hit the callback button on the last number that had called me.

Tally answered and I said without preamble, "Tally, I wanted to know if you understood the documents in the envelope labeled three? The contents were puzzling to me."

"I thought I made myself clear," she said in a

clipped voice. "I didn't look inside. Carl just said that if something were to happen to him, to retrieve the briefcase from his office and give it to you."

"He never said anything as to why he wanted me to have the documents?"

She sighed. "No. All I know is his father kept documents in his beach house. Carl had them all moved out to that abandoned marina. Except for the ones he set aside for you. He didn't elaborate and I didn't pry. Listen, I don't mean to be rude here, but I really can't help you. Good luck."

I sat there pondering my next move. "Carl had wanted me to have the documents. Why?" I asked Izzy.

She cocked her head to one side.

"Was it because his father had started this whole thing by choosing me? Carl would have caught wind of that info, surely."

She whined. Why couldn't there just have been a copy of the file in the folder that matched the sequence I had? Cracking the code that the burned folder belonged to Ms. Sally was easy. *Sally Porter 06/17/1979.* But only because I had snooped at the beach house and now that I knew the files had been relocated, I really wanted to take a drive out to the marina.

"What should I do, Izz?"

She rested her head on her paws.

"Right. I should try Eddie again."

Why wasn't he picking up? What was I supposed to do? I chewed on my bottom lip and debated my options. Surely Tally had informed Rainey Lane of her husband's disappearance. And surely Rainey

Lane had called the police. That would have them calling Peach Cove Sheriff's Department. But not before twenty-four hours were up. Alex would undoubtedly be questioned.

When my phone vibrated on the table next to me, I jumped. "Why haven't you called me back?" I snapped.

"Marygene?" Calhoun asked.

I'd been so lost in thought I hadn't even checked to see who it was before answering. With the assumption that it was Alex, I'd not answered politely.

"Calhoun." I took a second to readjust my expectations. "Hey, um, I thought you were Alex."

"Sorry to disappoint."

"That's not what I meant. I'm just up to my eyeballs." I began stuffing the documents back into the folders.

"I had the strangest phone call from Tally Waters."

My hand froze mid-stuff. "She called me too. Then I received a visit from her."

"What are you planning on doing, Marygene? I'm thinking that since the authorities are involved, we need to stay on the sidelines." He didn't sound like himself. Either he had lost interest, which I doubted, or he had other concerns he wasn't willing to share.

"You're right, of course. Back to Tally," I paused to consider my words carefully. "Did she have some documents delivered to you?"

"Is that what she brought you?" Calhoun answered my question with his own.

"Why are you evading my question?"

"I'm not. Why are you avoiding mine?"

"This is stupid!" I tired quickly. "Yes, I have a briefcase full of documents that just happens to be missing the most important one. Or at least what I perceive will be the most important."

Silence on the other end.

"Calhoun?"

"Turn them over."

"I will. I'm calling Eddie the second we hang up."

"Good."

We sat in silence for a couple of beats.

"I know you were upset with me the other night, and I understand completely. I wouldn't even bring it up again except, in the spirit of full disclosure, I felt I owed you this information."

"I'm listening," I said.

"I had a conversation with your ex-husband while I was in town."

My pulse raced.

"He was in the hospital, recovering from an attack."

That I hadn't expected.

"He was coming out of his office building after working late and was jumped. He has three broken ribs, a fractured jaw, and a lot of bruises and scrapes. Not enough damage was inflicted, if you ask me."

I kept silent.

"The reason I'm telling you this is because the person responsible threatened to end the man's life if he even thought about coming near you again. That tidbit of information he withheld from the police. Apparently, the attacker was convincing."

My fingers went to my parted lips.

"Peter also claims to have gotten in a couple of good jabs to the attacker's midsection."

My eyes welled up with tears. *Oh Alex . . .*

"Thank . . ." I cleared my throat. "Thank you for telling me." I swallowed hard.

"I owed you that much. Take care of yourself."

"You too." I guessed that was the last I'd hear from Calhoun.

Chapter 37

After yet another call to Eddie went to voice mail, I desperately needed something to focus on after the bomb that Calhoun had dropped. I spread the documents back on the table. I kept going over them, looking for anything I might have missed. I found it highly suspect that Carl would include blank sheets on purpose.

"Unless," I said to Izzy, "he was instilling suspicion." That would be a smart move. It might throw the investigation off. "What if Carl staged his own disappearance? Spread his blood at the scene before he vanished? And, instead of having Tally turn over all of this to the sheriff's department, he had her bring a copy to me and possibly one to Calhoun, giving him the time he needed to set things in motion?"

Izzy had tuned me out in lieu of a nap.

"I'm calling Felton," I said to myself, since Izzy had abandoned me.

He answered on the second ring. "What do you need?" Wow, Felton sounded stressed.

"Sorry to bother you. I tried Eddie and Alex first." I tried to sound apologetic. It came out more annoyed.

"Alex is being questioned by the police. Eddie is standing in as his rep."

"Questioned about what?" Please don't say for beating up Peter.

"Listen, I'm not supposed to be talking to you, but I know you won't stop until you're in the loop as to what's going on." He was right about that.

However, I had a pretty good idea what Alex was being questioned about and, now that I considered it, it couldn't be about my ex. What I wanted to be privy to was how the police were even involved. Carl hadn't been missing for twenty-four hours and, even if he had been, Tally would be the only one who could have reported it. She was adamant about not getting involved. Unless, Rainey Lane had called.

"I'm just really worried because neither of them have returned my calls. What kind of trouble is Alex in?" I asked.

"There seems to have been some sort of struggle at Carl Ledbetter's place in Savannah. Someone called in an anonymous tip and identified Alex as the one they saw leaving the apartment. I'm going to be honest with you, Marygene. Police brutality isn't a charge Alex wants slapped on him."

"Is Carl . . . did they find . . . ?" I couldn't finish the sentence.

"There isn't a body at the scene, if that's what you are asking."

"Alex isn't being charged, then?" He and I both knew that if there was no body, there was no crime.

"No, just questioned."

"Okay. Thanks, Felton. How's Heather doing?"

"She's recovering. She's strong," Felton said.

"She is. Have you arrested anyone yet?"

"Not yet," his tone hardened. "We're trying to keep this situation hush-hush. We don't want to cause an all-out panic on the island. Handling this quietly is best for everyone involved."

I agreed with that. Though, I didn't want anyone else to fall victim. Vigilance would be the key. I debated whether I should tell Felton about Tally.

"You still there?" Felton asked.

"Yeah. I was just wondering. Should the department at least issue a statement instructing all citizens to exercise caution? Keep their doors locked?"

"That won't be necessary. We think Heather was targeted for a reason."

"Like all the recent crimes are linked? It's mighty convenient that all the incidents revolved around the Ledbetters. All of them, except for Heather's." Felton had been doing most of the legwork. Digging into the family's background and business affairs. He also was the one who had a confrontation with Carl.

"Oh God! Someone was sending you a message."

The silence on the other end was deafening.

"You were getting too close."

"Careful, or I'll think you've been doing some legwork of your own." His tone was cool.

"Right." I half-laughed then changed the subject to more important matters. "Listen, Tally Waters dropped by here today. She said Carl wanted her to bring over some documents."

"What were they?" he asked tersely.

"Some legal documents. Power-of-attorney papers. That sort of thing."

"I'm going to need those," Felton said. "Was there anything else?"

"Not really. I can drop them by the precinct later."

"No. You stay put. I'll swing by later. Or if you must go into the diner, just leave a key under the mat for me." He sounded out of breath. Almost like he was running.

"Yeah, okay. Hey, Felton, it really gives me peace of mind to know you're looking out for Alex. Stay safe."

"You too." The call ended.

Chapter 38

The sun was going down, and Felton had yet to come by. Alex had called and said he and Eddie would be tied up for a few more hours. I wanted to mention what Calhoun had told me, started to, but, in the end, I decided to have that conversation in person.

Yvonne had come by for Izzy an hour ago, and I was already missing her company. I was glad to hear that the deal was going through with Yvonne's new business venture, and we would be able to catch up in the coming weeks. She was excited about her future and had already lined up a few clients. Not wanting to rain on her parade, I kept this whole mess to myself. She deserved to enjoy her moment.

Now, alone with my thoughts, something didn't feel quite right. It hadn't felt right for—well, for I don't know how long. So, I did what I always did when I needed a pick-me-up. I baked. I was pulling a batch of my lucky overnight chocolate almond cookies from the oven. The chocolaty aroma filled

my senses. Whenever I needed a little extra good
juju, I made a batch of these. Call me superstitious.
Some people had lucky charms, socks, a rabbit's
foot, or crosses. I had my overnight chocolate almond
cookies.

As I scooped the fragrant puffy beauties up one
by one with a spatula and placed them on a cooling
rack, I wondered why Felton wouldn't want me to
drop the documents by. He had a motive to harm
Carl. Well, at least he had reason to hold a grudge
against him. I wasn't sure how deep the hate between the two men ran. It was obvious there was
something between them that didn't sit well with
those who'd taken notice. Although, Felton certainly wasn't the one behind Heather's assault. The
pieces weren't adding up.

"Wow, those smell great!"

The cookie I had on the spatula went flying as
I shrieked.

Betsy guffawed. "Sorry. I thought you'd hear me
drive up."

"Betsy Myers," I huffed and panted, "you're lucky
I didn't have Mama's revolver in my hand."

The back door closed behind her.

Tears were running down her cheeks as she continued to laugh. "Jena Lynn asked me to swing by
and check on you." Betsy finally managed to pull
herself together.

"Why? Nothing happened to me."

Betsy shrugged. "Guess she figured you might
be broken up or somethin'." She leaned on the

counter and took a hot cookie off the rack. "She ain't as tough as us. Oh yummy. I sure could use one of your good luck cookies." She bit into it and her mouth dropped open. "Hot, hot, hot!" Her bottom lip was covered in gooey chocolate. She rushed to the sink, turned the faucet on high, and stuck her face in the cool water.

"Serves you right for scaring me the way you did." I put the last cookie on the rack and untied my favorite rose apron, then hung it on the hook inside the pantry door.

Betsy patted her face dry while I closed the door. "Where's Izzy?"

"Yvonne came by and picked her up."

"Oh. She bought the Palmer house then?"

"She did."

"Maybe she can help you out here. This place needs a complete remodel." Betsy pointed to the old home interior paintings on the walls and the condition of the dining room table. The counters were the worst of it, in my opinion. She hadn't even referenced those.

"I'll talk with her about it. It's high time I made this place my own. Since I'm going to be living here indefinitely now." I took a sip of coffee from my now-full mug.

Betsy pointed to the table. "What's all that junk?"

I sighed. "You're not going to believe this, Bets, but Tally Waters dropped it by. It seems Carl Ledbetter is missing. Or suspected to be missing. I don't know."

"No way!" Betsy made her way over to the table, and I filled her in on all that had transpired.

"I'm not all that concerned about Alex," I told her. "He can explain why he was there. The investigation being ongoing and all. Eddie can confirm his statement."

"That makes sense." Betsy thumbed through the paperwork. "It would be low for someone to go after Felton's girlfriend. But that's the MO we're dealing with." She flipped through the stack of blank pages.

"It is, and whoever it is didn't want whatever was in that third envelope brought to light." What could be so damning that Mr. Ledbetter kept it hidden all these years?

"Did you consider that maybe there is something hidden between these blank sheets?" Betsy continued to flip through them.

"No." I moved next to her as she flipped through them several more times. When nothing was found, I patted her on the shoulder. "It was a good thought."

"Yeah, it was. Stupid Carl should have thought of it." Betsy dropped the paper on the table.

We both sat. "What if Carl didn't know the file was blank?"

"Say what?"

"Indulge me for a minute."

She nodded.

"What if he just pulled the files from the cabinet that he believed contained the documents in their entirety? Maybe his dad replaced the file with blank sheets and perhaps the actual documents are still exactly where he left them."

"You mean at his house? You looked there."

"I mean hidden. Under another file name. Now all those files are at the marina."

Betsy leaned back. "They have to be there. Old man Ledbetter was an old coot but a smart old coot."

I stood. "Listen, Bets—"

"Don't you dare to try and cut me out, Marygene!" Betsy was on her feet. "There's no way I'm going to stay behind while you go off to the marina on your own. Not only is that out of my character, but it's also downright stupid on your part. We have a killer on the loose." Betsy was indignant.

"I'm not helpless and I'm certainly not stupid!" I pulled Mama's old revolver out of my bag and she stepped back. "See." I grinned and put it back into my purse.

She pulled an old Smith & Wesson out of hers. "Two guns are better than one."

Bayside Marina had never reopened after the storm. It felt like a ghost marina now.

We parked back a good distance from the usual lot. There was a small broken-down shack that was barely standing. An old worn-out sign read LIVE BAIT AND COLD BEER.

"This place is what nightmares are made from," Betsy said as I shut off the engine.

She was right. The moss-covered wreckage, broken

pieces of old vessels, and destroyed docks looked like a scene out of a horror movie at this time of night.

"We should probably tuck our guns in the back of our shorts, like they do in the movies. Hauling around a purse would be mighty inconvenient if we have to make a run for it."

I swallowed hard as we got out of the car and placed the gun against my lower back. The more I considered the location, the colder I became. It was one thing to investigate when you didn't have any idea if you would stumble on any perpetrators. It was a completely different scenario altogether when you might have a confrontation with a hardened criminal. Most people wouldn't have any reason to venture out to the deserted marina, and those who did wouldn't at this time of night. I wanted to face-palm. I'd searched all the properties belonging to Joseph Ledbetter except for his boats and fisher-man shack.

"Where should we check first?" Betsy whispered.

Even though no one was around, that we knew of, I whispered back, "That old boathouse." I pointed to the only floating boat on the water. It certainly was worse for wear, and, by the sight of it, it was surprising it hadn't sunk like all the others. It certainly didn't look seaworthy.

Betsy swallowed hard. "Roger that."

We moved quietly through the dark marina. All the old broken-down boats added to the eeriness. I had to hop onto the only poor excuse for a dock that remained. I held out my hand to Betsy. We clasped hands, and she jumped. We lost our balance and both nearly tumbled into the murky water. I grabbed onto her diner-issued polo shirt, and we somehow managed to remain upright. More surprisingly, we managed that without a peep.

Betsy's sweaty palm gave my hand a squeeze of thanks, and we continued to move as silently as possible past all the skeleton fishing boats that had once been the pride and joy of all the old fishermen.

Laboriously, I climbed over a pile of roping covered with seaweed and barnacles next to the barely floating vessel that now belonged to Carl Ledbetter. I gave Betsy a *wait* sign. My heart was fluttering in an odd rhythm, and I needed a second to right myself. I had a light-headed, almost-dizzy feeling.

"You okay?" Betsy asked.

I nodded and bent over, placing my hands on my knees. Something hit against the side of the boat, and the two of us shrieked. My hand went over my mouth.

Vacillating momentarily, I searched around for some sort of a weapon that wouldn't be quite as dangerous as my gun. I didn't quite trust myself to not blow holes in some innocent bystander. You never knew if kids were lurking around somewhere and, as much as I doubted it, I'd rather be safe than sorry. I found an old gaffing hook and gripped it in my hands before slowly hoisting myself up on wobbly legs to peer into the window. It was too dark to make anything out.

Another thud against the wall nearly caused

me to lose my nerve. A couple of deep breaths, or wheezes, later, I steeled myself for the unknown. Slowly and cautiously we moved down the side of the boat.

Betsy extracted her phone from her pocket, and we peered inside. The light reflected over the top of a large ice chest. There was ice scattered all over the floor, along with a sleeping bag and what appeared to be Coke cans.

"You think someone is living out here?" she asked in a shaky tone.

"I don't know about living, but someone has definitely been here. I just hope they're gone."

"Me too."

We moved inside and, after a quick recon, let out a sigh of relief that, at this moment, we were alone.

"Probably kids," I said.

"You think they've been fishin'?" Betsy lifted the lid of the chest and screamed.

What I saw next I would never ever be able to erase from my memory. After a quick intake of air, a part gasp and part sob left my lips. I swayed on my feet, gripping tightly to Betsy. The two of us were horrified. It was confirmed. I was on the precipice of something dark and deadly. Carl Ledbetter lay in the ice, his eyes frozen in widened shock. No one had even attempted to cover him. Blood had crystallized against his face from a little round hole in his forehead, and a few tears had frozen against his cheeks.

Bile began to rise in my throat. I clamped my hand over my mouth. We hightailed it out of there.

I managed to hold back until I made it to the water. When I'd finished, I wiped my mouth with the back of my hand. Betsy took the hook from my hand and tossed in in the water, then she went back inside. To wipe down the lid of the chest, I guessed. Betsy was no fool. We didn't want our prints or DNA anywhere in that boat.

Chapter 39

The night was quiet. The sounds of waves lightly rocking the boat remnants and the wind were all that we heard. The moon was high in the sky over the water. Betsy and I stood in stunned silence against the car. I had to call this in and, as bad as it looked for the two of us, there was no way around it. My thoughts drifted to Rainey Lane and how devastated she would be. I wished I could help somehow.

"Do you think Tally killed him?" Betsy asked.

"I don't see what she would gain by that," I said. Tally alerted me of his disappearance and had even sounded concerned. But what did I really know? Here I stood. Another dead body to add to the body count. I closed my eyes. Did Carl want me to find his killer? Was he somewhere lurking around waiting for me to do something?

"Give me a sign, something, Carl? Help me!" I whispered.

Betsy wrapped her arms around me. "I think

you're cracking up. Carl is the dead one. He ain't gonna help nobody."

"No, Bets." I gave a hoarse laugh and relayed everything that Mama told me about the dead and my aura. She freaked out a little and said something about getting her a cross and some holy water to keep with her.

Time passed slowly while Betsy and I managed to get our story straight. We needed to be on the same page. I was about to tell Betsy we should leave, my hand on the door handle, when we heard the sound of a car slowly rolling toward the marina to my left. Betsy and I locked gazes and, as if we were able to read each other's minds, both of us darted toward an old barge. The mammoth wreckage had been thrown on its side, burrowing into the shells and sand. Hidden from sight, we heard the vehicle come to a stop.

My leg muscles tightened. Adrenaline thrummed through my veins as I crept to the edge of the barge. Every single ounce of me was ready to run. I peeked around the side. It was too dark to make out the vehicle. My stomach clenched. I took a couple of deep breaths. A man, or I thought it was a man, was heading for the old fisherman's shack. Betsy's lips and chin were trembling in the moonlight.

"It's okay, Bets. We're going to be fine." I reached for my phone. It wasn't in my pocket. I'd left it in the car. Slinking back, I instructed Betsy to call Alex.

Betsy patted her shorts pockets, front and back. She didn't have her phone either. "I must have dropped it in the boathouse!" Betsy's eyes bulged as she wrapped her arms around herself. "What are we going to do?" She stumbled and bumped into the barge.

A loud thud echoed across the marina. We both held our breaths.

"We should have driven away the minute we found Carl. We are so stupid!" Betsy whisper-shouted.

"Stay calm." I put a finger to my lips. The last thing we needed was to be discovered skulking around this godforsaken marina. I pointed toward the car. "On three we make a run for it."

Betsy nodded eagerly. I began the countdown. Before I could get to three, Betsy took off around the barge, her arms flailing wildly as she ran. I followed.

Before I made it a few feet, pain radiated from the back of my head, and I fell to the ground hard.

I came to on a splintered floor. Slowly, my eyelids obeyed my command and opened to slits. My view was darker and cloudier than it should have been. When I attempted to swallow, I found the process difficult. The drumming going on inside my head was a majorly painful distraction. Where was I? The air was musty and thick. Sweat poured down my face, stinging my eyes.

My hand went to the back of my head. It was wet. When I brought my hand to my face, squinting through the pain, I saw blood. Noises. Breathing. Someone else was here. I attempted to focus on the face looming above me. A bottle was placed to my lips. The room-temperature liquid quenched my parched mouth and throat.

"Thank you," I managed before I lost consciousness again.

"Wake up!" Mama was patting my face. "You can't sleep! You have a serious head injury." Her high-pitched tone, intense with emotion, demanded my attention. When I was finally able to focus clearly, or clearer, Mama was gone. Had I dreamed that she was here?

This time I could sit up when I lifted my lids. The room spun and, a second later, my stomach revolted. An old bucket was beside me, and I vomited in it repeatedly. My head was pounding. Nausea, vomiting, and double vision. It didn't take a brain surgeon to diagnose I had a concussion. I shoved the bucket away and managed to scoot over to lean against the shabby wooden walls. Smoke, I smelled smoke.

Weathered walls with cracks of light shone through. A small folding table and chair were nestled against the wall on the other side of the room. The floor was broken in several places, the ground beneath visible. Seagulls were calling to one another. It was morning then. They were diving for their breakfast. There was a flicker of light against the door.

Slowly, I began to recall what had happened. Someone had hit me. Hard. This was the bait shack I'd spied from the barge. Oh God, Betsy! Where was she? Had she made it? Driven away? Called Alex? Left me here? I shivered convulsively.

I had to get out of here. Somehow, I managed to half-crawl, half-scoot across the floor toward the door. I focused on the peeling red paint. My knees and shins were picking up splinters. Some were painful. *I can do this.* I had no idea what I was going to do when I made it outside. I just knew I had to get out of here. I was forced to stop several times and catch my breath, nearly losing whatever bile was left in my stomach with each advancement.

"You're awake," a man said. I recognized that voice.

I sighed with relief and turned. He was wearing a baseball cap. I found that odd. I'd never seen him in one.

My lungs burned. "Felton, help me," I croaked. "I've been hurt."

He smiled at me, a sinister smile that chilled the blood in my veins. He was in the doorway between this room and the next. A filing cabinet was to his left. Documents were burning in a barrel. He held a file.

Pieces began to fall into place.

"I wasn't sure if you'd come to anytime soon. I didn't mean to swing that hard."

That day at the diner. The day my car was re-possessed. He was out front with Mr. Ledbetter. *The old man had said, "I've had just about enough of this."* Naturally, I assumed he was talking about my display.

But then there was Bonnie's account. She said they were arguing . . . Oh God . . .

I blinked several times. *He's the one who hit me.* The room began to spin. I nearly vomited again while Felton watched me with interest. Mr. Ledbetter must have suspected Felton would take revenge. He had the file number on him that day. It made sense now. The *A* wasn't an *A*. It was an *H*, written in a hurry. *HP 08/15/87.* F. Helen Powell had given birth on August 15, 1987, to a son, Felton Powell. He was the illegitimate son of Joseph Ledbetter.

My skin crawled. *Where is my gun?*

Felton tossed another file into the flames. "I see you're figuring things out."

I didn't say anything, shocked that the man before me had been capable of such horrific acts.

"I never wanted to hurt you." He closed the distance between us with two long strides. His hands shoved underneath my arms and hauled me away from the door. Sweat dripped off his face onto mine.

My teeth chattered. *No! I am never going to be a victim again!* I fought against him, my nails digging into his forearms. I let out a scream.

Felton shook me once. "Stop that!"

That was all it took. I ceased fighting. He propped me up against the wall near the doorway between the rooms. Jerking several boards from the front window, he let some light and air in. A waft of salty air made its way to me. I could taste it on my tongue.

I was exhausted—Lord help me, I was completely exhausted. As much as I tried, I couldn't force my teeth to stop chattering.

Felton sat down on the floor and put his Glock on his leg. He removed his cap and dumped a bit of water from the bottle on his bald head. He put the bottle to my lips. I wanted to refuse. To spit it in his face. Instead, I drank it down.

The malevolence wafting off him made my stomach churn. I feared I might vomit again. How had I missed the crazy glint in this man's eyes? The pleasure he derived from inflicting pain? "You look like a scared little bunny. It didn't have to be this way. I always thought we were alike."

He and I are nothing alike.

"Both of us are bastards. At least Eddie claims you. Joseph never claimed me." Felton's lip curled when he said his father's name. "You know, he's the reason Mama left the island. He used her up and threw her away for the next woman that got him hard."

"That's awful, Felton." I swallowed. "I'm sorry."

"I don't want your pity," he snapped, and I flinched. That gave him a laugh.

I dredged up the courage to ask, "You didn't hurt Betsy, did you?"

"She's in the trunk of your car. I put a couple of air holes in it for her. She never did anything to me." It came out as an absentminded answer. He used the barrel of his gun to scratch his cheek.

At least she was alive. But, in this heat, for how long?

"And you know, that asshole who raised me . . ." he continued down his memory lane.

He must have believed we were alike to confide in me the way he was. I could use that. I focused intently on him.

". . . my dad, he knew I didn't belong to him. He made me pay for it every day of my life." He turned his head away from me.

For a split second, I debated trying to get the jump on him. Maybe even wrestle the gun away. Reality set in. I was in no condition to fight him one on one.

His head whirled back around. His voice raised. "You know, I was doing okay in Savannah. Sure, I'd not been killing it financially or anything, but I was working. Then one day I saw Carl. I spoke to him." His face contorted with rage. "He glared at me as if I was lower than shit dust. I saw red. After that, he found out about me. Joseph had to tell him. He had a choice, drop the charges or I would have blown up his entire life. I hated Joseph. He never accepted me. I gave him a chance. Told him the day he died that all he had to do was keep his word and add me to the will."

My scalp crawled. I was dangerously close to crying. I swallowed the lump that was in my throat. "You poisoned him."

"Yeah, but it didn't go exactly as I planned. I paid a teen to call and cancel that order. That was a breeze. But, I wasn't sure how much Jena Lynn would use for his cake. Charlie let me in the night before. Joseph said something to Heather about Rainey Lane's intention to order a cake. I took the risk she would order a freshly baked one. You know her." He'd made a good bet. "Heather said she always did that. He was supposed to eat it at home. They all were." Felton wanted all three of them dead. "Charlie had a heart attack, so I didn't have to bother with him." At least he hadn't killed Charlie.

"What if Rainey Lane had changed her mind? Someone else could have been killed or several people." I rested my head against the wall. My head throbbed.

He spat on the floor.

"But what about Heather? She was so glad to see you the day she was attacked."

His face contorted in outrage. "I didn't hurt her. I'm not a monster."

I begged to differ.

"That half-brother of mine, Carl. He sent someone to rough her up. Lowlife piece of shit. He knew I had the proof to contest Joseph's will. He was sending me a message. He paid for it. The prick." He sure did. With a hole in the head.

"What about Judy?" I was unable to hide the pain in my tone.

His eyes hardened and he stood. "I told her to stay out of it. Stupid woman pined after Carl like he was something wonderful. Her life was on Carl." He leaned down and poked the barrel of the gun to his chest and shouted, "Not me!" Spittle sprayed my arms. This man was a raving lunatic.

"She fought?" My tone was shaky by the realization that was why her nails were torn. She had fought Felton, while he made the murder look like a suicide. That's why he had been first on the scene.

"I volunteered to be the lead on everything Eddie would let me." He snorted. "He didn't see what was right in front of him. Neither did your lover boy Alex. Idiots." He began pacing. "That nosy reporter." His eyes flamed with rage. "You almost cost him his life, baiting him the way you were, while you coaxed him to stay around by flaunting yourself."

A defiant scream welled up within me, but I clamped my mouth shut. He was waiting for me to provoke his rage. That was evident.

Wild eyes searched my face. "You see? If you had stayed out of this, you would have been spared!" He grabbed my face and squeezed until I feared my eyes might burst from the sockets.

"I'm sorry," I said softly when he released me.

Fueling his anger would only prevent me from getting to my friend, and I had to get to Betsy. She needed water.

"Me too." He raised his gun and pointed it at my head. "I'll toss you in with Carl. Guess I'll have to do Betsy too. Then I'll torch this place, and no one will suspect me. There will be no evidence of the kind of woman my mother had been. No evidence I was the product of her lascivious behavior."

"But what about the property? Isn't that what you were after in the first place? Your rightful inheritance?" I wanted to get his mind back to Carl and his dad. Let his anger burn for them, instead of me.

He lowered his gun and began to pace. The sun was rising higher in the sky, and I could see the uncertainty in Felton's eyes. Anger and bitterness had been eating him from the inside out his entire life. If pure evil hadn't been emanating off his body, I could possibly feel sorry for him. No. He killed people. Innocent people.

"We can figure this out, Felton. Maybe Carl was after you. Maybe he killed his dad because Mr. Ledbetter wanted you to have your share of the inheritance." I began to move toward the doorway. A small scoot at a time. "Carl was having an affair with Judy. That makes him the prime suspect. Say I called you after Carl attacked me. Hit me over the head. It could work." Another couple of scoots toward the door. I didn't want to die here today. I didn't want my friend to die either.

Felton turned toward me and gave a bark of bitter laughter. In that moment, I knew all the humanity left within him was gone, like someone flipped a switch in his brain and he became one hundred percent sociopathic.

"No." He raised his gun.

Involuntary tears leaked down my cheeks. I thought of all the things I should have said to everyone, and I hated that Betsy would pay for my idiotic mistake of driving out here. I sent a silent apology and love her way. My love was sent to Eddie, Alex, and Jena Lynn. Finally, I sent out to Mama, wherever she was, my forgiveness.

"Ah, Marygene, you brought this on yourself."

A giant flash of light filled the room, blinding me. A loud thud rattled the dilapidated building. Through squinted lids, I tried to focus as I scooted toward the door, kicking away the debris in my path. I managed to make it to my knees. When I turned back, Felton was lying unconscious on the floor. His gun was still in his hand.

I struggled to my feet. I had to get the gun. He could come to at any moment and still kill both me and Betsy. That was when I saw Mama standing over his body, her dainty hands folded in front of her. She was smiling.

"You saved me," I breathed.

"Yes, I did."

We both gazed at the body.

"He won't wake up," she said.

"Still, he doesn't need to be near a gun. The police might shoot on sight. Way too easy. This man belongs in a cage."

"Agreed," she said and I kicked the gun from his hand. The force sent me falling forward, bracing myself for the impact with the floor. Mama caught me, and I sobbed with relief.

"Eddie and Alex will be here in five minutes." She stroked the hair out of my face. "You're going to be okay. I set Betsy free. She was gagged and her feet tied, but her phone is with her. Her hands are free now."

I wondered if Betsy felt her aid.

"If I could get to that ex-husband of yours, I'd do worse than Alex did."

"That might hold you back from crossing over," I said through a half-laugh, half-sob.

The room began to go dark, and I was fully aware I was losing consciousness again. Before I did, I felt my body being gently laid onto the floor on the porch, the fresh salty air a welcome change from the stuffy moldy air of the shack.

I whispered, "Thank you, Mama."

Chapter 40

The EMT moved me to the stretcher and rolled me toward the ambulance. My head lolled to one side, and I caught sight of Felton in the back of the squad car. That would have made my day, any other day, that was. I caught sight of Betsy. She was breathing into an oxygen mask. She slid off the back of an ambulance when she saw me. The EMT treating her helped her sit back down when she swayed. I held up a hand. She did the same as I was lifted into the second ambulance.

The next couple of days were a blur. I woke in a cool hospital room to see different people sitting at my bedside at different times. Alex was holding my hand and whispering how sorry he was. Guilt was drifting off him. Dark circles were around his eyes. I managed to squeeze his hand before losing consciousness again. Eddie was there when I woke up another time. I think I overheard him saying he didn't want to lose me and that he wanted to make up for all the mistakes he'd made as a father.

Jena Lynn was there, flowers in hand. It was possible there may have been a few others.

Felton sang like a canary. He was proud to have been the one to torment the Ledbetters. He was a real piece of work. He asked for a visit from Calhoun. Probably hoping he could get some sort of psycho book deal in the future.

The day I was released, I still had a splitting headache. But, with no more brain swelling, I was on my way to recovery. My brother drove me home. He was fussing over me the best he could. Making sure my pain pill prescription was filled and helping me into bed. "You feeling any better? Your coloring isn't very good."

He placed a glass of water on my bedside nightstand and handed me two of my pain pills. I gladly took them and swallowed them.

I gave him a sarcastic smile. "Thanks. You sure know how to make a gal feel great."

His face flushed. My brother certainly wasn't Florence Nightingale.

"I'm just glad to be out of the hospital."

He took the glass from me.

"Thank you, Sam."

He sat on the edge of the bed beside me. "Sure. You need anything else before I go?"

I smiled, feeling the pain pills taking effect. It happened fast on an empty stomach. "No. You go on. Thanks for driving me home."

He stood to leave. "It wasn't a problem. My shift doesn't start until two." That Sam, such a softy. I had to laugh. "Jena Lynn should be by in an hour."

"I don't know what I would do without the two of you to care for me. I'm going to be a better sister to you moving forward," I said.

"Don't get all mushy on me." Sam rose. He was always uncomfortable showing his emotions.

"No worries about that." I smiled.

"I'll be back after my shift."

As soon as I heard him drive off, Heather arrived. "Marygene, you awake?"

Sighing, I threw the covers aside and stumbled down the stairs. I needed a shower in the worst way. I tucked my hair behind my ears as I reached the bottom of the steps. The trip had taken a considerable amount of effort. "I'm up." I was thankful for the pain relief.

Heather's eyes widened. She stood there in the doorway between the kitchen and the living room, mouth agape, casserole dish in hand.

"God Almighty, Heather, do I look that bad?" I asked in amazement.

She immediately closed her mouth. Tears welled up in her eyes. "I'm so sorry. So very sorry."

When I shook my head, I instantly regretted it. Nausea hit me. "You have nothing to be sorry for." I walked over to her as if in quicksand and took the casserole dish. "What happened wasn't your fault."

"It's chicken, rice, and broccoli," she said meekly.

The casserole was the standard delivery on occasions such as births, deaths, and illnesses. I thanked her and put the dish in the refrigerator.

"I didn't know. I swear to God, I didn't know." She was on the verge of sobbing now.

I felt like I should comfort her. I just didn't have the bandwidth to deal with any of this today. I was sure she'd been through the wringer. Eddie would have torn into the relationship, looking for some sort of connection between Heather and the case.

"Of course you didn't." I leaned against the counter. My equilibrium would be off for a while. "Felton was incredibly clever and a man with nothing to lose. No one blames you."

She sat down at the kitchen table. "I just feel so stupid. All the signs were there, and I never saw them. He was around my children." She broke down.

I let out an involuntary sigh. "I know you're hurting, Heather, and I wish I could help. I'm just too exhausted. I don't mean to sound heartless, it's just—"

She abruptly stood. "No, you're right. You're the one that's been through it." She wiped her face dry with a napkin from the holder. "All you need to do is pop that casserole in the oven at three hundred fifty degrees for twenty minutes," she said absently. "Try and get some rest."

"Heather," I said before she left out the back door. She paused.

Slowly, I made my way to her and embraced her. She seemed surprised. I could tell by the stiffness in her frame. But a couple seconds later, she relaxed and embraced me back.

"We're going to get through this," I said, "and when we do, we're going to be forces to be reckoned with."

When I released her, she gave me a rueful smile. "Take care." She left.

I caught sight of my reflection in the mirror as I turned on the shower. Surreptitiously, I inspected the damage. Both my eyes were bruised a bluish yellow color, and my hair was a total mess under the white gauze wrapped around my head. The nurses had done their best to clean me up, but I did look a fright—an all too familiar sight. Something inside of me woke. Violence should never be tolerated. Bullying on every level needed to be terminated. I knew what I had to do. I would call Doc Tatum first thing in the morning.

I hated the idea of another person going through abuse alone. Perhaps my story could help others. This wasn't just about me anymore. All victims, male and female, needed an advocate, a voice when theirs was nonexistent. Arms of comfort even when they feel numb. Someone to cry for them and with them. Assurance that there is no time limit on healing and they will get there. Together, we could stand up against domestic violence. Put an end to silent suffering and march into the future as stronger, more independent beings who demand change.

"Tomorrow will be better," I said to my reflection. "One foot in front of the other. You can do this."

The diner was hopping once again as I circled the block in Rust Bucket. The Mini Cooper had bullet holes in the trunk, and the tires had been slashed. Plus, after Betsy was trapped inside, I could never drive it again, repaired or not. Eddie had it towed away, and I was thinking I'd find something more suitable next time.

The door tinkled, signaling my arrival. The aroma of diner food was a welcome one. I was starving. Betsy waved at me as she served a table in the back section. Jena Lynn was smiling and placing peach rolls on the decorative display plate. She hadn't noticed me yet, but Heather had. She came up and gave me a hug before refilling a few mugs with coffee. She had a more normal countenance today, and I was glad to see it.

Calhoun had sent flowers and was on another assignment somewhere.

I gazed around my diner, so darn proud of my Peach family. We were a resilient bunch.

I sat down next to Alex, who was seated at the counter, eating a potato waffle. He'd been by to check on me several times but had respected my request for space to heal.

I bumped his shoulder with mine. "That's my recipe, you know."

"You don't say," he said around a mouthful of cheesy potato goodness.

Jena Lynn said he'd been in turmoil over what had happened and that he was obviously in love with me. *Love* was a word I wasn't sure I trusted these days, but I was warming to it.

Mama was MIA. Perhaps she had crossed over.

"I do, indeed." I reached behind the counter for a mug and held it up as Heather passed by.

"Today a good day?" he asked, and I knew then that Jena Lynn had been keeping in touch with him.

I smiled. "You know, today is one of my better days. I think it's going to improve from here."

"That's good," Alex said as I glanced over my shoulder at the framed prints on the wall, halting momentarily at the one of Alex and me. Time was still marching on. "You know," Alex said softly in my ear, "I hear that's you and your old high school sweetheart."

I hid my smile behind the mug as I took a sip.

"I also hear," Alex continued, "that he was an idiot who didn't appreciate what he had when he had it."

"That's true. I am historically undervalued."

"Hey, sis," Sam peeked through the serving window. "You want to go out on the boat with Dad and me this weekend?" Sam was really trying.

My heart warmed.

"That'd be great, Sam. I'll have to check with my boss first and see if I'm on the schedule."

Jena Lynn chuckled. It was good to see her back to her old self. She was still in counseling, and I was glad to see it was doing her a world of good. She informed me the other day that she and Tim would postpone the wedding. I adamantly rejected that idea. She wasn't going to put off her happiness for one single day because of me. With a half hour of assurances I was up to the task and glad to hold down the fort, she agreed to keep the dates as scheduled.

"Let me know what the old biddy says." Sam made a face behind Jena Lynn's back.

Jena Lynn turned and threw a couple of sugar

packets at him through the window. He batted them away with his metal spatula.

"You know what else." Alex leaned in close to my ear and whispered huskily, "I heard he's still madly in love with you and is dying for another chance."

Our gazes locked.

"He isn't concerned he'll end up with a swift kick to the privates and be tossed overboard?" I asked.

"Yes," he laughed, "but he's willing to risk it."

I took another sip of my coffee. "We'll see."

**Please turn the page for recipes
from Marygene's kitchen!**

THE PEACH DINER POTATO WAFFLES

2 pounds yellow or red potatoes, shredded and
    squeezed dry
3 tablespoons melted butter
1 cup shredded cheddar cheese, plus extra for
    garnish
¼ cup diced onion
¼ tsp garlic powder
1½ teaspoons Himalayan salt or sea salt
½ teaspoon ground black pepper
¼ teaspoon thyme
2 eggs, lightly beaten
½ pound cooked and chopped bacon
¼ cup chopped chives for garnish

Preheat the waffle iron according to the
manufacturer's instructions. Spray the waffle iron
with cooking spray, if required.

Toss the potatoes with butter, cheese, onion, garlic
powder, salt, pepper, and thyme in a bowl until
evenly coated. Stir eggs into the potato mixture.

Spoon some potato mixture onto the preheated
waffle iron; cook until the potatoes are tender and

golden brown, 5 to 8 minutes. Repeat with the remaining potato mixture.

Garnish with crispy bacon, chives, and extra cheese.

To Die For Chocolate Mango Beer Cake with Chocolate-Coconut-Raspberry Frosting

1½ cups Blue Moon Mango beer
1½ cups unsalted butter
1 cup dark chocolate cocoa powder
3 cups Swans Down cake flour
3 cups brown sugar
2¼ teaspoons baking powder
½ teaspoon salt
4 large eggs
¾ cup sour cream

Preheat the oven to 350°F.

Spray two 8-inch cake pans 3 inches deep with baking spray. Line the bottoms with parchment paper circles.

Place the mango beer and butter in a large saucepan. Heat on medium until the butter melts.

Remove the pan from heat and add cocoa powder. Whisk until smooth. Set aside to cool to room temperature.

In a ziplock bag or bowl, combine flour, sugar, baking powder, and salt.

In a mixing bowl fitted with the paddle attachment, beat together eggs and sour cream.

Add the cool beer-cocoa mixture and mix on low. Scrape down the sides and add the flour mixture. Mix for about a minute and divide between the pans.

Bake 30 to 35 minutes or until a cake tester comes out clean. Don't overbake.

Cool on a rack in the pans for 10 minutes before turning out and allowing the cakes to finish cooling on the rack.

For the frosting
2 cups heavy whipping cream
1 pound semisweet chocolate
2 teaspoons vanilla extract
Shredded sweetened coconut
Raspberries

Heat cream in a saucepan or microwave and bring it to a simmer. Place the chocolate in a large heatproof bowl. Pour the hot cream over the chocolate and stir until the mixture is completely smooth. Stir in the vanilla. Refrigerate a minimum of 1½ to 2 hours, stirring occasionally.

Remove the parchment paper and trim the cakes to a flat top. Assemble by spreading frosting on the bottom layer and topping it with shredded coconut. Top with the remaining layer and frost the entire cake. Top with raspberries around the

perimeter of the layer and coconut in the middle.
Chill until ready to serve.

Bacon, Dill, and Gouda Cheese Scones

3 cups self-rising flour
1 teaspoon salt
½ teaspoon cracked black pepper
½ cup cold butter, diced
2 large eggs (1 for egg wash)
1¼ cups buttermilk
10 slices bacon, cooked crisp and crumbled
1½ cups grated smoky Gouda cheese
2 tablespoons chopped dill

Preheat the oven to 425°F.

Add the flour, salt, and pepper to a bowl of an
electric mixer fitted with a paddle attachment.
Add the butter and dill, and blend on low until the
flour resembles corn meal.

Add in the egg, buttermilk, bacon, and cheese.
Mix until just combined. If the dough is a little
stiff, add a splash or two more of buttermilk.

Turn the dough out onto a lightly floured surface.
With a rolling pin, roll the dough into a ½-inch-
thick rectangle. Cut wedges of dough out to a
preferred scone size and arrange on a half sheet
tray lined with parchment paper.

In a small bowl, beat the egg and brush each
scone with the egg wash. Sprinkle with a little

coarse sea salt and pepper, and bake until nicely browned, about 15 to 20 minutes.

SAM'S SURF AND TURF BURGERS
WITH LEMON AIOLI

For the lemon aioli
 ¾ cup mayonnaise
 ½ tsp Dijon mustard or to taste
 Zest of 2 lemons
 Juice of 1 lemon
 1 clove garlic, minced
 1 tablespoon olive oil
 2 teaspoons chopped chives
 1 teaspoon chopped parsley
 Salt and pepper to taste

Mix all above ingredients together and refrigerate until ready to use.

 5 pounds ground chuck
 1½ tablespoons Montreal steak seasoning
 1 teaspoon Worcestershire sauce
 2 cups lump crabmeat
 1 teaspoon Old Bay Seasoning
 2 tablespoons mayonnaise
 1 teaspoon horseradish mustard
 1 tablespoon freshly chopped dill
 2 green onions, chopped
 Zest of 2 lemons
 ¼ cup panko bread crumbs
 6 slider buns
 Bibb lettuce

Season the ground chuck with steak seasoning and Worcestershire sauce. Divide into 12 slider-sized patties.

Make the crab stuffing: combine crab, Old Bay Seasoning, mayonnaise, mustard, dill, green onions, lemon zest, and bread crumbs.

Divide the stuffing among six patties, leaving ½ inch around the edge. Place the remaining patty on top of each stuffing-topped patty and crimp the edges with a fork or your finger. Reshape the patties by hand.

Grill to medium well or desired doneness. Serve on slider buns with lemon aioli and Bibb lettuce.

*Black and Blue variation.
Add crumbled blue cheese to the ground chuck before shaping the patties.

MARYGENE'S BERRY CRUMB BARS

For the dough
    3 cups all-purpose flour
    1 cup brown sugar
    1 teaspoon baking powder
    ¼ teaspoon salt
    1 cup (2 sticks) unsalted butter, cold and diced
    Zest of 1 lemon
    1 egg, lightly beaten

For the filling
    5 cups berries, (strawberries, raspberries, and
        blueberries)
    1 tablespoon lemon juice

1 teaspoon lemon zest
1 teaspoon vanilla extract
½ cup all-purpose flour
1 cup granulated sugar
¼ teaspoon salt
½ teaspoon ground cardamom

Preheat the oven to 375°F. Grease a 9 × 13–inch baking pan.

In a bowl of an electric mixer fitted with a paddle attachment, combine the flour, sugar, baking powder, salt, butter, and lemon zest until the mixture resembles cornmeal. Then add the egg. The dough will be crumbly. Pat half of the dough into the prepared pan. Place the pan and the remainder of the dough in the refrigerator while you prepare the filling.

In a bowl, mix gently together berries, lemon juice, zest, and vanilla extract. In a large ziplock bag or bowl whisk together the dry ingredients. Pour over the berries and fold gently.

Spread the berry mixture evenly over the crust. Crumble the remaining dough over the top.

Bake in the preheated oven for 45 minutes, or until the top is slightly brown. Cool completely before cutting into squares.

PEACH ROLLS

For basic sweet dough
⅔ cup whole milk
5 tablespoons brown sugar, divided

1¾ teaspoons active dry yeast

3 large eggs, room temperature

2¾ cups unbleached all-purpose flour

1 teaspoon kosher salt

2 teaspoons vanilla extract

½ cup unsalted butter, room temperature and diced

For the peach filling

¼ cup melted butter

1 cup peach preserves (homemade or store bought)

2 tablespoons cinnamon

½ teaspoon allspice

For the icing glaze

½ stick butter, room temperature

2 cups confectioners' sugar

1 teaspoon vanilla

Hot water

Heat milk in the microwave until an instant-read thermometer registers 110°–115°F. Transfer milk to a 2-cup measuring cup; stir in 1 tablespoon of brown sugar. Sprinkle yeast over the milk and whisk to blend. Let it sit until the yeast is foamy, about 5 minutes. Add the eggs and whisk until smooth.

Combine the remaining 4 tablespoons of brown sugar, flour, salt, and vanilla in the bowl of a stand mixer fitted with a beater. Add the milk mixture. With the mixer running, add ½ cup room-temperature butter, 1 piece at a time, blending well between additions. Mix on medium speed for 1 minute. Knead on medium-high speed until the dough is soft and silky, about 5 minutes. If the dough appears dry, add a couple splashes of milk.

Brush a medium bowl with some melted butter and place the dough in a bowl. Brush the top of the dough with the remaining melted butter and cover with plastic wrap (this can be made 1 day ahead) and chill.

Let the dough rise in a warm, draft-free area until it doubles in size, 1 to 1½ hours (or 2 to 2½ hours if the dough has been refrigerated).

Preheat the oven to 350°F.

Roll the dough out on a floured surface into a 15 × 9–inch rectangle. Spread melted butter all over the dough. Spread preserves over the buttered dough and sprinkle with cinnamon and allspice. Beginning at the 15-inch side, roll up the dough and pinch the edges together to seal. Cut into 12 to 15 slices and place on a cookie sheet lined with a slip mat or parchment paper and let rise for 30 to 45 minutes.

Bake for 30 minutes or until lightly browned.

Meanwhile, mix butter, powdered sugar, and vanilla. Add hot water 1 teaspoon at a time until the glaze reaches the desired consistency. Spread over the slightly cooled rolls.

MARYGENE'S LUCKY OVERNIGHT
CHOCOLATE ALMOND COOKIES

2 cups Swans Down cake flour
1½ cups all-purpose flour
½ cup dark cocoa
1½ teaspoons baking soda
2 teaspoons baking powder
1½ teaspoons coarse salt, sea salt
3 sticks unsalted butter
2 cups dark brown sugar
½ cup light brown sugar
2 eggs
2 tsp vanilla
3 cups semisweet chocolate chips
6 ounces sliced almonds (about 1½ cups)

Combine the cake flour, all-purpose flour, cocoa, baking soda, baking powder, and salt in a bowl. (A large ziplock bag can come in handy here. Throw all the ingredients in, seal, and shake around to combine.)

In the bowl of an electric mixer, beat together the butter and sugar on high until light and fluffy (about 3 to 5 minutes). Add the eggs one at a time, making sure to scrape down between each. Add vanilla and mix.

Add all the dry ingredients to the bowl and mix to combine. Then, add in chocolate chips and almonds, mix for 30 seconds or just until combined.

Cover the bowl with plastic wrap and refrigerate overnight. (Trust me, it's so worth the wait.)

When ready to bake, preheat the oven to 350°F.

Line three baking sheets with slip mats or parchment paper. With a small ice cream scoop, scoop out balls of dough and roll in your hands for a few seconds to shape. Place each ball on the cookie sheet 2 inches apart.

Bake cookies 15 to 17 minutes. Cool for 5 minutes on the sheet before moving with a spatula to a cooling rack to finish cooling.